LOVE ONE LAST TIME

He didn't see her when he entered the apartment. She was in the dark. The wall switch controlled only one lamp, and its bulb threw a faint glow that reached only slightly beyond the table on which it stood. She was on the couch, facing him.

"Hello, Ben," she said.

His skin prickled in the stinging electric shock of surprise. "How the hell did you get in here?"

"Please, Ben," she murmured softly, "just five minutes."

Again he looked at her. Something was peculiar. Different. He pulled her to her feet. This was a new Sharon. True, he had loved the old Sharon very deeply but the differences he now detected made her more exciting. Now she was even fascinating.

After a moment, his hand went out slowly. And Sharon took it . . .

THE
TRESPASSER

MELVIN WEISER

AVON
PUBLISHERS OF BARD, CAMELOT AND DISCUS BOOKS

THE TRESPASSER is an original publication of Avon Books. This work has never before appeared in book form.

No novel is completed without the assistance of many people. Two who may not go unrecognized are my agent Barbara Rhodes for her steadfast commitment and my editor Susan Moldow for her inspiring sensitivity.

AVON BOOKS
A division of
The Hearst Corporation
959 Eighth Avenue
New York, New York 10019

First Avon Printing, June, 1981

AVON TRADEMARK REG. U.S. PAT. OFF. AND IN
OTHER COUNTRIES, MARCA REGISTRADA, HECHO EN
U.S.A.

Printed in the U.S.A.

10 9 8 7 6 5 4 3 2 1

DEDICATED

To my beautiful wife Isabelle with love and gratitude for her patience and helpful interest

AND

To Ann and Sam Weiser who are also beautiful and supportive.

PART I

The Transition

There is no real American theatre today, and there never will be until you people address yourselves, once again, to the timeless questions of Man.

Alexander Weintraub, Broadway producer.
From "Death of a Theatre," an address delivered to the New Playwrights Group at the Golden Theatre in New York City, February 17, 1975.

1

She had been dead three days when she started to move.

Something within a single cell of her right eyelid was working powerfully to take shape. At first it was an imperceptible flutter. Then it rooted and swelled and finally burst from its solitary confines. Neighboring cells were ignited. Infinitesimal explosions. They sprawled and fused across her face until her entire head, her brain, her senses were joined in life.

She was propelled into contact with her surroundings. Her ears picked up the muted conversation of mourners in the next room. Her lips twitched at the light touch of a passing fly. She worked her jaw in quick, snapping movements and listened to the click of her teeth. A smile of satisfaction pulled at the corners of her mouth. Then she opened her eyes and saw for the first time since that day, one week ago, when everything had dissolved suddenly in flashes of searing light.

She had suffered a devastating cerebral hemorrhage. There was no recovery. For four days she had lain in a coma. And despite the monumental efforts of the best doctors in Phoenix, her bodily processes had stopped, and she was pronounced dead.

Now she was looking at the soft folds in the lining of the casket's lid. She studied them for a moment. With sensual delight she was reminded of satin sheets in another place.

The lid was up. She could see the dark ceiling of the dimly lighted chapel. She forced her sight into the darkness and discerned hairline cracks in the aging paint. This made her smile again, a smile of strange satisfaction.

3

Then closing her eyes she directed herself to the task of bringing the rest of her body to life.

The explosions began again. This time they were in her diaphragm. Her entire midsection was suffused with a liquid warmth. It tingled upward and soon her lungs began to function. It washed through her pelvis, down her thighs, into the soles of her feet. Her legs throbbed. She bent her left knee. *God, she was alive again.* And then her heart began to beat. At first the rhythms were erratic. There was a disturbing bubbling sensation in her throat. She let her attention focus upon the spot. She rejoined the severed vein and artery ends. The problem persisted. There was an obstruction within her neck. She concentrated harder. The embalming fluid was forced against the blockage. She felt a series of soft clicks. The obstruction eased, and the fluid flowed through. The gurgling subsided, and the heart pumped—slowly but evenly. She could have made her entire body function without a heartbeat, just as she had controlled her head and her lungs, but that would have required total and continuous concentration upon every one of her organs. And that would have been too costly and dangerous to her purpose. The more she could get her body to work on its own, the more attention she would be able to give to the realization of her objectives. Just getting her fluid to flow past that obstruction in her neck had taken valuable effort. Now, she set aside a portion of her consciousness to sustain her heart's rhythm, and she gave herself to the joyous fact that she was alive again.

Alive.

2

Howard Demerest was attending the few mourners in the adjacent room. Mr. Demerest was the director of Calvary Chapel.

"Mr. Demerest . . ." Curtis, his young assistant, had edged close.

Mr. Demerest's attention was centered on a slight, middle-aged lady.

"Reverend Nelson is ready."

Mr. Demerest nodded. "I have to leave now, Mrs. Rouche," he said. "We'll be starting the services soon."

He turned toward his assistant. Together they moved toward the chapel just as Sharon Kane was easing herself to the floor near her casket.

"Curtis, ask Reverend Nelson to meet me in my office. There's something he should know about Mrs. Rouche before we start."

"A problem, sir?"

"Perhaps. She's extremely distraught. Tell him I'll be there in a moment. I just want to check a few details in the chapel first."

"Yes, sir." Curtis left to deliver the message to the handsome, young minister of the First Evangelical Church of Christ.

Mr. Demerest paused at the chapel door and glanced in the minister's direction: he was standing as if framed by the room's only large window.

"He's a picture, all right," the mortician thought. He smiled at the idea and entered the chapel.

As he turned to close the door, he heard a soft, female voice speak his name.

"Mr. Demerest."

Oh, Lord, had someone slipped into the chapel to be alone with the deceased? These were the only moments he found truly difficult. He knew solitary mourners. Sometimes they were desperate souls. Sustaining the bond between themselves and the departed was often their lifeline to sanity.

"You really shouldn't be in here," he said, turning to face her.

But he saw no one. Only rows of empty chairs standing neatly in the half-light. He glanced quickly toward the coffin. Still no one. Only a sedate floral arrangement dressing the familiar setting.

"Mr. Demerest." Again. So distinct. So precise.

Was someone actually hiding in the chapel? He couldn't believe it. Good God, children's games in a funeral parlor! "Whoever you are," he said, a bit vexed, "you really ought to be in the anteroom."

"Please sit down."

"We'll be starting in a minute. I do wish you'd—"

The sight of her was like an electric shock. It drove his tongue to the roof of his mouth. He felt his throat tighten as if a powerful hand were clamping off his breath. What was happening?

She stood in the shadows against a far wall. Her hands were clasped before her face, forefingers pressed together and against her lips. From her head, outlining the contours of her hair and shoulders, a soft, blue light radiated and pulsated like a supercharged neon sign. Her gaze was shooting through her eyebrows. And the downward tilt of her face caused the lower part of her eyes to gleam like white holes. She raised her head and lowered her hands slowly. A pale luminescence detailed her features clearly in the darkness.

Howard Demerest fought for control. His heart was pounding in his ears. His thoughts were scrambling in a red blur of confusion and fear. "This is a disgusting game!" he growled. And he rushed down the carpeted aisle toward the casket.

"Please . . . I haven't completed my transition." The voice was velvety soft, but there was an urgency in the plea that made it more command than request.

"I don't know who you are, miss," Demerest continued, his voice rising, "but this kind of foolishness is insanity. And if you've done anything to Miss Kane's body—!" He had reached the casket. He looked into it. Its emptiness was a bludgeoning confirmation of what he was still rejecting. "What have you done with her body?" he croaked.

"Wait . . . wait . . . one . . . more . . . moment . . . one more . . . moment . . ."

He saw the blue aura weakening. The head began to move toward him. My God, he thought, it's really she! He was paralyzed. A dark gauze began to envelop his brain. He was losing control, but he couldn't tear his eyes from the advancing figure.

She emerged from the shadows, moving with a bizarre grace, a soft, soundless glide.

"You arrived too soon," she said coldly. "You almost ruined everything."

"You're dead . . ." It was an incredulous whisper.

"Really?" She was smiling peculiarly at him.

It was then that Howard Demerest realized the last shock that his system was able to sustain at that moment: her lips were not moving. The words were coming from somewhere within his own head. His eyes rolled upward into the gauze, and he fell backwards heavily, tumbling the casket from its supports and sending the folding screens and floral decorations sprawling.

The noise was deafening.

She looked at his unconscious figure for a moment. Then she turned calmly toward the door.

It swung open sharply, smashing against the wall. Curtis burst into the room followed by the Reverend Mr. Nelson and the few confused and anguished mourners.

She stood in the middle of the narrow aisle.

They ran past her, around her, pushing, rushing toward the wreckage at the end of the room. No one touched her. No one saw her.

She remained perfectly still, staring straight ahead in deep concentration. It was only after everyone had passed her that she relaxed a bit and smiled that peculiar smile again. I can do it, she thought with a sigh of satisfaction. Then as pandemonium swirled around Mr. Demerest and the empty coffin, she walked slowly from the room.

3

"Howard, do you honestly, actually, expect me to believe that a corpse got up and walked out of this mortuary?" Police Chief Wheeler asked incredulously.

Mr. Demerest raised his eyes and looked at him in helpless affirmation.

"She couldn't have been dead," the chief insisted.

"Please, Matt . . ." he pleaded weakly. There was nothing more he could add.

They were alone in Howard Demerest's office. After he had regained consciousness, Mr. Demerest had waited there for the police, stubbornly refusing to see anyone or to answer any question until he was alone with Wheeler himself.

"All right, all right." The chief put up his hands apologetically. "That may have sounded as though I'm questioning your professional integrity. I'm not, Howard, believe me."

There was a slight pause as he waited for a response, but Mr. Demerest only waved a hand as though it didn't matter, as though nothing mattered. He slipped back into his armchair. Trembling fingers pulled at his lower lip.

The chief liked Howard Demerest. They had been friends for years.

Now, as he looked at him, he wondered how he could get some reasonable answers from a friend without adding to his obvious distress.

"I don't want to upset you, Howard," he said gently, "but none of this makes sense."

"I know," Demerest said simply.

Wheeler drew up a hassock and sat before him.

Demerest's head was bowed; he was staring at private images.

The chief's voice was a gentle prod. "Howard, is it possible you were mistaken?"

The funeral director shook his head.

"Not about what you saw," Wheeler added quickly. "I mean about her being dead?"

Another shake of the head.

"Why are you so sure?"

"The doctors at Good Samaritan signed the death certificate . . ."

"They're not infallible . . ."

". . . and I embalmed her."

Chief Wheeler threw his head back and stared at the ceiling. This is ridiculous, he thought. There has to be some explanation. An idea occurred to him suddenly: perhaps the embalming hadn't even taken place. "Did you embalm her personally?" he asked.

"What?"

"Did you do the embalming personally, or did you assign the body to one of your assistants?"

"I did it . . . personally."

Matt Wheeler exhaled sharply and ran a hand heavily over his face. Each of his doors was being closed. He stood and crossed to the desk. His mind raced. "Then the only thing I can think of at this time," he said, "is that someone stole the corpse and is now playing some insane game trying to make you believe she's still alive."

"That's what I thought while I was waiting for you, but it's impossible," Mr. Demerest countered.

"Why?"

"Because Curtis and I cosmetized and clothed her this morning and brought her into the chapel about an hour before anyone arrived."

"It doesn't take an hour to steal a body."

"But the chapel has only one entrance, and I was in the anteroom all the time after we brought her in."

"You didn't leave at all?"

"No."

"And you didn't see anyone go in or come out?"

Mr. Demerest looked at him helplessly. "Just the minister, Matt, and I was with him."

If anyone but Howard Demerest were telling him this

fantastic story, Matt Wheeler would have made arrangements immediately for hospitalization and observation. But he was sufficiently acquainted with his friend's personality to know that he would never, under normal circumstances, permit himself to become this disturbed over anything or to become involved in any kind of weird game.

He was at a loss.

"Tell me about the embalming," he groped.

"What's there to tell?" Demerest shot back. "I cut the vein and artery, pumped the fluid in until all the blood was out, clamped the ends and closed the incision."

"Standard procedure, right?"

"Why?"

"I don't know. I'm just asking questions, Howard. I don't know what the hell to think about this!"

Demerest fidgeted for a moment. "It's standard procedure for me," he answered finally.

"What does that mean?" Wheeler was puzzled.

"Nobody uses clamps. I do."

"How's it usually done?"

"After the fluid is in, the vein and artery are usually sealed with a glue and then sutured. But a number of years ago, I developed a special clip. Small. About the size of an index fingernail. It snaps closed. I find it easier than glue and stitches."

"You're the only one who does it this way?"

"To my knowledge."

"Where do these clamps go?"

"It depends on the circumstances." Demerest was becoming exasperated. "Sometimes in the groin, sometimes in the arm . . ."

"Where are they in the Kane girl?" Wheeler interrupted.

"In her neck."

"Her neck? Why there?"

"No special reason," Howard Demerest snapped impatiently. "I just decided to do a neckline job, that's all."

"So what did you do?"

"I've already told you, I opened her neck, did the job and closed the incision."

"And the clamps are . . ."

"Inside her neck, for God's sake!"

"Then nothing's flowing," the police chief concluded erroneously. It was almost a whisper. "Dear Jesus, even if there were blood in her, nothing would be flowing."

There was a long silence after that.

"All right, Howard," Matt Wheeler murmured finally, "you say a dead girl's come alive, but I'll be goddamned if I'll tell that to anyone else." He was still holding on to the probability that the body had been stolen and that someone was impersonating the dead girl for some crazy reason.

Demerest asked, "What are you going to do?"

"I'll have to put something in the report while I look for her. . . . I'm going to say the body was stolen." A thought occurred to him. "That's not going to be very good for your business if the newspapers pick it up . . ."

Mr. Demerest waved off such meaningless concern with an impatient gesture.

"Meanwhile," Chief Wheeler said, "I'll question all the others. Maybe someone saw something else after you passed out—" Suddenly he exploded. "Jesus Christ, Howard, you're telling me that somewhere in Phoenix there's a woman walking around with formaldehyde in her veins instead of blood! Do you realize what that means?"

Mr. Demerest stared at him. "I don't want to think about it," he whispered.

4

"Felicia, honey, you've got a problem," Alex Weintraub sighed. "You wake up every morning not knowing whether to put on your brassiere or your Jockey shorts."

"Your problem's worse, Alex," she countered angrily. "You put on your Jockey shorts every morning and know you don't have enough balls to fill them."

"There's enough there to kick your pretty little ass out of this show," he warned softly. It was an empty threat and she knew it.

"Stop acting like a fool, Alex," she fumed, "and get rid of Dandy Maynor *now*."

"Not a chance, doll."

"He's a clown," she spat. "He's a long-haired, freaky clown! You know what he did yesterday—in the séance scene? He *farted!*"

"I heard . . ."

"I wouldn't doubt it. It was loud enough to be heard in Los Angeles."

"Felicia . . ."

"And those friends of his—Neanderthals! What does he need them around for anyway?"

"Maybe to protect him from his leading lady." He smiled.

"Go ahead, Alex, think it's funny," she snapped ominously, "but you'll stand around with your thumb up your ass, waiting for me to go on that stage again with Dandy Maynor."

"Felicia, honey," he said soothingly.

She raged, "Don't try to con me, Alex!"

And she started to leave.

He touched her shoulder as she passed. It was a concil-
iatory gesture. But she swung around and her hand came
up in a sweeping arc that would have rattled his brains if
it had connected. Instinctively, though, he blocked it with
his forearm and countered with a stinging smash across her
own face. It was the first time in her life she had been
struck that way. The force of it had never even happened
on stage. She staggered off-balance and fell over an arm of
the sofa, her face sinking into one of the soft seat cushions.
There were tiny, bursting lights veiling her vision. Her head
rang strangely, and her body went suddenly and crazily
weak.

Alex moved fast when he saw the blood. He rushed to
her side as she tried vainly to push herself into a sitting
position.

"Felicia! Felicia, baby, I'm sorry. Believe me." He was
helping her to sit. "MARILYN! MARILYN, WHERE
ARE YOU?"

His secretary came bursting into the room, her expression a mixture of perplexity and fear. She had never heard
him shout quite like that.

"What is—"

"Get some water, quickly."

"What happened—"

"Some water!"

She charged out and returned almost immediately with
a small cup of ice water from the office cooler.

Alex had one knee on the couch. He was holding Felicia's hand and cradling her head against his chest. Her
nose was bleeding profusely, and a dark purple stain was
spreading quickly across his blue shirt. "You'll be all
right . . . you'll be all right," he was mumbling.

"What happened, Mr. Weintraub?" Marilyn asked in a
trembling whisper.

He took the cup and put it to Felicia's lips. Blood ran
into the water.

"Felicia . . . Felicia . . . please."

"What happened? Should I call the hospital—"

"No."

"But she needs a doctor."

"She'll be all right. She just fainted. Get me some ice
cubes."

Marilyn hesitated.

"Get a move on. *Quick.*"

The young secretary bolted from the room.

Felicia allowed him to coax her into a reclining position. Her head was beginning to clear. She became aware of the blood running into her mouth and down her throat. She coughed and tried to sit up again.

"No, no . . . stay there . . . for Christ's sake, don't move!" He jumped from the couch and ran to his desk for a handful of Kleenex. Quickly folding one into a small, thick pad, he placed it under her upper lip, murmuring, ". . . get some pressure under there . . . that'll stop it . . ." And all the while, he dabbed gently at the stream of blood.

Marilyn reentered with a tray of cubes.

"Give me those." He grabbed two and wrapped them in his handkerchief. He spaced them so that one would lie on each side of the nose.

"Is there anything else I can do?" Marilyn asked.

"Leave us alone now," he mumbled, applying the ice gingerly.

After a pause the secretary withdrew uncertainly to fret at her desk and to wonder about the large, red impression on Miss Ohrman's face, a mark that so much resembled the outline of a hand.

"It's slowing down," Alex observed. He examined the nose carefully. "I don't think it's broken . . . I think I caught you here near the bridge . . . probably a ruptured vessel, that's all . . . but I want you to go to a doctor and have it checked."

"All right," she said meekly. The bleeding had shifted her emotional gears. She saw his concern. She sensed a deeper significance behind the violence. She couldn't make out what it was, but she felt a bit responsible for having triggered it.

"I'm sorry, Alex," she apologized softly.

"*You're* sorry? I nearly break your nose and you're—" He smiled and shook his head. Checking the handkerchief, he saw with relief that the bleeding had slowed to a trickle.

"Sometimes I'm such a miserable bitch you'd be justified in killing me." It was said so simply.

He stopped his ministrations and looked tenderly at her. "You know," he said with a gentle smile, "when you're not being an actress, you're the most beautiful thing in this world." Then he bent and kissed her lightly on the corner of her mouth. And in a voice that was little more than a whisper, he added, "I'd give five years of my life to wipe out the last five minutes. You know that, don't you?"

Her hand came up slowly and touched his lips. He kissed her fingertips. Then he took her hand in his and stared absently at it for a long time before he finally spoke again. When the words came, they floated in softly on a troubled sigh. "Leesh, there's a problem . . . I can't give you the particulars now . . ."

She started to respond, but he cut her off. "No, listen . . . I can't drop Dandy. . . . I could lie and give you all kinds of reasons except the real one. Just believe me: I can't drop him. I know he's a pain-in-the-ass sometimes, and I wish he had more stage experience . . . it's a sure thing that being a rock star is no substitute for acting talent . . . but I think he'll make it, I really do. . . . he'll be playing himself, that's all. . . ."

There was a lengthy silence. They simply looked at each other.

"Will you ever be able to tell me what the trouble is?" she asked gently.

"I don't know."

"Is there anything I can do?"

"Just stay with the show. Please. I'll talk to Mike Ross and see if we can do something about Dandy."

A simple honesty was passing between them, creating that rare moment when two people are real with each other. It wasn't new to them; they had experienced it many times before. But it was something neither had expected to come out of this meeting.

She sat up and picked the pad from under her lip. She toyed with it before dropping it into an ashtray. She seemed nervous. Finally, she confessed softly, "If this hadn't happened today, Alex, I doubt if I'd ever have said this aloud: it isn't Dandy . . . Oh, he's no actor and he's a fool but you're right, he'll be fine . . . It's me . . . I won't be able to get what you need." She stood and crossed to his desk, keeping her back to him.

That surprised him. He knew she had been having difficulties with the part. He expected as much. It was a most challenging role, and Felicia was a totally dedicated actress. She wouldn't be happy until she had mastered every nuance of every line. He could appreciate concern on her part, but he never expected to hear her express defeat.

"I don't understand what's happening," she continued. "It's the play. . . . It scares me. . . ."

"It's only another role, Leesh. You've done all kinds."

"I know . . . but I still can't get into it . . . every time I get close to the character, I get very scared, and I feel as though I'm screaming inside . . . Look at this. Look." She showed him her hands. "I just talk about it, and I start to tremble and sweat."

"Have you discussed this with Mike?"

"He's only a director, Alex, not a psychiatrist." There was a long pause as though she were mustering courage for her next words. She crossed to the couch again and sat near him. "Alex," she said finally, "I've been afraid of this play from the minute I started to read it . . . and as I read on, I developed the oddest feeling that something was going to happen . . . not in the play, but to me. . . . Suddenly I heard my heart beating, but it didn't seem to be inside my body. I began to perspire. I lay perfectly still, hoping, if I didn't move, everything would be all right again. And that's when it started . . . at first it was a peculiar, tingling sensation on the edge of my hand, here near the little finger. It became very intense and then radiated slowly up my arm. Soon it reached my neck, and I could feel the hair prickle at the back . . . and then . . . Alex, I swear to you . . . I saw a . . . something . . . I swear it . . . a light . . . a blue, undulating light . . . like a ball. . . . It just hung in the air . . . and rolled and quivered. I knew it was all in my mind, but it was as real as you are right now, and I couldn't turn my thoughts away from it. And even worse, I couldn't shake off that feeling of imminence, as though my body were going numb because something very important was about to happen . . . and then I heard words . . . There was no face, no mouth, but words came from it so clearly, and all I could think of was *NO!*"

"What did you hear?"

" 'Let me through . . . please . . . let me through.' "

"Then what happened?"

"I panicked. I threw the script across the room. I turned up the radio on my nightstand. I waved my arm around and even began to beat it on the mattress to bring back my normal sensations."

"And the light?"

"It lingered, but it didn't speak again. Eventually, it dissolved, and the tingling and heartbeat seemed to go with it."

There was a silence in which he could hear her breathing.

"But all of this has nothing to do with the play," Alex insisted.

Felicia didn't speak, but her expression told him she was having difficulty accepting that conclusion.

He read the expression correctly. "Did this ever happen again?"

She glanced at him. A flicker of trepidation edged the look. She dropped her eyes to her fingernails.

"Well?" he persisted.

She nodded. "Once more . . . and it was while I was reading the play again . . . only it wasn't as strong. . . ."

"And did it speak?"

"No . . . it was only in a kind of transparent outline this time. I guess I didn't give it a chance. As soon as I heard the heartbeat and started to feel that strange sensation, I forced myself to move around quickly and to think of something else—anything else!"

There was a deep silence.

"What do you think it all means?" Alex asked her.

She shrugged her shoulders helplessly.

"Well," he murmured with a heavy sigh, "this whole story makes me very unhappy."

She felt an unexpected tremor of apprehension. "Why did you say that?" It was an anxious whisper.

He looked directly at her with an intensely troubled expression. In the thick silence, they could hear the whir of the electric clock on his desk. Then he broke suddenly into a wild, ridiculous grin. "Because I'd love to get that light—cut my electric bills down to zero." And he roared at his own silly joke, hoping that something so unexpectedly nonsensical would shatter the morbidity of the moment.

Felicia, however, was not fooled by his performance. She heard the faint, hollow note within his laughter.

"Alex," she said quietly, "you believe me."

"Oh, come on, baby," he protested, still grinning broadly. "Of course I believe you, but I don't think the experience is anything to get upset about. You had a dream, that's all."

"With my eyes open?"

"Yes, with your eyes open. And your reactions to it were as legitimate as anything connected to a sleeping dream. Haven't you ever imagined something for a moment with such clarity that you were sure you'd actually seen it?"

"But this wasn't a moment, Alex."

"So, two moments, three moments—what the hell's the difference how many moments? The point is, we all have these weird experiences. Look, last month I thought I felt a thread between this tooth and my gum . . ." He indicated his lower right canine. ". . . Under the tooth, right in the gum. It was so real. I saw myself drawing the damned thing out slowly until it was four inches long. Then I tugged a little too hard to pull it free, and my gum crumbled, and the tooth came out with part of my jaw. Scared the hell out of me, and I wouldn't chew on this side of my mouth for three days. But was there really a thread? Was there really a shattered jaw? And I was awake when it happened, Leesh, wide awake. Don't ask me why these things happen, but they do. Maybe we daydream crazy things because we're basically masochistic, who knows? At any rate, I grant you it's very unpleasant, but Christ, it's nothing to become permanently upset or scared about."

She stared at him, wanting to believe his explanation.

"Maybe the answer is really very simple," he added gently. "And no one has to be a psychiatrist to understand it: the pressure's on, it's a bitch of a part you're doing, you're an artist who'll settle for nothing short of perfection, and you're tired, baby, very tired."

"I wasn't tired before I started rehearsals . . ."

"Of course you were!" he interrupted. "What's the matter, have you forgotten how you didn't even want to read the play because you wanted to go on a six-month vacation after wrapping your last film?"

That was fact. She had been in Wyoming for eighteen weeks. And the rigors of such a heavy shooting schedule on location in an extremely primitive area of the state had drained her to the point of exhaustion. If the picture hadn't ended when it did, she was certain she would have been a case for hospitalization.

She considered this for a moment. It wouldn't be the first time someone's hallucinated in exhaustion, she thought, so he's probably right. There was a yielding sigh as she smiled acceptance.

She leaned against him. Everything felt all right again. She was glad she had told him.

"Why don't you take the day off and relax," he suggested lovingly. "I'll tell Mike to work around you. After what you've been through here—what I've done to you—you deserve it."

She looked into his eyes and smiled her approval.

He kissed her lightly on her nose; she flinched. "Oooo, sorry," he apologized quickly, examining the tender area. "See a doctor about this, please."

"It'll be all right, Alex."

"Please, Leesh." It was a sincere plea.

"All right," she agreed and snuggled closer.

"And if it'll help you," he added softly, "I'll work with you on the part. I don't think Mike will mind. It'll be like old times. Remember when you couldn't get Lydia in *Time of the Harvest?*"

She nodded.

"Don't you worry; we'll get this one too."

She pulled back and studied his face. "You know something, Alex Weintraub?" she said in that playfully matter-of-fact way so familiar to him. "I love you."

In answer, he brushed his lips lightly across her mouth.

"Mmmmmmm," she murmured, closing her eyes.

Her pleasure was terminated abruptly by the ringing of his telephone. Raising his hands in a gesture of helplessness, he pulled his head back and smiled at her.

"Let it ring," she whispered, pressing against him.

He tried, but the persistent jangle destroyed all further enjoyment of the moment. Easing away from her, he went to his desk.

"Mister Ross is on the line, Mister Weintraub."

"Put him on."

Felicia made a blowing kiss with her fingers and moved to leave. But Alex raised a hand, signaling her to wait one minute. She sat on the arm of the sofa.

"Hello, Mike," he said when Ross's voice came through, "I'm glad you called."

Felicia scowled comically at him.

He laughed and corrected himself. "Well, actually, I'm not glad you called at this particular moment, but as long as you did, we can talk because I was going to get to you in a few minutes anyway."

She nodded her approval.

"No, nothing serious. Felicia won't be at rehearsal today. She has a doctor's appointment. . . . No, really, it's not serious. Can you work around her, maybe do something with Dandy?" He jumped up. "What? . . . Well, where the hell is he?" Anger flashed through him. "Didn't he at least call in? . . . That irresponsible sonofa— Well, look for him. The last thing in the world I need is Dandy Maynor running around loose in Arizona. I'm coming down to the theater. . . . No, I'll be there in a few minutes. And look, if that character shows before I do, I want you to put him in his dressing room and to lock him up if you have to, but I want him to stay right there until I've had a chance to talk to him! . . . Right . . . O.K., see you soon."

He eased the receiver back into its cradle and traveled somewhere on an anxious and distant thought.

Felicia approached. She was concerned too.

Maynor was totally unpredictable. His aberrations were almost legendary. For one thing, he was frenetically promiscuous, desperately trying, in his own words, ". . . to ball every chic in this world before I'm thirty-five!"

She could easily imagine some teenage groupie jumping out of her drawers for the questionable thrill of being rammed by one of America's leading rock idols. And here in Phoenix, authorities would probably fall all over themselves pressing charges in so commonplace a matter as statutory rape. She asked a bit helplessly, "Is there anything I can do?"

He murmured, "No . . . thanks."

She sensed accurately his desire to be alone for a few minutes before going to the theater. She leaned in and kissed him gently on the mouth. "I'll call you tonight," she whispered.

When she had gone, Alex crossed to a small closet in a corner of the office. There he removed the bloodstained shirt and dropped it into a hamper. From there he went into his private bathroom and washed his hands and face. After replacing the towel on the rack near the sink, he combed his hair. Then he returned to the closet for a fresh shirt. He was so deep in thought that during all of this, there was absolutely no awareness of his movements. Finally, in the middle of stuffing his shirt into his pants, he dropped to the couch with an exasperated growl. This whole thing with Dandy Maynor had gotten to be too much. It was complicating everything. But there was no way to get rid of the bastard.

For the hundredth time he tormented himself: "Why did I ever undertake this production in the first place?"

For fourteen months prior to receiving the manuscript, he had refused to have anything to do with the theater. He wouldn't even talk to anyone connected with the stage. He had just traveled. And read. And eaten good food. And relaxed. It had been a trial run for retirement. And he had felt great. But then this play had come in the mail, unsolicited. Not even from an agent but from the author himself.

All factors considered, it was incredible that he should have read it. But read it he did. And he loved it instantly. All the former retirement decisions evaporated like a spot of alcohol in a summer sun. And he was committed. Totally, irrevocably committed. Despite the fear, despite the strange beating of his heart and the peculiar tingling that made his arm go dead, despite the light that he saw—the undulating blue light—the light that spoke to him without a face, without a mouth, Alex Weintraub knew that he was going to do this play, regardless of any and all obstacles that could possibly stand in his way.

5

When she left the mortuary and stepped into the warm, blazing, Phoenix morning, Sharon Kane experienced startling sensations. "It's cold," she thought aloud, "and everything's so silent and gray." But why? What was wrong? She didn't remember it this way. She remembered heat and clarity and color and sound. Has everything changed so drastically since I left? she wondered.

She stepped carefully off the sidewalk onto Calvary Chapel's diagonally slotted parking area. And it occurred to her suddenly that she was not feeling the action of her body. Strange. Inside the mortuary, she had felt her body. She had worked her jaws, used her eyes, concentrated on the movement of her organs as she had come alive. What was wrong? Certainly, that was it. "It's incomplete again," she murmured. "The process is incomplete."

And that was it. She had redirected her thinking as the people came charging into the chapel. She had directed her awareness to the task of blinding them to her presence.

Out here, she reasoned, that redirection is still in effect.

The correction was simple. Something like the fast shifting of focus through a camera's lens. Consciousness gathered; consciousness concentrated. Instantly, the sun felt warmer on her skin. Colors leaped at her. The smallest sounds of life came crashing at her eardrums. She looked at the activity going on everywhere.

"Oh, yes," she whispered, "this time it's going to be very different, indeed."

22

Her thoughts were interrupted abruptly. The Reverend Mr. Nelson came charging from the building, throwing the plate door open so forcefully that the air was slashed by the sounds of smashing glass. She turned her head sharply in his direction. Splinters floated and glistened in the sunlight like millions of brilliant prisms filling the morning with flashing spectrums. And behind it all, the minister—looking about, totally indifferent to the damage he had just caused. He turned toward her.

She allowed him to see. However, not as she actually appeared. He saw another form, another face. He saw a man.

As he hurried over, the scuffing and crunching of his shoes on the broken glass crackled like electricity inside her head.

"Excuse me, sir, has anyone come out of this building?" He was breathing hard.

"Only you."

"You haven't seen anyone else—? Anyone?"

"Only you."

"Have you been here long?"

"Yes."

"And you haven't seen *anyone?*"

"Only you."

"Stay here . . . please . . . don't leave. . . ." Then he broke away and charged around the west end of the building to the delivery entrance.

She remained where she was with no movement other than the slow turn of her head as she watched him go.

He was back soon. His right hand was pressed down hard against the top of his head; his mouth was a thin, tight line.

"You have cause to be distressed," she said.

"What?"

"I said, 'You're distressed.' "

"Look, sir, we've just had a—" He stopped abruptly. What was it? An accident? A theft? An occurrence? A *what?* "Look," he started again, "something's just happened inside, and it's hard to believe no one's come out . . ."

"You're the only one I've seen leave the building."

"Come inside with me, sir." It was almost an order.

"No."

The response startled him. No "I'm sorry" or "I'd rather not" or "I have an appointment"—none of the usual amenities. Just a cool, flat-out no. It irritated him. "I'm afraid I have to insist." He gestured toward the door and turned impatiently.

Sharon remained impassive, silent.

When she didn't respond, he turned sharply toward her and said, "See here, sir, I'm Reverend Paul Nelson and I'm . . ."

"I know."

"Know what?"

"Who you are."

"Well, then, come . . ."

"No."

He had never felt so uncomfortable and tense in another person's gaze. What was the matter with this man?

For the Reverend Mr. Nelson, this was a rare moment of impotence. He became curt. "Your name and address, please." As though a sudden demand could help him to regain the initiative. "This refusal to cooperate is absurd. I'm sure the police will want to speak to you about your attitude." He pulled a small pad and a felt pen from the inside pocket of his jacket and hoped his reference to the police would generate alarm.

Silence.

He looked up from his pad. "Now see here—"

"Revenant." Watching him evenly.

"What?" The voice had surprised him.

"A. Revenant." It was deep and almost a monotone now. "My name."

A chill went through him. "Oh . . ." He wrote quickly and in his confusion misspelled it *Revanint*.

"And your address," he snapped.

Silence.

"Your address, sir!"

His tone, sharp as it was, made no impression whatsoever. The heavy silence continued for another moment before the deep voice said, "I don't have an address in this city."

A thought occurred to the minister. "Mr. Revenant," he challenged suspiciously, "exactly what were you doing out here in this parking lot?"

And then there was a smile. For the first time, a slow, secret smile. "Some people might say I've been trespassing," she said. It had come in almost a whisper.

"Reverend Nelson. *Reverend Nelson!*" The cry screeched from the doorway.

He looked quickly toward the caller. It was Mr. Demerest's assistant, Curtis. "Please, hurry . . . It's Mrs. Rouche."

He glanced again at the stranger and withdrew slowly a few steps before turning to run.

She watched him until he was gone. As he entered the building, she murmured, "Soon, Paul . . . very soon." Then she gave her attention again to the stimuli that were still bombarding her senses. In an ordinary person, they would have prompted desperation and panic with their crashing, horrendous complexity. But in Sharon Kane, instead of being a shattering assault upon the nervous system, they were simply absorbed. Collectively. Individually. Simultaneously.

It was enjoyable. But it was time, also, to leave. She bowed her head and there was a moment of incisive concentration. As she touched each of her senses with a thought, she noticed an immediate reduction of stimuli. Soon, all five senses were regulated. She had blocked out a major percentage of each one's operating efficiency, exactly what normal people do unconsciously.

Calvary Chapel was located on Bethany Home Road, east of the Black Canyon Freeway. It was deeply recessed in a private, gently landscaped cul-de-sac. And magically it maintained an air of quiet seclusion, despite its proximity to two of the busiest traffic arteries in the city.

Without a second thought, she stepped directly from this serene seclusion into the hustling, febrile activity of Bethany Home Road.

Later, an eyewitness would recount excitedly to Chief Wheeler how this ". . . crazy broad causes the whole five car smash-up. It's a miracle nobody was killed. She walks right into the traffic. I'm tellin' ya, I seen the whole thing. She comes off the sidewalk like she's the Queen of England or somethin', like everything's supposed to stop just 'cause she plants her ass in the gutter. Wildest thing I ever seen.

I swear! She steps right in front of this gold and black
Porsche—guy's doin' about fifty—an' she turns an' looks
at him without battin' an eye. She just stands there. She
don't put up her hands, she don't scream, she don't move
her head an inch. I damn near shit in my pants an' this
broad's standin' there like she's at a church picnic. Well,
this guy in the Porsche . . . What? Yeah. 'Bout twenty-five
I guess. Goodlookin'. Long hair, blond, rich . . . whataya
talkin' about, he's gotta be rich. Who else drives a Porsche?
Do *you* drive a Porsche? Do *I* drive a Porsche? Huh? Oh.
Yeah, well—the guy in the Porsche slams his brakes so
hard he goes spinnin' right up on the sidewalk. Goddamn.
If anybody'd been standin' there, they'd be dead. Missed this
broad by an inch but is she bugged? No, man, she walks
right up to the car, gets in an' slams the door. I swear it.
Meanwhile, the Toyota right behind the Porsche? It crosses
those lines in the middle of the street . . . what're they
called . . . y'know what I mean . . . median . . . yeah that's
it, median . . . well, it crosses those lines in the middle of
the street, an' the Ford pickup goin' east knocks the livin'
shit out of it. Then the Corvair rams into the pickup, the
Mercury sails into the Corvair an' the Riviera comes bar-
relin' along like it's trying to fly over everything. But that
ain't the kicker. No. Wait. You won't believe this. The
broad an' the guy in the Porsche, y'know what they do?
They rip past that whole pileup an' head west like nothin'
ever happened! I mean, they go off together like she never
done nothin'. Crazy! The girl?—Pretty. In her twennies.
Blond. Round face. Good build . . . nice set o' lungs—I
always notice things like that—an' she had on a nice dress.
Red. Could have been a little shorter but it was nice. What?
Oh, hey, listen, I'm glad I could help. But I tell ya, that
was the wildest thing I ever seen. Hey, man, that broad's
a menace. You catch her an' you do everybody a favor if
you put her away for life . . . or at least keep her the hell
away from where *I'm* drivin'."

And that's exactly the way it had happened.

When she got into the Porsche, the young driver was
shaking with fury. "YOU FUCKING CRAZY BITCH—!"
he screamed. But she turned and showered a smile on him
that was golden. Her eyes were wide and flashing. Her

entire manner conveyed a sparkling effervescence that was totally disarming.

"Hi there."

"What?"

"Hey, we'd better get out of here before you find yourself in a lot of trouble." A simple observation.

Something like a metal door clanged inside his head. His fury was sealed off. For a moment, his throat bulged with choked invective. But that smile—that smile. It was so light and carefree—a laser beam of contagious merriment that immediately destroyed his resistance. The incongruity of the situation suddenly swept over him. Here was the cause of it all—a bitch who nearly got herself killed and who probably did get half a dozen other guys killed or at least wracked-up—telling him in the craziest, cool way that he ought to get moving before he found *his* ass in a sling. He threw his head back and laughed like music.

He shouted happily, "O.K." and then slammed the car into gear. "Let's split." And they gunned past that whole incredible disaster before anyone, besides that one witness, really understood what had happened.

The Black Canyon Freeway was only blocks away.

The speedometer needle hit seventy. They were there in moments. All the while, the young driver's fingers tapped the wheel rapidly in the excitement of escape. And the girl kept her eyes on the rear, urging him on with shouts and laughter.

"We're doing it. We're doing it! No one's behind us."

"Stay cool, baby, stay cool."

"You're fantastic, you know that?"

"You noticed, huh?" He was pleased.

They entered the freeway at eighty-five, heading north. He wove adroitly through heavy traffic until they broke into a stretch of clear highway. Then he dropped to sixty and looked at her for the first time with keen interest. He was impressed: short, shaggy, blond hair, a sweet face with a perky nose and glittering blue eyes, a full and marvelously curved body. Nice. This was the kind of woman he liked. He grinned at her as though his cheeks were being drawn behind his ears.

"Did you see it?" she was shouting excitedly. "Did you *see* it? There were five of them in that pileup!" She was laughing. Melodious staccatos. (He would remember later how he had caught an image of glass chimes being loved by a breeze.) Her hands were pressed together, forefingers between her teeth. And her head was thrown back in what seemed to be a moment of joyous prayer.

It made him laugh too. His head bobbed quickly in answer to her question. A visual chatter.

"It was unbe–liev–able! And the way you cut by it all—" Rippling, chiming laughter, hooking him deeper, pulling him in. "Did . . . did you notice that fat guy?"

"No . . . no . . ." Between spasms. "Which . . . which one?"

"The one near the bench . . . the one with the cigar . . . I thought he was going to choke on it." Laughter swelling from chimes to chords. "He . . . he couldn't believe what he was seeing . . . and . . . his eyes. His eyes! They . . . they were popping around like . . . crazy Ping-Pong balls."

From chords to melody. A wild song of hilarity. And he was caught completely in its rhythms. Rising on her crescendos, dropping on her breathless diminuendos.

Man, she made him feel like singing.

"Hey, baby—" he shouted an improvised gut-blues melody. "You're gonna stay with me."

"If that's the way you want it, baby," she shot right back, imitating, "that's the way it's gonna be."

It was so totally unexpected and yet so perfectly right. He gasped in delighted amazement. "Jesus, you're too much. I meant what I said, you're stayin' with me."

"And I meant what I said," she grinned and belted the line again: "If that's the way you want it, baby, that's the way it's gonna be."

"But first I'm takin' you to . . ."

". . . your house," she finished the sentence.

"No, first I gotta go to . . ."

". . . your house."

"What?"

"You're taking me to your house."

He found himself unable to refuse, even liking the idea. He laughed louder. He had just found a jewel. "You're out o' sight, you know that?" he exploded. "What's your name?"

"Sharon Kane." She was still bouncing and jerking to the silent beat of their improvised song.

"Bee–yoo–tee–ful! Mine's Dandy Maynor."

The bouncing didn't stop. It didn't vary a jiggle or a beat. But her voice dropped to an ominous murmur as she fixed him from the corner of her eye.

"I know."

PART II

The Meeting

WHICH WORLD

Which world do we live in—
        You and I?
Breathing what air?
Under what sky?
Fighting to live,
   But living to die?
Which world do we live in?

Which world do we live in—
        You and I?
Loving what truth?
Hating what lie?
Trying to laugh,
   But laughing to cry?
Which world do we live in?

Summer sun—
   And joys and years;
Autumn leaves—
   And tender fears;
Winter cold
   Brings death and then
New-born spring
   Says, "Try again!"

Which world do we live in—
        You and I?
Feeling what love?
Breathing what sigh?

Living a wish,
  But wishing life by?
Which world do we live in?
Which world do we live in?

Music and Lyrics by Dandy Maynor
Abelard Music Publishing, Inc.
  Copyright 1975
From the LP Album: "Dandy Maynor
  and the Fire And Air sing
  'Where And Why?'"
Eagle Records—Album #1803c

6

"I don't care what any English instructor has told you or will tell you," he was saying with an intensity that riveted his students, "if it's not what I'm about to say, it's wrong. Now I know that sounds cocky. I mean, after all, who's this Krozier to set himself up above everyone else? What makes him think he knows so much? Well, lovely people, I didn't make it up. It's just something that I happen to know along with a few thousand other students of literature, and it's fact and undeniable.

"Now if you're going to understand literature, then you've got to eliminate confusion at the outset. Know, first of all, that there are only two types of literature in existence. One is called *escape* and the other is called *theme*. Simple. Escape literature has nothing to say. It can be good or bad depending solely upon the imagination and skill of the author. What does it do? Only one thing. It attempts to take us away from our everyday lives and, for a few minutes, excite and entertain us.

"The other type, theme literature, attempts to immerse us in the realities of life in order to present some insights which, in the *lofty* wisdom" . . . (He touched the word with irony and drew the expected smiles from most of his avid listeners.) ". . . in the lofty wisdom of the gifted writer, will allow us to put together a little more of life for ourselves and maybe even achieve a little more happiness. Pretty good objective, right? Right."

Anthony Krozier: intelligent, drivingly energetic, forty-three and certain that he looked thirty-four.

And his students loved him. "Hey, man, get Krozier

35

for Lit 201. Work your ass off, and you'll be glad to pull
a B, but he's something else. Great teacher."

"For the rest of the semester, ladies and gentlemen,
you're going to be concentrating on the techniques of literature interpretation, and we'll start that the next time
we meet. Thank you and have a good weekend."

In a gesture of dismissal, he turned his attention immediately to the papers on his lectern.

The class began to fragment as he slipped a wide rubber-
band around the folder that held his notes. He was in a
hurry to leave. He hoped no one would come up to speak
to him today. Luck was with him; no one did.

Now, he strode across campus to the faculty parking lot.
From there he would drive directly to the Sunset Playhouse
to fret through another rehearsal of Alex Weintraub's new
production. However, although the rehearsals had started
a little more than three weeks ago, this new routine in
Anthony Krozier's life had actually started months before.
It had begun with a voice:

"Oze . . . Oze . . . Oze . . . zosezose . . ."

He had been reading *The Metamorphosis* again, preparing his notes for the next day's lecture: "Kafka understood
the forces that play upon us, the effects of lifeless routine,
the insensitivity of those we love—*these* are the major
contributors to the dehumanization and the death of
Man . . ."

"Kafka . . . Oze . . . Kafka . . . Oze . . . Kafffffff . . .
Koze . . ."

It had been so clear. He actually jumped as he heard
the words. No whisper. No eerie, distant and distorted
voice floating on dissonant melody. Nothing so gothic. Only
a clear sound—neither male nor female—and just a little
throaty.

"Oze."

He felt the skin prickle over his entire body. A cool
breath spread across his back to the nape of his neck. He
turned his head sharply with a quick intake of air. No
one. And then something else. Instantly, his head was filled
with pictures. Fragments of scenes. Flashes of objects. Bent
coins. Musical instruments. Ecstatic, screaming people. A
young singer. A desperate woman. It was a jolting profusion of knifelike images that seemed to lacerate his brain.
His hands came up quickly to hold his head together. But

the quick picture-pain lasted only a moment. Suddenly, it became totally meaningful. He started to write:

> Mrs. Oze is experiencing something she herself cannot understand. Objects are disappearing in her hands. She has no idea why or where they go or what happens to them. Sometimes they return, appearing in midair and dropping to the floor. Coins now bent with unrecognizable markings. Keys with new ridges, no longer capable of opening their locks but suggesting, now, nonexistent doorways. Sculptured figurines, their features reassembled, the nose where an ear should be, a hand protruding from the brow, an eye below the mouth . . .
>
> Although this began outside her control, Mrs. Oze finds now that she causes the disappearances to take place. It takes only a fleeting thought as she holds the object. At this point she becomes trapped by fear and desperation: fear itself causes the intrusion of the terrible thought—the less she wants to think it the more often it occurs—and desperation flares when nothing she does can cause the objects to reappear. . . .

He wrote through the night. Kafka was forgotten. It was a prodigious inspiration. The words flowed from him, outpacing his ability to get them on paper. It was as though he had to write as quickly as possible or they would disappear from his mind. Sentences slashed across the pages, sometimes leaping over lines. He was using long, yellow legal pads, tearing the pages off fiercely, scattering them at random over the table. Some floated to the floor; others creased or tore as he pushed them aside frantically. By morning he was exhausted. But after rubbing his bleary eyes with the heels of his palms and stretching the cramps from his bent body, he collected his night's work and counted sixty-three pages. Sixty-three pages! Where had it all come from? What could have prompted it? He was amazed and exhilarated. At various times in his life, he had planned to write something—Anthony Krozier was a man who felt he had much to say—but he had never actually undertaken a project. Until now there

had never been the right confluence of dramatic ideas.
But now, *now* . . . it was actually being done.

He looked at the pages and realized with a shock that
he held in his hands a full outline and the first act of what
could be a very exciting and compelling drama. At this
point, he didn't bother to consider the source of his inspiration. He merely marveled at its existence. Then, putting the
pages lovingly into a long pale folder and setting the folder
neatly on top of his desk where he would be certain to see
it immediately upon entering the room after school that
day, he jumped into the shower and washed the weariness
away with coconut-scented liquid soap and a cold, jet spray.

For the next five nights, the ferociousness of his creativity did not diminish. He couldn't wait to get to his desk.
And by the end of the week, he sat back in his chair and
gazed with numbed pleasure at a fully typed manuscript
that bore the title: *The Trespasser*.

"My God," he whispered ecstatically as he kissed the
manuscript, "I've done it. I've actually done it."

And then he danced around the room with a whooping
joyous abandon that he rarely permitted himself.

After a minute of this self-indulgence, he collapsed
on a couch. There he spent the remainder of the night,
staring at the light in the ceiling with a faint, slightly
twisted smile on his lips, the manuscript lying on his chest
and thoughts of grandeur floating disconnectedly around
in his head.

No less startling than the quickness with which the
play had been completed was the quickness with which
Alex Weintraub had accepted it. It was sent to Weintraub
because years ago Weintraub Productions, Ltd. had done
the works of Miller and Williams, whom Anthony admired
immensely. And because recently Anthony Krozier had
accidentally come across a *New York Times* interview in
which Alex had discussed his retirement and, among other
things, lamented the paucity of serious American playwrights.

Two weeks later, a letter of acceptance had arrived.

Three weeks after that, he received a two-thousand-dollar
option check and a signed Dramatists Guild contract.

Now, in his Toyota, he raced toward the Sunset Playhouse for another rehearsal of his play. Quickly down
Olive, staying on it as it changed into Dunlap, gunning

from Dunlap onto the Black Canyon Freeway to Camelback Road and racing east across Camelback to Sixteenth Street.

On the way, his mind raced as well: Don't think of Maynor today. . . . School . . . think of school. . . . Have to present a lecture for the book review series . . . Something good the old folks from Sun City will enjoy. . . . He smiled suddenly. Wonder what they'd think of *The Trespasser*. . . . Sex Scene alone would give them a collective seizure. . . . Oh, that Ohrman . . . a very special woman. . . . Must be thirty-six now . . . very juicy . . . and God, what a talent . . . Not like that idiot Maynor. . . . She's the play. . . . The play . . . the play . . . amazing how a whole thing like this gets put together . . . incredible. A formless drift of energy, an idea, is transformed into living personalities, wanting things, reacting, interaction. . . . A home is designed for them to live in. . . . Clothes are prepared for them to wear . . . and a veritable army of helpers, pamperers and attentive specialists all work their asses off—and for what? For nothing more than that original formless drift of energy with its incomprehensible and infinite capacity to stimulate and to excite. . . . Incredible!

He slammed his palm against the steering wheel suddenly with such intense emotion, the car veered sharply and almost went out of control.

The driver in the cruising Ford at his right pulled away quickly in near panic.

"Easy . . ." Anthony cried aloud to himself. He gripped the wheel tightly. "Easy, Tony my friend, easy. . . ."

7

"Ross. Mike Ross. Where the hell is my director?"

Alex's voice nearly echoed in the emptiness of the Sunset Playhouse.

"ROSS. MIKE ROSS."

"He's in one of the dressing rooms, Mr. Weintraub."

"Thank you, Richard."

Richard was the show's gofer, a gentle nineteen-year-old who was more than willing to run all errands, do all menial tasks and accept all kinds of abuse for seventy-five dollars a week and the questionable excitement of being close to a real live, Broadway-bound production. He stood stage center now, having run from the wing at the sound of his master's voice.

"Richard, has Dandy Maynor come in yet?" Alex hurried past him to the upstage stairs that led to the dressing rooms.

"No, sir."

Alex mumbled, "Junky-freak."

"Yes, sir."

"Not you, son."

"I know, sir."

Alex stopped on the stairs and smiled at him. His voice softened. "If he comes in while I'm with Mr. Ross tell him to join us, will you please?"

"Yes, sir." Richard grinned as though he were sharing a secret with God.

Alex turned and continued up the stairs.

Good kid, he thought. Should do him a favor and fire him. A light thought but he meant it. "Ross? Mike Ross?"

"Here, Alex." The voice was crisp and businesslike. "I'm in Elliot's room."

Alex strode down the dimly lit, dark-green corridor. He breathed self-consciously. The mildewed walls gave off a fetid dampness not unlike that of a public urinal. "God, it's always this way: behind the stage is the Behind of the Stage!"

"Elliot, we don't have time for that—!" he heard Ross demanding.

"Mike, I know what you want. Don't worry, you'll have it."

"But I *do* worry because you haven't shown me one shade of it yet." He wasn't shouting, but his tones were unmistakably severe.

"Gentlemen. Problems?"

"Hello, Alex. No. No problems. Just trying to get an understanding here."

"Hello, Elliot."

"Hello, Mr. Weintraub." Elliot Dark looked sullen. He was half-sitting, half-leaning against his makeup table. His hands were at his sides gripping its edge, his ankles crossed in affected casualness. A picture of poorly concealed tension.

"Am I intruding?"

"No, we're finished for now. C'mon. Let's go out to Gerard's for some coffee." He turned to Elliot. "Look, I'm sorry if that sounded strong to you, but we can't keep diddling around . . ."

Elliot pushed himself forcefully to his feet. "Jesus Christ, Mike, if you think I'm diddling . . . !"

"I didn't mean it that way," Ross cut in quickly. "Poor choice of words. I'm sorry. I just meant, we've got to nail this scene down—now."

"I told you we will!" He was the indignant artist now for Alex's sake.

Ross dropped a half-note of syrup into his voice.

"You're right, of course, El." Now exactly the right touch of capitulation. "It's just that I've had so many problems with this production, I'm afraid I get a little anxious when I see something missing that I feel should be there by now. I don't doubt your talent for a minute. You're one of the finest actors I've ever had the pleasure of working with. You'll give it to me, I'm sure."

After a beat Elliot grinned a bit sheepishly. He took Ross's extended hand. "You've gotta have faith, Michael."

"I have . . . in you—not in too many others, but I have in you."

Elliot gripped his hand a little harder and a little more warmly for that.

And Alex put his touch to the scene by concluding it. "I'd ask you to join us, Elliot, but there are some things I have to discuss with Mike. . . . I hope you don't mind."

"Not at all, Mr. Weintraub. You two go on. I was just going home anyway. Got some line study to do. I'm not as sure of the third scene as I'd like to be."

"Fine. I'll be seeing you again."

"Sure thing."

"See you tomorrow, El."

"O.K., Mike."

Chez Gerard was one of those small, elegant restaurants. Good food. High prices. Quiet gentility. Efficient service. It was almost always crowded. Now it was filled with luncheon trade. Nevertheless, Ross and Alex were shown immediately to a corner booth—a special attention that acknowledged the director's penchant for absurdly generous tipping. It wasn't until their coffee was before them that Alex finally spoke: "So why can't you handle Maynor that way?"

Ross stroked an eyebrow absently with a forefinger and studied his coffee.

Alex continued, "Elliot's going to kill himself now to give you exactly what you want."

"We'll have that scene tomorrow," Ross agreed.

"I know. You handle him like he's your personal puppet. You handle them *all* that way . . ."

"They're not puppets, Alex . . ."

"O.K., they're not puppets. Who cares what you call your actors. The point is: one way or another you get them to give you exactly what you want."

"So?"

"So what the hell's wrong that you can't keep that freak Maynor under control?"

"You've just said it, Alex—he's a freak. He's no actor—"

"Come on, Mike," Alex interrupted sharply. "No cop-out please."

"I'm not cop—"

"I've seen you handle every kind of situation, every kind of character this business can throw at you." Alex pressed. "Maynor's just another problem, and I refuse to believe he can't be controlled."

Ross flared. "Just let me lay this out for you, Alex, because I don't think you see the full picture."

"I see everything that I . . ."

"No you don't!"

"Would you like to order now, Mr. Ross?" The maitre d' was smiling down at them. He knew they wanted only coffee. But their voices had begun to carry, and it was his way of alerting them. The director was in no mood to side-step Alex's attack, and the maitre d's gentle reminder became an unwanted intrusion. "No, Henri," he said curtly, "we're just having coffee I told you."

Henri responded with a smile. "Yes, sir." But the slight pause before he said it and the slow condescending droop of his eyelids made the point of his interruption quite clear. He retired. Nothing more was necessary.

Ross lowered his voice. His anger was a muted snarl as he swung his attention back to Alex.

"Something's been wrong with this whole thing from the start, Alex. There's no rehearsal laughter. No camaraderie. No eagerness to approach the climactic scenes. It's as though we're being forced to step up to a mirror from which different faces are liable to stare back. It's weird! It's the weirdest piece of writing I've ever seen, and I'm doing every damned thing I can think of to make it work."

"Calm down, Mike."

"Then don't accuse me of copping out."

Alex's elbows were on the table, his hands folded just under his mouth. His eyes were fixed on Ross. The words came almost in monotone: "Poor choice of words. I don't doubt your talent for a minute. You're one of the finest directors I've ever had the pleasure of working with."

The cold humor in this expressionless parroting of his own manipulative speech to Elliot Dark checked Ross abruptly. There was a frozen moment as they stared at each other. Then Ross lowered his eyes and shook his head slowly, snorting a soft laugh.

"Christ, I'm *your* puppet."

"You're no puppet."

He looked up sadly. "Why did you do that, Alex?"

Alex relaxed, and his manner warmed perceptibly. "Because I realize we're both like Elliot Dark, Mike. We have a problem . . . both of us . . . and neither one of us has faced it the right way."

Ross let that register. Finally he nodded his head slowly in agreement. "All right, Alex, what do you want?"

Alex crossed his arms on the table and eased slightly forward on his elbows. His tone was measured. The words were spoken evenly: "I want to know why you can't control Dandy Maynor and whether or not he can do this role."

Mike Ross lifted his cup and took a mouthful of hot coffee before answering. The cup rattled slightly as he returned it to the saucer. He didn't look up.

"To begin with," he said with a sigh, "he can't be controlled."

"Yes he can."

"Well, then *I* can't control him, O.K.?"

"Why haven't you told me this before?"

"Because it was meant for this moment to make me realize it, I suppose."

"What do you propose, then?"

"Get rid of him."

"That's impossible."

"Why?"

"That's not your business."

"Then get rid of me."

"Is that what you want?"

"Jesus no! We have a play here—I don't know what to call it: drama, mystery, science fiction, horror—I can't identify it, but I do know it's very special and I have no intention of leaving it willingly. If you want me out, you're going to have to dump me."

"That's unthinkable. I happen to believe you're the one to do this play the right way."

"Then you have a dilemma," Ross said evenly.

"Not really. He can be put into line."

"If you can do that, Alex, you're a better man than I am."

Alex Weintraub smiled for the first time, a slow grin that said, "Was there ever any question of that?"

Ross understood. After a moment he shook his head slowly and broke into a grin of genuine appreciation.

"Now the second part of my question," Alex said.

"What was that?"

"Can he do the role?"

"It's not a matter of *can*. The question is *will* he. He's a strange kid, Alex. He's not interested in anything that's imposed upon him. Totally undisciplined that way. He hasn't put down more than a dozen lines. But if he decides to be interested in something, I imagine he can be quite dedicated. I've been trying to arouse that interest. But the play doesn't seem to excite him. Do you know where he is now?"

"No idea."

"That's my point. He's going to do things his way. Actually, if he ever decides to do the part, he won't be bad. It's as though the words were written for his mouth."

"That was Felicia's appraisal, too."

Alex made a quick decision. He would put a call through to the source of his problems and force an acceptance there of some responsibility in getting Dandy Maynor to conform to the demands of a stage production.

"Mike," he said determinedly, "we're going to end this nonsense right now."

"I'll be grateful, Alex." It was said very simply and honestly.

They looked at each other in silence for a long while, sharing some indefinable secret.

"I'm glad we've had this talk," Alex said. He felt sure about this director.

"It should have happened sooner," Ross responded. "I'm sorry."

"No apologies. But from now on we keep our lines open . . . and above all, you stay with this thing because, like-it-or-not, you're one of the master keys to whatever is going to happen."

They shook hands as though they were sealing a pact.

Back in his office, Alex hurried past his secretary. He shrugged off the enumeration of calls that had come in during his absence. "Not now, Marilyn, please." She was left protesting and nonplussed as he closed the office door in her face. He removed his jacket and flung it in the direction of the couch. Then his tie came open and his collar was loosened quickly as though he were preparing himself psychologically for a difficult moment. He had forced his energies to run high, and he was moving now on their crest.

Behind his desk, he flipped the intercom switch.

"Yes, Mr. Weintraub?"

"Marilyn, I don't want to be disturbed for any reason whatsoever, understand?"

"But Mr. Lehman called from New York, and he wants . . ."

"Later," he cut her off.

He opened the top drawer of his desk and removed a small, green, leather-covered box. He set it down gingerly as though it contained a bomb and, for the first time, allowed himself to slow his movements. Looking at the box, he wondered for a moment if he should talk to Maynor before making this call. Then, annoyed by his indecision, he snapped open the lid. Inside, there was a small assortment of personal jewelry and a gold-colored, leather address book. He flicked aside the jewelry and removed the book. He opened it to listings under the letter *J:*

V. J.
(212) 555-2433

He dialed the number and heard three signals before a man's voice answered with a repetition of the last four digits: "2433."

"I want to speak to Mr. Victor Jordan."

"Mr. Jordan is not to be disturbed now."

"Tell him Alex Weintraub is calling."

"I'll see if he'll take the call, sir."

He waited through a lengthy silence, snapping the box shut and impatiently tracing his fingers over the gold design.

"Mr. Weintraub." It was the quiet voice of a strong man, a man filled with imposing self-confidence.

"Mr. Jordan, matters here have taken a sudden and disturbing turn," he began quickly, intentionally omitting a greeting in a move to convey urgency. He waited for a response. There was none. "It's Dandy," he continued, and he was annoyed with himself for the quivering he felt in the pit of his stomach. "He's disappeared. Didn't come to rehearsal at all today and can't be found."

Silence. From surprise? If so there was no indication in his voice. The response when it finally came was as cool as before.

"What does that mean, 'can't be found'?"

"Exactly what it says: we don't know where he is. Possibly he's just decided to disappear, and if so, it's one more problem he's created in a long list of problems."

"I regret asking that question, Mr. Weintraub. My asking it automatically involves me more directly in your relationship with Dandy Maynor than I had intended."

"You *are* involved, Mr. Jordan."

"Oh quite, but not with its particulars. They're your concern. I've told you Dandy is your responsibility throughout this project. Nothing must happen to him and he must succeed. It's really quite simple."

It was a tacit threat. Said so casually.

Alex felt a light sweat spring to his back.

But he replied quickly. "That's not good enough, Victor." The man's Christian name was used for the first time in their association. It was a move to create imbalance. Had it worked? Had he heard something? A slight breath? "No one is capable of controlling your property," he continued without a pause, "no one—not the director, not his fellow actors, not even myself—and there's nothing more simple than that. You've admitted a mistake to me. Well now I'll admit one to you: it was arrogant of me to think I could fulfill my part of our agreement without some outside assistance. You're that assistance, and this whole thing will fall apart if you don't accept some responsibility yourself." He was moving. He wouldn't give Jordan a chance until he had completed the performance. "We're a week from previews and Dandy hasn't seen fit to memorize more than a dozen lines. There's no success possible in light of that kind of attitude. No one can open his head and pour the words in, Victor. And the list of other detrimental actions on his part that I could relate to you would keep us on this phone for an hour, something I'm sure neither one of us would enjoy. The next step is yours, my friend, despite our agreement, despite your clearly stated intentions. Nothing of the past applies now. Everything is on a different level, and that is a level of potential failure. Now, if the urgency of this situation isn't significant enough for you to modify your position, if the possibility of this project's failure isn't upsetting enough to cause you to make one concession that could easily avert it, then you must be prepared to accept the consequences of your remoteness. There is no one who can control Dandy Maynor except you, and without that control—and I mean *right now*— you can forget all of your carefully conceived plans for him, and you can be prepared to look defeat in its face."

It was a very bold speech. His palms were wet. His mouth was dry. A muscle in his cheek quivered. And he waited for a response.

There was a vacuum. The silence seemed interminable. For a fraction of a second, he was tempted to speak Jordan's name, to ask if he were still there. But such a move, he knew intuitively, would be a serious blunder. He clamped his teeth so tightly, his jaw muscles bulged. Fully another ten seconds passed before Victor Jordan responded. When he did, his voice—though cool and controlled—was unusually low.

"I'll be there tomorrow, Mr. Weintraub."

Nothing more. He heard the receiver slip gently into its cradle. There was an overwhelming sense of relief as he settled back into his chair.

"He's coming. He's coming."

He still held the telephone in his hand, tapping it lightly against his lips.

"I can't believe it."

His entire face became suffused with a bright and marvelous smile of self-satisfaction.

"Alex Weintraub, you dog, you handled that whole thing magnificently. Now we'll get this goddamned show into shape!"

And that's when it happened.

The first thing he felt was a searing, stinging slash across the palm of his left hand. It was as though the telephone were cutting him like a hot knife. He dropped the instrument instantly and clutched the injured hand before his face, gagging on the excruciating pain and expecting, of course, to see blood. There was none. Then as quickly as it had appeared the pain was gone. What remained was a wide, ugly purple welt. He began to pant.

He looked in bewilderment from his hand to the telephone.

It was writhing like a snake toward a small ebony figurine on his desk.

Alex gasped and leaped to his feet. The sharp movement upset his chair and sent it clattering behind him toward the window. He swung his attention in that direction. But he heard a brittle, peculiar explosion, a mixture of breaking glass and burning, sizzling wires that jerked him around again to the telephone.

The receiver had stopped its slithering. Now in the center of his deskpad, it stood slowly on its end. It quivered and vibrated like a living thing in agony.

Alex was transfixed.

"Look what you've done. . . ."

There was a voice coming from it. Strange, heavy, thick —not unlike that of a record on a very slowly revolving turntable. It didn't sound distinctly male or female. It could have been either. Or both. But the words were clear.

"Look what you've done."

Alex gasped and backed away after the initial shock. But he was unable to tear his eyes from the instrument.

"Aaaaggghhh . . . oh God help me."

He froze.

The receiver fell to its side and thrashed about in short snapping movements. Suddenly it brightened in color, intensifying, heating steadily, quickly, until it glowed a pulsating, fiery red. It began to melt. First the receiving end.

"Help me . . . Help me!"

It shriveled and twisted and ran slowly like a wax figure in a flame.

Then the handle, bending, drooping, joined by the mass from above, ran down to cover the mouthpiece.

"Look—what—you've . . ."

The voice became garbled and muffled as the receiver collapsed. Soon there was nothing left of the instrument but a charred, twisted lump of unrecognizable matter, smoldering like wet grass after a fire and filling the room with the acrid odor of burned plastic.

Alex retreated around and away from his desk. He inched backwards, never taking his eyes from the offending residue. He bumped into a nearby armchair and settled trancelike into its softness.

He was ashen.

8

"Hey, where are you, baby?" Dandy laughed brightly. "Lost you there for a minute. What were you thinkin' about?"

Sharon Kane turned dazzling blue eyes upon him. She answered peculiarly, "A telephone."

The Porsche was far from town. They had left the freeway, stretching a trail of dust behind them as they cut across unpaved desert roads.

The land was lean and tough: distant mountains and hills but mostly a bare, flat face with gully scars and pimples of volcanic rock. Attractively ugly. Strangely fascinating. Deadly.

Sharon crooked an arm over the open window frame of the car door and rested her chin on the back of her hand . . . attractive . . . fascinating . . . deadly.

They rode in silence. Only the rhythmic hum of the engine and the steady crunch of the tires intruded.

Sharon was looking at nothing in particular. She was feeling the totality.

"Gets to you, doesn't it?" he observed finally.

Without moving, she murmured, "More than you'll ever know." Then she turned sharply and added with a twisted smile, "You knew what I was thinking."

"Wasn't hard. Gets to me too."

"Wait'll *I* get to you," she offered cryptically.

He laughed. "Lady, you're something else, you know that?"

"Uh huh," she agreed.

The strangely simple way she had said it tickled his insides. He laughed delightedly. "Great God Almighty, you're never gonna get away from me alive, you know that?"

"Uh huh." That same peculiar agreement. Again it in-

51

fected and, this time, he broke into ringing laughter in which, slowly, she eventually joined.

By now, Dandy was completely taken with his passenger's remarkable self-assurance. She wasn't fawning. Apparently, his accomplishments meant nothing to her. He had earned five platinum, and fourteen gold, records. He mentioned them to her. There was no response, and he found this very intriguing.

Another thing: She was a welcome relief from the tedium of that goddamned play. That play—

Why had Mr. Jordan done this to him anyway? Everything was goin' along so fine. Last single bustin' the charts . . . twenny-nine weeks . . . ten weeks in the number one spot . . . "Liza's Love" . . . Oh, what a sweet song. An', man, that last concert in Chicago . . . forty-eight thousand climbin' all over themselves . . . $600,000 gate . . . eighty percent his . . . the sounds, the space, the lights, the bodies. . . . Man, when he sang "I Knew a Manchild," there wasn't a sound in that whole fuckin' stadium. . . . Man, that quiet was like the whole world holdin' its breath an' he was so on, his voice was a velvet knife, cuttin' through all their shit an' spreadin' him softly over their souls— An' they knew it too, man, they knew it. An' they *told* him they knew it. When he finished those last lines:

> I never could see the manchild;
>   Never could see . . . never.
> Alone,
> Unknown to my empty eye,
> Coloring gentle, coloring shy,
> There to be known;
>   But I passed him by . . .
>   Dull . . . blind!
>   Dull . . . blind!
>   But, now, in my later years I find
>   The face of the manchild touching
>   my mind,
> And I cry . . .
> Softly, in myself, I cry;
> There to be known
>   But I passed him by . . .
> So, now, my friends, too late,
>   I cry. . . .

that whole stadium had welled slowly, an imperceptible ripple that grew and ran and swelled and surged and topped itself, building, feeding itself, growing quickly into an all-obliterating tidal roar of understanding and appreciation. And he could see the people beyond the lights. He could see their glistening faces and their damp sparkling eyes, and he could see the adoration, he could actually *see* it—girls, boys, men, women—everybody. And, goddamnit, if there'd been cats and dogs and horses and copulating elephants there, he'd have had them too. Because it was right. The night was right. An' it was so out-o'-sight, so all-fuckin' powerfully, fantastically out-o'-sight that . . . oh, shit, how he missed it!

"Longing's always the first step in making things happen," she murmured mysteriously.

"What's that?"

"Nothing."

But he had heard her. And the words dug into him. He looked at her from the corners of his eyes.

"Hey, you were inside my head."

"What's good for the Dandy gander . . ."

They broke into laughter.

"I think we're gonna have some very interesting times together," he grunted happily.

Her answer was simple: "I promise you that." Then she turned away to rest her chin upon her hand again.

They had turned a bit sharply off the road, taking a narrow, almost totally hidden path that now jounced them over large river rocks in the bed of a dry wash. On the other side, they drove slowly up a steep rise.

"We're here," Dandy announced.

The Porsche passed behind a section of a hill. It completed its climb and rolled to a stop at the rear of a large old house. Four scrubby-looking mongrels, instantly howling and yapping, came charging toward them from another building. Dandy leaped from the car to greet them. He made loud, playful dog-sounds. Then he dropped to his knees and let them drive him to the ground where he rolled in the dirt and laughed wildly as they danced all over him.

Sharon watched.

"Dan the Man!" The voice came from a distance.

Dandy got to his feet without bothering to brush the

dust from his clothes. "Hey, Goose, how's it goin', man?" He was looking toward a strange tall structure approximately fifty yards away.

It was something like a watchtower with a partially completed shingle roof, one end of which tapered into a suggestion of an eagle's head.

"You ever gonna finish that thing?"

"Don't really matter much, does it?"

"Guess not." He turned toward Sharon. "Goose Berneau. Fantastic lead guitar. C'mon, I'll show you the house."

"Hi, Dandy."

He turned to greet two lovely young women who had just come from the big house. They were dressed in faded jeans, T-shirts and sandals. One was blond with long straight hair parted in the middle. The other was obviously the younger—a sweet, oval face with wide-set, alert brown eyes, full lips, and a perfectly straight little nose. Her hair was very short and as jet black as her skin. The blond was about thirty; the black girl, nineteen.

"Good to see you girls."

They approached the car. Each stopped and brushed Dandy's mouth with a light touch of her tongue. Nothing sexy. As innocuous and meaningless as a peck-kiss.

The dogs were still barking and yapping and climbing all over each other to get at him.

"Nolan! Beau! Stop it now," the black girl ordered. Despite the force of her tone, though, she didn't sound harsh at all.

"Sheba . . . Angel . . . get away . . . all of you," the blond girl added.

At the sound of the two voices the dogs seemed to hesitate.

"Go on . . . go on now . . . get on over to Goose. Goose. Hey, Goose, will you call them, please?"

"Here, Beau. Nolan. Angel. Sheba. Come on, babies! Come on to Goose."

They tore off in his direction with a thunder of barks.

Dandy was grinning.

"Nancy, Lorna, this is Sharon . . . she's gonna be my lady." The announcement was clean and simple. Sharon accepted it. "Nancy an' Goose are makin' it, an' Lorna goes with Josh. You'll meet him later; he's busy fixin' up the bunkhouse like a goddamned recording studio."

"Hi," the salt-and-pepper beauties greeted her. It came out brightly, warmly, overlapping so closely it seemed almost in unison.

"Hi," Sharon answered.

"Goin' somewhere?" Dandy asked them. They were carrying shoulder bags, and he knew they tolerated these encumbrances only when they left the immediacy of "The Ranch," as the place was called.

"Pioneer Village. Want to come?" Nancy asked.

"Nope."

"O.K., see ya."

As they climbed into the cab of an old battered pickup, Lorna shouted back, "Hey, what happened, no rehearsal today?"

"Somethin' better came up." He grinned and glanced at Sharon. "Oh, hey," he added suddenly, "try to be back early. We're goin' to the Sorry Spike for steak an' lobster." Now, why had he said that? He didn't know where the Sorry Spike was. As a matter of fact, he had never even heard of the place. Obviously, from his words, it was a restaurant, but he had never been there. That realization struck him just as soon as he had said the words. For a fraction of a second, he wanted to call the girls to cancel the appointment. But something stopped him. It was nothing he could understand—just a sudden swelling of the larynx as though the idea had solidified and lodged there. Instead of calling, he coughed lightly four or five times. By then, the pickup was trailing away in the usual swirl of desert dust.

That was troubling. He was stroking his throat with two fingers when he turned toward Sharon. Her wide blue eyes were watching him with such seemingly innocent interest that his concern dissolved instantly, and the lump in his throat went with it.

"C'mon," he said brightly. "Show you the house."

The tour began.

He walked her past a rear door with a badly torn and bent screen. To the right was the kitchen.

Sharon's interest took in everything. She fingered vitamin bottles. She even opened one to study and to squeeze a resilient E capsule as though it were an entirely new and strange object. She smelled an orange rind. A tentative flick of her tongue at the pulp produced a deep, throaty sound of pleasure. She opened closet doors, counter drawers, jar lids. Wherever she could inquire, she poked and studied and tested.

When she had finished investigating the kitchen, Dandy grinned at her. "You're crazy, you know that?"

"But you like me."

"You're right, I like you."

They held each other in a gaze for a few moments.

"C'mon, there's more house," he said suddenly. And, laughing, he pulled her from the room.

They went down a long carpeted corridor.

At the end, the hallway forked into two bedrooms. Both were models of disarray. And proximity to the first one—even before she entered it—jolted her so strongly that she actually gasped. It was the smaller of the two, and it was called the D.D.D. (Dynamite Drug Drop), the H.H.S. (Happy Head Shop), the F.F.P. (Friendly Family Pharmacy)—naming the room this way had become a game, and each day produced a new series of letters.

This was where all of the members of the Maynor clan dropped in to drop out: a stereo system provided music, and assorted jars held a wide assortment of drugs.

He was watching Sharon closely now. "What d'ya think of the place so far?" he asked cautiously.

"I get feelings."

"Like what?"

"Things are seething in this room."

Seething. He had never thought of it that way. This was supposed to be a place of relaxation. Seething?

She stared at him. He began to feel warm in her gaze. Suddenly, he felt like jamming his fingers between her legs, sliding them in and out of hidden orifices. He felt his pulse quickening. But he checked himself when he thought he heard the word "later" somewhere in his mind, and all he did was extend his palm to invite the smooth, soft touch of her hand. Their fingers entwined.

"Show me more," she whispered.

He nodded.

Dandy's room was across the hall. It was spacious with an entire wall of windows admitting the brilliant Southwest sunshine. And it was even more of a disaster than the small, drug room.

Sharon ignored the litter. She walked directly to the small, electric piano in the far corner.

Although he hadn't written a song since becoming associated with the play, he couldn't bear to be without his instrument.

She touched it, feeling his intense love for the music it had produced. Yes . . . this would be her handle—her means of manipulating him—this and her body.

"Show me more," she said.

He extended his hand again, and she took it.

It took two full hours but, in the end, she had seen and studied the entire ranch, a fifteen-acre spread with three adobe buildings and a collapsing wooden structure that had once been a blacksmith's shop.

Now, with the tour completed, he looked at her and said simply, "O.K., you've seen it all. Like it?"

"Uh huh," she answered, gazing steadily into his eyes.

"Have I missed anything? Is there anything else you'd care to see?"

"Only your body."

"It's yours," he answered happily. "Let's get into the sack."

And they did—for the rest of the afternoon, almost to the minute when it was time to leave for the Sorry Spike.

9

"That's right," he was trying to keep his voice down, "I want every man on the force looking for her, but I don't want a single word of this to leak to those reporters outside."

"Right, Chief, but what's she done?" Sergeant Clemmens insisted.

"You heard me, she's a missing person."

"We've had thousands of missing persons, Chief, but there ain't a one that's been singled out this way—"

"Cut it," Matt Wheeler snapped angrily. "Just do what you're told."

"Yes, sir." Clemmens spun about and raced from the office.

Alone now, Matt sagged back against the high rest of his swivel chair with a troubled sigh. He rubbed the weariness from his eyes and face and then took a notebook from his desk. He scoured its pages as though he were searching for a key—a missing point—something that would connect everything magically into an understandable and acceptable explanation of what had occurred. It wasn't there. His notes covered every question he had asked of everyone at the mortuary. According to the black booklet before him, no one had offered a thing of real value.

"It doesn't add up," he growled.

He riffled quickly through the notebook until he came

to a page headed: Joe Lamspock. He read the account again. It was the eyewitness description of the five-car pile-up outside the mortuary. It contained an accurate description of Sharon Kane as the party who had caused it all.

So the dead girl was seen walking inside and outside the mortuary. Ridiculous. Someone's got to be impersonating her, and the corpse has got to be hidden somewhere inside that chapel.

There was a knock at the door.

"Come in."

It was Sergeant Clemmens. "Chavez just brought this in. Said you wanted them immediately."

He laid some papers on the desk and exited.

On leaving the mortuary, Matt had asked Chavez and two other patrolmen to inspect every inch of that chapel. This was their report.

He ran through it quickly, praying there would be the all-important reference to a corpse discovery.

Of course, there was nothing. A complete, minute description of every foot of the room, tests for loose flooring, hidden compartments, secret chambers. But there was nothing.

"Conclusion," he said aloud. "If there is no body and Sharon Kane was seen by reliable witnesses to be walking around and talking . . . I can't accept it!" But the inference swept over him again. "If this is true, then in some way, death has been altered."

Suddenly he was struck by a startling question. Suppose she *has* come back to life, how did she get through that waiting room without being seen?

The answer took the implications of his reasoning into deeper dimensions. He was shocked by his own insight. He sank into his chair. Holy Jesus, if a dead girl can walk around with formaldehyde for blood and with clamps in her throat that won't even allow it to flow, then there's no end to the things she can do. And whatever else they are, they'll surely go beyond any understanding of life that I've ever had!

It took him a while to recover from that. He tried to imagine things that a dead Sharon might be able to do, none of which he could actually grasp. They were like wispy shadows, slipping away before he could ever give them the substance of understanding.

"If this is true, I'm afraid to think what may happen if and when I find her," he admitted softly.

His telephone rang.

He jumped.

"Chief Wheeler here."

"Matt, it's Howard."

"Yes, Howard." He felt concern immediately. "How are you?"

"I'm still not sure. . . . I keep seeing her face."

Matt could feel his friend's fear.

"I wish there were something I could do to help you."

"Put her back in her grave where she belongs."

"If that's where she belongs, that's where I'll put her, Howard." He made it clear that he still didn't believe.

There was a weighty silence.

"Howard, what's the matter?"

"Nothing. . . . I just feel stupid asking it."

"What?"

"Nothing. . . ."

"Ask it, Howard."

"Well . . . will you . . . are you . . . what are you planning to do tonight?"

"It's my anniversary. Why?"

"Never mind. . . . It was nothing. . . . Congratulations. How many years is it? I've forgotten."

"Twenty-seven. And thank you. Why did you want to know what I'm doing tonight?"

"It doesn't matter."

But Chief Wheeler knew it did matter. It mattered very much. Because Howard was terrified and not strongly enough recovered to endure being alone.

"Why don't you join us?"

"No, no . . . thanks anyway, Matt."

"Come on, don't be silly. We'd love to have you help us celebrate. Both of us."

There was hesitation, a relenting pause.

"You sure you won't mind?"

"Howard, believe me, if I did I wouldn't ask you."

"Thank you, Matt," with a short sigh so intense, its relief was almost palpable.

"Tell you what, Howard, you meet us at seven o'clock, O.K.?"

"Gladly."

"You know where the Sorry Spike is?"

"I'll find it."

"Good. See you there."

10

"It was uncanny, Leesh," Alex was explaining softly to Felicia Ohrman. "I'll remember it for a long time. That telephone was alive."

"I'll tell you what you told me, Alex—you're tired, tense . . ."

"That's true. But still I saw it, and I heard it." He took another slow sip of his vodka tonic.

They were hidden away in a corner booth.

It was a quaint bar. Waitresses in abbreviated western outfits whipped their order pads from little holsters like fast-draw gunfighters. And the two bartenders, looking like grizzled prospectors, filled glasses with a pleasant dexterity that was inspiring.

After recovering from the initial shock of his telephone experience, Alex had left his office quickly. He wanted distance from the incident.

Marilyn his secretary was disturbed and puzzled by his subdued yet urgent instructions to call the telephone company for a replacement of the smoldering instrument on his desk.

In the elevator, going to the lobby, he stood in a corner, something he rarely did. He preferred always to be the first one out. Now he seemed light-years away. And when the car reached the lobby he hurried past dawdlers and pushed the glass doors of the building open as though fresh air were salvation.

Outside, Alex paused under a palm tree to collect his thoughts. He stood there for almost ten minutes, reliving the experience. There was no way he could make any sense of it. And the more he dwelled on it the more perplexed he became.

Suddenly, he felt a strong desire for company.

He thought of Felicia. He needed to talk with her. However, the prospect of using a telephone just then was not particularly attractive. Instead he drove to her apartment, preferring to take a chance on finding her at home.

She wasn't.

He cruised all the way to the eastern end of Tempe with his radio on loudly. He was passing time. Periodically, he examined his palm. The purple welt was disappearing. By the time he finished driving around and then back to Felicia's apartment, it was gone completely. And it was seven o'clock.

He pressed the door button. The chimes rang softly.

"Be home."

This time she was.

"Alex, how funny. I had a feeling you'd be here tonight." Her greeting was warm and loving. "I'm glad I was right."

She kissed him. His response was decidedly less than expected. Stepping back, she looked at him quizzically.

"How's your nose?" he asked a bit uncertainly.

Her fingers went to her face. "Fine," she answered. "The doctor said I'm all right." She studied him for a moment. "But you didn't come here to ask me that, did you?"

"Offer me a drink," he said.

"Certainly." And she hurried to a cut-glass decanter of scotch that she kept inside a corner highboy.

"Water?"

"Please."

He inspected his hand once more. Nothing. He couldn't believe it. He felt his nerves going taut again. However, when the scotch was seeping through him, giving him a feeling of spreading substance, he relaxed enough to look straight at her and say, "Either I'm going psychotic or I've just had the most amazing experience of my life."

She sank wordlessly to the hassock before him and listened with rapt attention as he related the main points of the incident. His description was vivid and detailed. When he was through, she stood before him and said simply, "Take me somewhere."

"What?"

"Come on." Her manner was cool and crisp.

"Leesh, don't you understand . . ."

"I understand that we should both go someplace where we can find noise and people and a good bartender."

"Felicia—"

She insisted, "Come on, Alex."

And as he protested, she led him from her apartment to her car.

She refused to discuss the matter further. Instead, she maintained a smooth running chatter about everything from the tenderness of her nose to the golden fingers of Mr. Norman, a marvelous beautician she had just discovered, a man ". . . with a sense of line that would have given Michelangelo an erection."

She knew exactly what she was doing.

He understood, too. He let her drive without any more protestations. And once inside the cocktail lounge, as the hostess was drawing out the table to enable them to slide into the booth, he whispered appreciatively, "You're an angel, and you could charm the balls off a gorilla."

"Patience, Kong, we'll get to that later," she had whispered with a seductive leer.

Now they were on their third drink.

For awhile, her banter had prevailed. At no time, though, did it ever completely blot out the picture of that telephone. And from time to time, the details emerged unexpectedly, flashing suddenly at an inadvertent word or phrase.

Eventually, the entire subject surfaced again. It had to. The final fillip was the incessant ringing of a telephone behind the bar.

When he first heard it, Alex's eyes jerked in its direction. He checked himself, though, and swung his attention quickly back to Felicia.

She had caught the movement and was watching him closely over the rim of her cocktail.

He tried to sustain the drift of their conversation, but the continual ringing worked like a jackhammer, cracking its continuity and lifting its veneer implacably to reveal the basic thought they were trying to suppress.

"It was uncanny, Leesh. I'll remember it for a long time. That telephone was alive."

"I'll tell you what you told me, Alex—you're tired, tense . . ."

"That's true. But still I saw it, and I heard it." He took another slow sip of his vodka tonic and seemed relieved when the bartender finally lifted the receiver. "There must be an explanation."

She knew from his tone there was no way to avoid the subject any longer. So she jumped in boldly. "Alex," she said, "I have a feeling that in some insane way what you've experienced is connected with the play."

He protested immediately. "Oh come on, Leesh . . . that's preposterous." However, the memory of his own strange play-reading visions hooked into the weirdness of the telephone incident now and wouldn't let go. He was looking directly into her eyes, weighing the connection.

She had no desire to discuss this at length, and she sensed that he was not in total disagreement with her. So, leaning forward in her intense way, she restated her conviction merely by insisting, "Let's just get this damned production finished and behind us and—"

"Care for another drink, sir?" It was their cowgirl waitress.

The interruption could not have been better cued or more genuinely welcomed if Felicia had conceived it herself. She turned and looked up at the young, pretty girl. "Has anyone ever told you, you have absolutely marvelous timing?"

The waitress nodded her head vigorously with a happy, comical grin. "My boyfriend. Three or four nights a week. God, he's an animal." Then with bubbling brightness she asked, "Want another drink now?"

They laughed appreciatively. The mood began to shift. Their surroundings were slipping into focus again.

"No. I think we've had it," Alex responded.

"You're kidding. You looked like you could stand a good time—both of you!" She said it almost like a chirp.

And they laughed again at her delightful effrontery.

"She's right, Alex . . ." Felicia agreed brightly. "Let's make a night of it."

Actually he was ready too, and her happy decisiveness was just the needed incentive. But he warned her playfully, "You haven't eaten anything, have you?"

"No."

"Neither have I. Two more of these and we could be on our respective asses, you know."

"Hey, that's great . . . 'respective asses' . . . I never heard it called that before," the waitress commented appreciatively. "Classy."

That was the clincher. They looked at each other and beamed.

"O.K.," Alex agreed, "get us a sandwich or something and another round of the same."

"Sorry. No food served in here. But if you want, I'll put your name on the waiting list for the dining room, and you can take your drinks in there with you."

"How long a wait?"

"I'll put it at the top," she offered with a conspiratorial wink. "After all, you've been here an hour already, right?"

"You're a very accommodating young lady," Alex said.

"And that's something my boyfriend *complains* about."

Felicia was surprised. "Why should he complain about that?"

"Claims he knows a hundred other guys who say the same thing . . . but he's always such an exaggerator! You said another round of the same, right?"

"Right," they echoed together.

"And the name's Weintraub," Alex added. "Makes no difference how you spell it as long as you get us a table."

"Great." And she was off in a hip-swinging skip of energy that brought smiles to everyone she passed.

Alex asked, "Can't you just see her in *Butterflies Are Free?*"

"Perfect."

He reached across the table and took both of her hands. "All right, Miss Ohrman, let's make a night of it."

"And I don't want to hear another word about the play or telephone or anything that won't lead us directly to bed." It was a velvet demand, warm with promise.

"Just one thing—"

"No."

"Please. I don't want it to come as a surprise. Just let me prepare you, and then we'll enjoy the rest of the evening, I promise."

She looked at him with playful skepticism. His smile was so reassuring, she had to relent. "O.K., mister, make it fast."

"The man I was speaking to when that telephone thing happened will be here tomorrow."

"So?"

"I don't know how long he'll stay, and there's a chance you may meet him."

"Again, so?"

"If you do, I want you to be ready for him."

"Why, is he a gargoyle?"

"In a way. He's the reason I can't get rid of Dandy Maynor."

"Ohhhh?" She was interested now.

"His name is Jordan—Victor Jordan—and I owe him."

"Owe him what?"

"I'll just give you a sketch now and fill in the particulars at another time. Four years ago when *Busy Baby* was a hit, I thought it would make a good film."

"It was terrible."

"True and that's part of the story. I went to the studios for financing, and I couldn't come to terms with them. For their money, they wanted everything, especially control. In effect, I'd be working for them. So, I decided to get backing elsewhere, and I went out scouting. The budget was a little over five million. And I was having trouble raising it. Well, I was having lunch with Fred Blauder one day— ever meet him?"

"I don't believe so."

"One of the vice-presidents of United Insurance. Knows everybody with money. Well, he asked me if I wanted the five million in bits and pieces or in one lump. And that's where I made a mistake. I said one lump if it were possible and . . ."

She concluded the sentence: "He introduced you to Victor Jordan."

"Exactly."

"But why was it a mistake?"

"Because when you have a lot of little investors, you're never deeply obligated. But the loss of five million dollars to one person is another story."

"Did you lose all of it?"

"The film went over-budget and came in finally at five million seven. Jordan put up the extra money without saying a word. After its full run and television sale, we were out three million eight."

"Alex," she asked suddenly, seeming to pick up a vibration of something, "are you afraid of this man?"

He leaned forward and toyed with one of her long fingernails. He wanted to be perfectly honest now—with Felicia
and himself—but he hadn't really faced that question yet,
and he wasn't quite sure that this was the time to do so.
Nevertheless, he offered the most honest response of which
he was capable at the moment.

"I don't believe so . . . he's a most unusual kind of
person, though, and I'd be lying if I didn't admit I'm being
affected in some way that I don't completely understand
or like."

She was surprised. "Alex," she whispered, "you *are*
afraid of him."

"What makes you think so?"

"Well . . . I . . . I've never seen you this way."

"Maybe you're right. I really don't know."

"Why are you telling me all of this now when you refused to discuss any part of it this morning?"

Again he took one of her hands. "Because I've made an
important decision. It happened only a moment ago when
you said, 'No more talk about anything that won't lead us
directly to bed.' I suddenly remembered all the bed times
we've had . . . and the good times."

"That's terrible," she said fondly.

He grinned and continued, "And I thought, 'You've always been so right together, Alex. Marry her.' "

She was stunned. Delightfully so. "God," she said, "you're
full of surprises tonight, aren't you?"

"So," he concluded, "when this whole thing is over,
we're going to be married and get into bed for one whole
year, and I want it all to start off cleanly and honestly
right now."

She laughed warmly.

"Oh, you marvelous nut!" And she squeezed his hand
hard. "I love you even more than Elizabeth Browning loved
Robert, and I'll get into bed with you for *two* whole years,
but we're never going to be married."

"Yes we will."

"No we won't."

"Don't you want to?"

"Nope." She was smiling. "And when the time comes,
you won't want to either."

He gasped playfully. "That only makes me wonder now

how well you really do know me. I said we're going to do it, and we will."

"Whatever he says you're going to do, Ma'am, you can believe you're going to do it. Truthfully, I couldn't say no to him for anything." The waitress had returned with their drinks.

Alex grinned. "How do you like that for an endorsement?"

Felicia was laughing beautifully.

"Guess what. I have a table for you in the dining room if you're ready."

Feeling particularly happy now, they eased from their booth, picked up their drinks and followed their sassy little waitress as she wound her way deftly through the crowded room.

11

Dandy and his friends were working on each other as they sat around their table at the Sorry Spike. They had been drinking double Margaritas since arriving. Their wits and spirits were well-oiled. And uproarious laughter punctuated every thrust.

Goose was complaining about Josh's fondness for toothpicks: "I've known this guy for five years now, an' I ain't never seen him without a fuckin' toothpick! More wood passes through his stomach than food! He got his ass thinkin' it's a goddamned lumbermill."

Josh fired back: "Could fart a forest roots an' all, man, an' it'd *still* sound better'n that shit you call singin'."

Dandy nearly slipped under the table, unable to catch his breath.

The Sorry Spike was a new restaurant. Its owner, Ben Canto, was almost feverishly dedicated to making it a success. Certainly, like any businessman, he wanted profit, but more than that, he wanted desperately to prove something.

Ben was part of a long tradition of restaurateurs. His great-grandfather, Guido Canto, had started it all in 1870 when he opened the Golden Spike, Phoenix's first, real restaurant.

Over the years, while the Golden Spike retained its distinctive character, it grew and expanded to become the most respected steak house in the entire West. There had never been discord in the family over the business . . . until Ben Canto urged his father, Jorge Canto, to open a branch in the northwest corner of the city because his own demographic study had indicated impressive movement in that direction. The older man had rejected the idea flatly. The northwest would never develop properly, he insisted. Besides, all store expansion would have to continue exclusively on the land of the existing facility. That's the way it had always been done.

Actually, there was another reason for this resistance: Ben was sustaining a relationship with a young woman "of questionable character." And Jorge Canto wanted an end to it.

Ben had met her during one of her infrequent trips to Phoenix to visit an aging aunt.

Jorge wanted to meet the girl. He arranged to meet her while on business in Los Angeles. And during that meeting, there was something about her that disturbed him—a subtle evasiveness, a barely perceptible uneasiness behind the pleasant, self-possessed manner. It was enough to arouse his suspicions.

So, either to support or dispel those suspicions, he had her investigated. The report: she was married; there was a year-old daughter; there was, also, another ardent admirer besides Ben.

To Jorge Canto, the family was sacred. A family woman with two lovers was definitely of questionable character. He presented the facts to his son and expected him to behave sensibly.

But Ben didn't respond that way at all. Instead, stunned by what he called his father's meddling, he was deeply resentful. He didn't believe a word of what he had been told; however, to calm things at home, he agreed to present these allegations to his girl. The next morning, he flew to Los Angeles.

And they talked.

In tears, she vehemently denied the existence of another lover, but she readily admitted having a husband and daughter.

What was this all about?

It was simple. Her husband was a violent alcoholic. They were no longer together. She had thrown out his belongings and changed the lock on the apartment door.

But why had she kept all of this a secret from him?

She wasn't sure of anything—the state of her marriage (she was in the process of divorce), the direction of her relationship with Ben (she didn't want to jeopardize that), the stability of her emotional condition (she vacillated between control and tears on a word)—anything. It was foolish, of course, not to have told him, but these days she wasn't behaving entirely rationally about simple things, let alone complicated matters of involvement.

He met the child, and he stayed with both of them for three days. Beautiful, gentle, tender days. And that was enough for Ben Canto.

So, despite his father's objections, he continued the relationship. And he fell more deeply in love every time he phoned or flew to the Coast to see his young lady.

Jorge Canto was amazed. His son was missing the point entirely. The girl had lied. Couldn't he see that? And she was still lying about her other lover. He had never realized what a fool his son could be. It was a sentiment he took no pains to conceal. And that candor precipitated what seemed to be an endless series of blistering arguments.

Finally, during one particularly heated confrontation over the future of the restaurant, the elder Canto charged rashly that his son's thinking was, no doubt, being affected by a preoccupation with that "whore in California."

Two days later, Ben left the family business, the only Canto ever to do so.

The moment of separation was filled with rancor. Jorge Canto predicted sweeping failure for a "blind, ungrateful snot-nose." And the last words that Ben heard shouted at him were: "Go on, marry the lying slut. Go ahead, try to open another Golden Spike. But you won't succeed at either one of them because you're a damned fool. And you'll be sorry. You wait and see, you'll be sorry about everything."

Later, in an act of bitter defiance, Ben was to name his new establishment the Sorry Spike.

But before going into business for himself—as a matter of fact, just as soon as he left his family—he moved to Los Angeles to be with his woman. He was there only five days. That's all it took to learn about that other lover, and the fact that he was still very much a part of her life.

This time, she couldn't deny it. He had found her own careless doodling on a random notepad, burning references to some gloriously gratifying sexual experiences. He left without creating a scene. He packed silently as she cried and swore repeatedly that she'd stop seeing her other man and remain true to Ben for the rest of her life. Within his pain, pictures of his father flashed in assorted attitudes of I-told-you-so. God, half of the prediction had come true so quickly!

Now, the Sorry Spike was two months old and to keep from being totally crushed, Ben Canto was singularly determined to make it a resounding success.

As for the girl, he hadn't heard from her or seen her since their separation. He had made no attempts at contact. Sometimes he thought of her, though—after all, he had loved her very much—and he wondered where she was or what she was doing. He would soon find out. She was in his restaurant.

She was Sharon Kane.

And what is more—she knew at this moment that Ben Canto was approaching her table, concerned about the raucous behavior of her companions.

"Good evening," he said pleasantly.

The group erupted in a babel of happy responses.

Then he saw her, and his smile froze and crumbled.

Merrily, Sharon made the introductions. "Glad you could join us, Ben. This is Dandy Maynor, that's Lorna Christianson, Nancy Williams, Goose Berneau, Josh Billings over there, and this is Ben Canto, the owner of the Sorry Spike. Right?"

Delighted exclamations burst from the others.

Ben looked only at Sharon.

She rolled on: "And you've come over to tell us we're making too much noise, right?" She reached and took his hand. "Well, you're right and we are and we want you to sit down and have a drink with us and we'll try to be a little more quiet if you do."

He slipped his hand free.

"Hey, move over there, Goose, an' give the man a piece of that seat," Josh directed.

Eagerly, Goose bumped Nancy in tighter and slid off his place to make more room. He reached up and grabbed Ben's arm to coax him into the space he had just vacated.

Ben's attention, though, was on Sharon. "Why are you here?" he asked her softly.

Goose was still tugging at his arm.

"Hey, man, don't abuse the guy like that." It was Dandy, laughing. "Goddamned re–tard!" Then he looked at Ben again. "Gotta excuse our friend, please; someone once told him, to be a success he'd have to learn to think. He thought they said *drink* an' he's been tryin' to drown himself rich ever since."

"Stupidest drunken failure in the world!" Josh shouted proudly.

The laughter rolled over Goose without touching him.

Obstreperous customers were not new to Ben Canto. One could hardly be in the restaurant business very long without meeting them. But these people were something else. They suggested an instability that could not be expected to respond to simple requests. This situation would probably require the police. He would have to get away gracefully to call them. But before he could move, everyone's attention was caught by the sound of musical felicitation.

> Happy anniversary to you.
> Happy anniversary to you.
> Happy anniversary, Mr. and Mrs. Wheeler.
> Happy anniversary to you.

The procession passed their booth: four singing waitresses slightly behind the restaurant's hostess. She carried a small, attractively iced cake in which Fourth of July sparklers sputtered a collective pink glare. The waitresses sang the sentiment repeatedly as the group snaked its way through the large room to a secluded booth. Their voices grew in volume and verve. And as they stood before Police Chief Wheeler's table, they blended in beautiful barbershop harmonies for a rousing finale.

Spontaneous applause erupted throughout the room.

It was a fine moment.

"Do you know that couple?" Nancy asked Ben in the flurry of applause.

"No," he answered. Then he thought again of his problem guests. "Look," he started to say a little more amiably, "this can be a pleasant evening if . . ."

But Sharon interrupted excitedly. "Dandy, do something nice!"

"Like what?"

"Pay for that couple's dinner."

"Fuck no. . . ." Dandy laughed.

There was an explosion of enthusiastic entreaties and friendly demands.

Dandy grinned and resisted and objected—but his manner was warm and friendly—and the coaxing went on. Finally, he wavered. "How much is their bill?" he asked Ben.

A waitress was passing.

"Mary," Ben stopped her, "who has the anniversary table?"

"I do, Mr. Canto."

"What's their tab?"

She looked at her pad. "Thirty-two forty-five."

"I'm payin' it," Dandy announced to the waitress, who smiled and promptly turned away to inform the celebrating couple.

The group cheered and applauded, and Dandy protested. But his wide, shy smile conveyed genuine pleasure.

"That's very nice of you," Ben said, trying to control the moment. "I'd like to buy the table a round of drinks."

This, too, was greeted with clamorous approval.

Ben looked at Sharon. And again she was looking at him steadily with that odd, little smile.

Chief Wheeler's face was aglow with friendliness as he introduced himself to Ben Canto: "My name's Matt Wheeler, and I want to tell you, you've given me one of the most pleasant surprises of my life. It was a beautiful, generous gesture, and my wife thanks you as sincerely as I do."

Ben made the connection. Police Chief Wheeler. Marvelous! Suddenly, but very mistakenly, he felt safer. "That's very nice of you, Mr. Wheeler, but you should really be directing it to that gentleman over there." He pointed at Dandy.

Matt was slightly embarrassed. "Oh, I'm sorry," he apologized to Dandy.

"Hey, that's O.K." Dandy was enjoying this immensely.

"Well, it was really wonderful," Matt beamed, "the kind of thing you read about in books or see in the movies."

"How many years have you been married?" Sharon asked, intentionally drawing his attention.

He grinned. "Twenty-seven." And he really looked at her for the first time.

"I know you from somewhere, don't I?" he asked.

For an answer, Sharon announced playfully, "Hey, guys, this is *Police Chief* Matt Wheeler. Right?"

"That's right," he acknowledged.

"Po—lice Chief . . . we–e–e–ell, least we rate the best." Happy agreement.

"Can't do nothin' to us, man, we just bribed you with a dinner." Pleasant laughter.

Matt smiled. But his sensors detected trouble.

"Hey, Chiefy, sit-on-down an' have a drink with us. Ol' Ben here's buyin." Goose blurted, pounding the seat.

Matt continued to look at Sharon. "We know each other."

"Not really."

"Not really?"

"This is the first time we've met." Still smiling.

Ben was starting to frown.

Matt persisted, "You look familiar."

"I am."

"Don't be a riddler . . . please."

"She ain't no riddler," Goose piped. "She am a fiddler an' a diddler, but the lady ain't no riddler." Cackling, he tried to bury his face in his glass. The others bellowed delightedly. Except Dandy. Dandy watched the exchange with growing uneasiness.

Matt asked once more, "Do we know each other?"

No response.

"What's your name, miss?" He cut into the file of pictures and descriptions that always crammed his head.

Sharon replied, "Soon . . . very soon."

"Matt, dear, are these the lovely people who . . . ?" It was Margaret Wheeler, arriving with Howard Demerest to add her own words of appreciation to those of her husband. Her question was never completed.

The connections struck simultaneously.

"For God's sake, Sharon, answer the man," Ben had snapped. And her name collided with a sudden identification of her fact sheet. *Sharon Kane.* Matt felt a chill. Precisely at that moment, Howard Demerest saw her.

Howard gasped and shouted, "Do something, Matt!"

And the implication that Sharon was in some kind of trouble provoked her friends into an uproar.

"Do what? What's he talkin' about?"

"Where'd *he* come from?"

Words tumbled over each other as Dandy and his clan rose to protect her from whatever it was going on.

Matt asked Ben, "May I use your office?"

And Dandy shouted, "Hey, man, she ain't done nothin'!"

Through it all, Sharon remained perfectly still.

Across the dining room, though, Alex Weintraub started as he heard Dandy's last, angry exclamation snap like the clear crack of a whip.

"Did you hear what I heard?" he asked Felicia uncertainly.

She nodded.

He muttered in disbelief, "He's here. That freaky clown is here." He looked imploringly at her.

With a sigh, she closed her eyes and nodded approval.

"Come with me," he requested. And he jumped to his feet.

She followed closely.

On reaching the area, they found bedlam. And into this caldron of ugly emotions, Alex threw his own fury.

"Maynor!"

It was a shout of ultimate resentment, and it came in tandem with a single, overriding command from Sharon Kane:

"Stop this—*now!*"

Strangely, slowly, silence took over. A heavy silence in which everyone seemed to be waiting.

She took her seat again.

"Everyone, sit down," she suggested quietly.

Hesitantly, and after some prompting, they found places near and around the table.

"This is no place for arguments," she insisted. Then, looking at Alex and Felicia, and Margaret and Matt, she murmured, "My name is Sharon Kane. I'm pleased to meet you." She was smiling faintly.

Matt felt cold again. He tried to speak, but found himself unable to make a sound. What was wrong? What was happening to him? He saw Margaret, Alex and Felicia smiling uncertainly, nodding, acknowledging the introduction; he felt Demerest's silent terror at his elbow; he heard Alex ask about the uproar that had drawn him to their table—but he couldn't say a thing. He looked at Howard Demerest, and he could see, immediately, that his friend, too, was struggling desperately. But no one else seemed to notice. Sharon was quietly dispelling concerns, shaping reactions, with the most innocuous and general kind of explanation. Good God, he thought, we're being controlled.

And they were. From the moment of her command, without their knowledge, everyone around that table had surrendered a portion of his will, his thoughts or his feelings to her.

"Just a misunderstanding," she was saying softly. "I seem to remind the Chief and Mr. Demerest of someone, and my friends didn't want to see me getting into trouble."

Alex was about to tear into Dandy Maynor for his outrageous behavior, but he checked himself abruptly when he heard her add pleadingly, "It's a shame to ruin such a beautiful evening."

"That's true," he found himself agreeing. "We ought to keep things down. There's been enough commotion for one night."

Everyone concurred.

It all seemed so natural, so reasonable. And yet strange. But what was most interesting was that no one except Wheeler and Demerest seemed to be even faintly aware of that strangeness.

Matt felt his guts churning and his throat bulging in his effort to express himself. Finally, he broke through. "What is it you want?" It sounded like an angry growl.

"Nothing," she said with captivating innocence, her grin broadening into a lovely smile.

She was the Picture of Honesty. But what she wasn't saying was that every person around that table would be playing a major role in this nightmarish scenario she was concocting, and that their participation was absolutely vital to her success. She suspected quite accurately that hours— and even minutes—were going to be a critical factor in her plans. And so she had structured this meeting to accomplish in one brief period all that would have to be done to get this project started:

Wheeler *had* to accept the fact of her death—and with an acceptance so dramatically effected that his anxieties would both keep him out of her way and, ultimately, contribute to his cooperation;

Canto *had* to feel the stirrings of his love for her because that love would be a marvelous weapon;

Weintraub and Ohrman *had* to become aware of her existence if their natural resistance to deep involvement with a total stranger were to be weakened;

And Demerest—well, Howard Demerest, for all of his fear and uncertainty, would start it all happening in just a few more moments.

"This is an opportunity for everyone to become friends," she was saying brightly. "Isn't there a bond between all people?"

"And what are you supposed to be, the Great Welder?" The voice cut in and rubbed like a rasp. It was Howard Demerest.

She didn't respond. She just watched him steadily. Something was going wrong. She was having trouble controlling all of them to the exact degree that she had intended. First Wheeler's breakthrough and now Demerest's. She would have to be careful. Very, very careful.

"What the hell's eatin' him?" Josh complained. "She's talkin' about bein' friendly. What's wrong with that?"

Demerest couldn't answer. His head was bowed, and he was being racked by the terrible pains of fear and frustration.

"Easy, Howard, easy," Matt heard himself cautioning.

"Hey, we got some drinks comin' on the house ain't we?" Goose reminded Ben. And there was an eruption of agreement.

Then before he could say anything else, Matt Wheeler heard a single sentence deep within his mind: *Victor Jordan will be here tomorrow.*

"What?" He was startled. "Did you say something?" he asked Sharon.

The sentence rang again: *Victor Jordan will be here tomorrow.*

She wasn't looking at him, though. She had turned her attention to the swirl of gaiety that Goose and Josh were now creating with their comical calls for that round of drinks. And her palms were resting on the table.

It was then that she threw a suggestion at Howard Demerest, and he moved instantly on it. His fingers had been touching one of the long, pointed steak knives. Now with an anguished cry, he sprang to his feet and brought the jagged blade down savagely, insanely, into the back of her hand.

Shrieks and screams of horror ripped the quiet of the restaurant.

"What's the matter with him."

"He's crazy."

"Kill that sonofabitch." Dandy was halfway across the table for the mortician's throat before Matt and Alex could stop him.

"Stop it. Stop it!" Alex was snarling.

And Ben Canto pushed a whimpering and confused Howard Demerest farther out of Dandy's reach.

It was a melee. But over the pandemonium, Margaret's voice pleaded: "Watch out. Watch out. You'll hurt her. You'll hurt her. Watch out!"

And that shocked Dandy into an awareness of the further damage his struggling could cause. The commotion stopped abruptly and then became a soft murmur as everyone stared at her hand.

"Oh, my God . . ."

"Je—sus Christ . . ."

It was skewered to the table.

She was dissembling pain, gritting her teeth, seeming to gasp. From the wound, a pale, pink fluid oozed steadily, spreading itself into the green tablecloth. Only Wheeler and Demerest were allowed to see that for what it was; everyone else saw blood.

"Help me," Alex muttered to Dandy.

Dandy jumped to assist him.

The blade was embedded so deeply in the wood beneath, it required considerable effort to force it loose. And the rocking movement kept cutting her flesh, making the wound and the stain larger.

All the while, she remained perfectly still, her eyes closed as though she were fighting agony. However, Howard Demerest, sitting apart and under the protection of Matt Wheeler, heard her cold, crisp thought: *Your fear is stupid, Mr. Demerest, but even stupidity can serve a purpose.*

Howard seemed to shrink in his skin.

The knife came free finally. Dandy dropped it to the table with a baleful look at the mortician as Mrs. Wheeler took the hand gently and quickly wrapped it in one of the napkins on the table. Sharon held the wrapped hand close to her chest.

"Well, what are you gonna do about this?" Dandy challenged Matt.

"How the fuck could he do that?" Goose muttered incredulously.

And Josh snarled, "Oughtta lock that crazy bastard up!"

Demerest's gaze flew from one to the other.

Matt was watching Sharon Kane, his thoughts a jumble. He found himself asking, "Do you want to press charges, Miss?"

And before Dandy could explode with "Goddamned right she does," he heard her answer calmly and emphatically, "No."

Her friends protested. But again she said, No, this time adding cryptically, "Mr. Demerest will be living with this for the rest of his life, and that's punishment enough for being stupid."

"Someone ought to get you to a hospital," Ben Canto urged quickly.

She looked into his eyes and saw the confusion of mixed emotions. Good, she thought, it's happening.

Dandy jumped at Ben's suggestion and broke around the table. "C'mon," he ordered.

His friends moved to join him.

"I'll go by myself," she said.

"Are you crazy?"

"You could be bleeding to death."

"You don't even have transportation."

"That's all right, I'll get there," she contended.

"C'mon, we're going to the hospital."

But she couldn't allow that. None of these people could be allowed to witness the next phase of her program. Quickly, she directed a thought at everyone, and the resistance to her wishes became a flurry of concerned pleas.

"I'll be all right," she insisted reassuringly. "Really." It was said so sweetly. And yet strongly. Their opposition wavered. "Why don't all of you stay and have that drink?" She looked at Ben. "That is, if the offer still stands."

"Well . . . yes . . . of course." He was thrown off guard.

Then she followed through with: "We'll be seeing each other again—now that we've all become friends . . ."

Her voice had done nothing special with those final words; however, they left each member of the group with a private and disquieting sense of calamity. Then before any further resistance could be regenerated, she turned quickly and left her colleagues and the Sorry Spike.

Only Howard Demerest reacted differently to those words. And it was a reaction she had never intended: "We'll be seeing each other again—" Well, maybe not, he thought, maybe not.

He had seen the flow of his embalming fluid when the knife went into her flesh. It had continued even as the napkin was wrapped around the hand. This meant something. Something important. But what? Realization engulfed him: her heart was pumping!

His own heart leaped. And he understood instantly that although she had seemed so terribly invulnerable only moments ago, she did have a weakness. Why, she could actually be stopped from completing whatever it was she was planning—and he knew exactly how that could be done.

PART III

The Play

EVIL MAN

I met a man once—
   Evil as can be.
He took me walkin'
   On the bottom of the sea
An' showed me treasures
   That he said were meant for me . . .

      Evil was, evil was,
      Evil was, evil was
         In his smile.

He tol' me, "Take it.
   Take it all away.
If you don' take it
   Someone else is gonna say
That you were crazy
   'Cause you blew yer lucky day."

      Evil was, evil was,
      Evil was, evil was
         In his eyes.

I stuffed my pockets—
   All that they could hold.
Inside my shirt I
   Pushed that jew'lry old an' cold.
An' in my shoes I
   Packed a hundred tons o' gold.

      Evil was, evil was,
      Evil was, evil was
         In his heart.

No way to move then—
 Hard as I would try.
"C'mon an' help me!"
 Were the words I had to cry.
But he stood laughin'
 Like he meant fer me to die.

  Evil was, evil was,
  Evil was, evil was
   In his soul.

I dumped my pockets—
 Ev'ry single dime.
Ripped off my shirt an'
 Kicked my shoes into that slime,
An' swam away from
 There in no amount o' time.

  Evil was, evil was,
  Evil was, evil was
   In this man.

Now if you meet him
 Think o' what I say:
He'll give you somethin'
 But he'll take yer soul away.
An' you may never
 See another sunny day.

  He was evil, evil,
  An evil man.
  Always doin'
  The worst he can.

Evil Man. Evil Man. Evil Man. E-vil Man!

   Music and Lyrics by Dandy Maynor
   Dolomin Music Publishing, Inc.
     Copyright 1975
   From the LP album: "Dandy M."
   Catalyst Records—Album #1865LP

12

It was Saturday and the first-class section of Flight 147 out of Kennedy International was half full. Seven passengers. The 707 had taken off promptly at 9:00 A.M. It was scheduled to land at Sky Harbor International at 10:53 A.M. Phoenix time.

Two men were engaged in pleasant conversation. One was small and enthusiastic; the other tall and self-important. Their voices were raised slightly in order to be heard over the steady sounds of flight.

Another of the seven passengers in the section left his seat after listening to some whispered words from an impeccably dressed gentleman at his right. He approached the talkers.

"Excuse me," he said softly.

They looked up at him and smiled blandly.

"My friend is trying to sleep. I'm afraid your voices are carrying a little too strongly."

They quieted instantly.

"Sorry about that," the small one whispered *sotto voce*.

The other offered his own apology: "Didn't think. Tell him we're sorry."

The man who had interrupted their conversation was a young, cool business-type. He smiled, nodded his head once in appreciation and turned to leave. But the small one touched his arm.

"Say, if your friend can't sleep, tell him to take a Nytol. I've got some with me if he'd like one."

"No. That's all right. Thank you very much."

The small one stopped him again. "Nytol's the best. Someone once told me to use Darvon but Darvon's got

87

caffeine in it. That may be good for killing pain, but it's not gonna get anybody to sleep, right?"

The young, cool business-type eased his arm away. He stood up straight and looked down at his fellow passenger. An odd look. After a beat, the small man slouched in his seat. Then the young, cool business-type turned and settled next to his traveling companion.

"Did you see that look he gave me?" the small one whispered.

"Strange."

"I was just trying to be helpful."

"That's what's wrong with flying," his friend sighed. "A person can't always control whom he's with."

But thereafter the pair was self-consciously subdued.

If the impeccably dressed gentleman with the closed eyes had heard that last remark, he would not have agreed. Generally, he did control his flight situation. It was done simply. He merely purchased all first-class tickets and kept the section exclusively to himself and his companions. This time, though, his decision to fly had come too suddenly to enable him to buy up every seat.

"They'll be quiet, sir," the young, cool business-type assured him.

There was no response.

Upon the black screen of his closed eyelids, Victor Jordan was watching a memory. . . .

Phoenix, Arizona . . . February, 1951 . . . He was twenty-five years old and within $90,000 of being a millionaire. He had made a promise to himself: within four years after leaving the army, he would be a millionaire. The four years would be up on March 21.

So far, he had killed three people in pursuit of that goal. One in Caracas, Venezuela. Another in Bogotá, Colombia. And the third in Phoenix. That is, three people directly. Two others had been subsidiary deaths. Unfortunate but necessary correlatives to the actual slayings.

Even in those days he was dangerous. A social mutant. There were no psychological-environmental reasons for his deadliness. No childhood deprivation. No parental cruelty. It just seemed to be in his soul. Oh, the war had given him ideas, of course. It had shown him how easily people could be made to die. Millions of people. Millions. Life was so tenuous. Only the earth and things lasted. *Things.* He would acquire things. A sophomoric conclusion—but then again he was only a schoolboy when he had enlisted. Seventeen. That was in 1943. And within months he was killing along with everybody else, adding to the final score.

By V-J Day, he had contributed eighteen of his own to those millions.

It never bothered him.

"Why does it bug you?" he once asked one of his buddies.

"Hey, man! What're you, some kind o' zombie? They're people. Don't you understand that, man, they're people!"

"So?"

"*So?* What kind o' question is that? Would *you* like to die? You like to have your brains splattered all over some foreign country?"

"No, but . . ."

"But, shit! Hey, man, people got feelings an' if you can't feel something when you kill one of 'em then somebody oughtta blow *your* head off an' I mean now!"

Almost everyone else seemed to be troubled by the death and violence. Some guys were even cracking up. Section eights. All he knew was that he felt a sense of satisfaction in putting bullets exactly where they were designed to go. And he was doing it well. Zapp. Dead center.

He collected many medals.

Shortly after his release from the army he had learned that stolen gems could be obtained rather simply in Venezuela. The deal had fallen into his lap. A friend who operated a small but exclusive jewelry store in Scottsdale, Arizona—one of the wealthiest cities in America—had shown him a small satchel almost filled with emeralds. Victor was impressed. He had never seen that many emeralds in one place. It was like a small treasure chest in one of the caves of Aladdin.

"How much is this worth?" he asked.

"I don't know yet. I have to appraise them."

Each stone was wrapped carefully in a soft protective tissue. Victor removed a green pebble and held it between his thumb and forefinger.

"That one should be in the neighborhood of eight thousand," his friend said.

"Then there must be . . . there must be . . ." He scooped

a handful and let the wrapped gems fall loosely from his palm. They rustled musically as they flowed back into the satchel. He murmured, "You've got over a million bucks worth of emeralds here . . ."

"No. I don't think so. A lot of them aren't too good. The cuts are wrong . . . the color's off."

"Then a half million . . . a quarter of a million . . ."

"Oh yeah a quarter of a million easily. I'll know better in a week when I've had a chance to study them all, but I'd say somewhere between a quarter and a half."

"Dollars . . ."

His friend smiled and nodded his head.

"Are they yours?"

His friend just looked at him.

"Well, are they?"

"Maybe," he answered with a cryptic grin.

"What does that mean?"

His friend returned the satchel to his safe before responding. The silence foretold a momentous revelation.

Victor waited patiently.

When the jeweler looked at him again it was with an expression of friendly conspiracy. He stroked his chin absently and smiled.

"Victor, how would you like to be a millionaire?"

In answer Victor Jordan's eyes went flat and his mouth pulled slowly into a cold, dreamy grin.

The jeweler went to the door and locked it. Then he signaled with a wave of his fingers.

"I don't want anyone interrupting this."

When they were seated in the corner where the friend usually did his custom-designing, he started with an inviting warning: "This could be a little dangerous, Vic, but no more dangerous than what you've already been through in the war. And dollars buy more than medals."

Victor Jordan lit a cigarette. "I'm listening, Bob."

"That little bag of emeralds came from Venezuela. Caracas. Lots of action in South America now . . . refugees, escaped war criminals, generals, politicians . . . you name it. Seems like everyone's trying to find some security in gems. Along with precious metals they're really the only international currency, y'know. And for conversion the United States is the best market because our dollars are the only cash that counts right now.

"Last month I met this Venezuelan consul at a dinner party in Tucson. When he learned I'm a jeweler he became very friendly. A few days later he showed up here in the store. After dancing around awhile he finally came to the point. He wanted to know if I could dispose of a large quantity of stones. Nothing in settings. Just plain stones. Emeralds. He wouldn't say where they'd come from, but I suspect he's tied up with someone in Colombia. Colombia's one of the main sources of emeralds in the world. In his position he probably knows some other official there, and they're looking out for themselves. At any rate, he wanted a conversion point, somebody who could give him cash for the merchandise and have it distributed throughout the States.

"I asked him if this was a one-shot transaction or if he'd have more later on." The jeweler paused for effect and then leaned forward. His eyes glistened with avarice. "Victor, the man's got his hand in the till and the shopkeeper's on vacation. Apparently there's no end to the supply, and he's all for setting up a connection."

Victor Jordan rolled the glowing tip of his cigarette in the ashtray on the desk until it separated from the butt. Dropping the butt near it, he said softly, "In other words, my friend Robert, you're getting into the business of fencing hot ice."

The jeweler's face held its expression. His response was a chiding challenge. "And if you say yes, my friend Victor, you'll be getting into the business of smuggling it."

Victor Jordan liked that. It had been said with a touch of style. There was a brief pause as he enjoyed it. Then he crossed his legs and eased comfortably back into his chair. "I'm still listening."

The jeweler beamed. "Good!" He was becoming agitated with anticipation. Standing quickly and coming from behind the desk, he pulled over a small chair and sat before his listener. He leaned forward eagerly. "Here's the story. He can't declare the stuff, of course. First of all, it's probably hot and, secondly, duties would cut the hell out of his returns. And he hasn't wanted to risk bringing in large quantities at once, either. That bag of emeralds is the result of two years' work—two trips a month. I'm guessing, but I think he's been afraid that with large shipments, one error would label the operation an international smuggling ring and bring the government into the picture. So, he's been bringing them in a few stones at a time. That way, in case he's caught, he can claim oversight, pay the duty on a few emeralds and still be safe."

Victor held up a hand to stop him. "Wait, wait a minute . . . I don't see why you want me."

"The schmuck's been caught. They're watching him now."

Victor nodded his head. "O.K. I think I see it all now. I skip between Caracas and Phoenix, a few stones at a time —by the way, how many is a few?"

"He was limiting himself to five."

"I see. So, I bring in five stones at a time, you buy them, pay off the consul and then sell them wherever you can."

"That's basically it."

The friendly smile dissolved from Victor Jordan's face. He leaned forward and tapped the jeweler's knee "I thought you asked me if I'd like to be a millionaire, Robert," he challenged softly without blinking.

"I did, Vic . . ."

He cut him off. "No, no . . . You're asking me to be an errand boy. And errand boys are nothing."

"I'd see to it that . . ."

"There's nothing there to see anything about!" he exploded. "You get your end on the buy. But after your consul buddy deducts expenses and takes his share from what's left, there won't be enough in it to make it worth my while to go to Tucson, let alone Venezuela!"

"You'll get something from my end, too, Victor."

"But none of this could make me a millionaire." He stood sharply and walked away a few paces. When he turned again his expression was more serious than the jeweler had ever before seen. "I don't take that word lightly, Bob. I've been out of the army two months now, and I'm going to have that million within four years. But this isn't going to do it for me." His voice shifted. "Unless . . ."

They watched each other.

"O.K., Vic," the jeweler relaxed finally, "now *I'm* listening."

He returned and stood directly before his friend. His voice was soft and certain as he looked down at him. "You tell that consul I'm not interested in his small shipments. I'll bring in a hundred at a time if he can supply them . . .

and he'll be perfectly protected . . . but for every five stones of his I want *one* other for myself. And you buy those from me."

The jeweler thought for a moment. "How will you do it?"

"None of your business."

"And you'll assume your own expenses?"

"Right."

The jeweler slapped his knees and stood. "I'll tell him. All he can say is no."

But the Venezuelan consul didn't say no. As a matter of fact he was more than a little interested. Since being discovered at customs almost six months ago he had brought nothing into the country. Ordinarily his limited operation would not have meant much in terms of accumulated stones. But there had been a slight and recent change in his situation. As the jeweler had accurately surmised his source was Colombian—General Miguel de Ortega. The operation was simple: General Ortega was the protector of a certain mineowner's son. The son was a notorious playboy. Each month the general received for his solicitude a few stones, which he passed on to a cousin who was an attaché with the Colombian embassy in Venezuela. The cousin conveyed them to the Venezuelan consul who then brought them to the United States. Very neat. Very simple. As long as no one became greedy. But something had happened to create the greed: instead of being court-martialed for the misappropriation of two truckloads of guns and ammunition, the mineowner's son was made the general's aide-de-camp. And for this increased service the general demanded considerably larger monthly payments.

In the eyes of the mineowner, protection now took on the shadings of blackmail. So, to guard his own position, he set into motion a number of dangerous forces—all directed against the general. Miguel de Ortega was in deepening trouble and he knew it.

Nevertheless, for the while, payments were being made and emeralds were accumulating rapidly now. They were hidden in a private box at Banco Comercial in Bogotá. But in view of his uncertain position General Ortega preferred, of course, to have cash—American dollars—in a private box at Credit Lucerne in Switzerland.

The Venezuelan consul was being pressured to do something. And Victor Jordan's offer to bring in larger quantities seemed to be heaven-sent. He questioned the jeweler carefully. What kind of man is this? Is he trustworthy? Is he intelligent? Self-composed? Resourceful? Has he ever experienced danger? If something should go wrong—customs officials are actually conducting body searches now—would he implicate others? Is he fearless?

With each response the jeweler was direct, thorough, detailed.

The consul was impressed. There was a long silence. Finally he said, "Very well." But then he added quickly, "For now. I shall want to meet him first . . . and only once. . . . Thereafter all matters will be transacted through you. Is that understood?" And as the jeweler nodded he continued, "I must tell you now though—his proposal is not acceptable. This is my offer: tell your friend I'm not sure how many trips there will be each month but he may have one gem for every ten stones delivered. Tell him he will receive it when he accepts the shipment in Caracas. If that is satisfactory then have him visit me here—alone—tomorrow evening at seven. If the terms are not acceptable I have no desire or need to meet him."

They met in a large and tastefully furnished house on the side of Camelback Mountain. The consul greeted him personally at the door. His name was Francisco Vargas, and he believed everything to have been settled. He was soon disturbed, though, and then just as quickly impressed by Victor Jordan's presumptuousness.

"There's no agreement yet."

"But I said . . ."

"I know what you said, but I always talk for myself. Fair agreements are reached only with some give-and-take. You and I must do this without a mediator."

It was a businessman's statement. No rancor or aggressiveness. Just a cool clean expression of position. It struck a responsive note in the consul. He softened.

"Would you like a drink, Mr. Jordan?"

"No thank you. First, talk. If we can't agree, drinking would be a waste of social grace. If we do agree, I'll have a little white wine."

The consul smiled. "Very well." He settled into a large leather armchair. "What is your next offer?"

"You get only one delivery a month to start," Victor

announced. "More than that at the beginning would be dangerous. Later we can increase the number. I want two stones for every fifteen delivered and I'll select them from each shipment at this end, not in Venezuela."

The consul laughed.

Victor's voice turned cold. "That wasn't meant to be humorous."

"Of course not. I'm sorry. That was merely a reaction to your audacity. Actually I like it." He studied his guest's unsmiling face for a moment and decided that this determined young man might be just the answer to his predicament. "All right, Mr. Jordan," he said, "I can agree to your first demands. But your desire to select your payment from the shipment is unacceptable. Why is it necessary? Why won't you take payment in Caracas?"

"At this end, I'll know what I'm getting."

"Yes, but what is to prevent you from choosing the largest and best stones?"

"No stone will be worth more than five thousand dollars." The answer was quick, sure.

The consul looked at him with interest. "Even so," he hesitated, "you would be getting . . ."

"About fifteen stones a trip with an appraisal value in the neighborhood of seventy thousand dollars."

"I don't know. That's a considerable sum of money."

"True. But only sixteen percent of what you'll be getting." It was said slyly. With a faint smile.

The consul smiled in return with added interest and respect. "And are you sure," he asked, "that you can bring in at least one hundred a month?"

"If you can supply them."

Señor Vargas thought for a moment. "I'm satisfied," he said suddenly. "But one last point: how do you intend to pass that many gems through customs every month without being detected?"

"With considerable caution. . . . A little white wine, if you please."

And that's all the information he would offer.

The next morning Victor Jordan visited his brother-in-law Jorge Canto at the Golden Spike restaurant and obtained a loan of ten thousand dollars from him for a business venture that would see the return of the money plus ten percent interest in the short space of four months.

The interest didn't concern Jorge at all. That was Victor's idea. He had insisted on it against Jorge's protests, to keep the entire matter businesslike. Of course he didn't tell his brother-in-law the true nature of the undertaking. But the project he did detail sounded interesting and promising enough to arouse Jorge's hope that Victor was finally finding himself. Jorge liked Victor. Very much. He saw him as a person with strong family ties. A man like himself in that respect. Oh, a bit on the quiet side perhaps, but that was always preferable to the empty-barrel sounds of his own loudmouth brother Emilio. Clearly, Victor was a man of sincerity. With genuine feeling. A person who cared.

He would never forget—even if he lived three lifetimes —what Victor had done on the day of his wedding.

During the reception, a colorfully costumed quintet of Italian musicians had made a marvelous and unexpected appearance on the scene. And the afternoon was suddenly lifted to new heights of pleasure. It was Victor's surprise gift for the newlyweds. Something a little different that would be remembered forever.

To Jorge it was a touch of brilliance. Feeling. A family gesture. When he found his new brother-in-law to thank him, Jorge was touched further by his embarrassment. Victor took him to one side away from some people with whom he had been standing.

"No, no, Jorge. We're brothers now," he had said. "No thanks are necessary. What I do I do for love and family. Marta's always been a beautiful sister, and it's easy to see that you're the man for her happiness."

Jorge had beamed at him and clasped him in a warm *abbraccio*.

"Just remember, Jorge," he said as they parted, "keep her happy with you." Then he looked at him most meaningfully and added a word he rarely used, ". . . please . . ."

From that day on Jorge Canto harbored warm and loving feelings for his relative. And when Victor returned to Phoenix after his discharge from the service he demonstrated this by making him a very attractive offer to work at the Golden Spike. Regrettably, as far as Jorge was concerned, the offer was rejected. Nicely but firmly. It was appreciated and he could understand why the restaurant business was right for the Cantos . . . but he, Victor, had other plans for himself.

The weeks passed though, and nothing seemed to arouse his interest.

Jorge and Marta's concern for him mounted.

So when Victor Jordan approached his brother-in-law for the ten-thousand-dollar loan, when it seemed as though he had finally found something he cared to do, it was with great pleasure and relief that Jorge Canto advanced him the money.

Now Victor moved quickly.

Immediately half the money was placed in a new checking account with the Equity National Bank. The other half was converted into Venezuelan bolivars and deposited through the ENB's International Currency Department with the Banca Primera de Caracas. This amounted to more than twenty thousand bolivars. The transaction would be completed within the week. Quickly Victor Jordan would become a man of means in Venezuela. And quickly people there would become interested in the day he'd make his appearance.

After he left the Equity National Bank he went directly to 30 North Central Avenue where Nick Chasey had just opened his newest store. Chasey's was special. Gentility. The finest in men's wear.

"Shirts," was all he said to the smiling clerk as he strode in.

"Yes sir. Did you have a particular brand in mind?"

"Show me what you have."

"Certainly." The clerk went behind a glass counter and slid open a walnut partition with a flick of his index finger. Withdrawing an attractive white shirt with quarter-inch vertical blue stripes spaced an inch-or-so apart, he laid the item with a slight flourish upon a small, red, velvet mat on the countertop. "We have many name brands but Wellsley is still one of our most popular."

"Do you have other collar styles?"

"Yes sir." And quickly two other shirts lay on the counter top flanking the first. "Tab. Button-down. And spread." He pointed at each collar as he identified it.

"Good. What sizes do they come in?"

Squinting slightly and cocking his head as he appraised his customer the clerk guessed. "Well I'd say you wear . . ."

"They're not for me. What sizes do they come in?"

The clerk grinned. "Oh they're to be a gift. Well do you know the party's size? I'm sure we have it if you'll . . ."

Again he cut him short. "Just answer my question."

The clerk started to lose his composure. The question was inconsistent with customary sales situations. What could this young man be getting at? Oh, Lord, was he stuck again with another browsing oddball? No sale. Only aggravation. His manner became cooler, crisper. "They start at fourteen-and-a-half, sir, and go up to eighteen, I believe. We don't carry eighteen in stock. Seventeen-and-a-half is the largest neck size I have now but . . ."

"Fourteen-and-a-half to seventeen-and-a-half . . . that means seven sizes."

The clerk sniffed a bit impatiently and rolled his eyes slightly. "Fourteen-and-a-half—fifteen—fifteen-and-a-half . . ."

Victor stopped him. "Seven sizes."

"Yes, I believe . . . seven sizes . . . yes."

"I want six shirts of each size."

The clerk was startled. "S . . . six of each?"

"And the six should consist of two of each collar style. Two tab, two button-down and two spread. Six. Is that clear?"

"Well, I . . . I . . . yes, sir." He brightened instantly. "You're ordering . . . forty-two shirts?"

"That's right. Now what arm lengths do they come in?"

The clerk began to fall all over himself. He worked on commission. Who would have dreamed this sale could have turned out this way—forty-two shirts! He sprang to the order like a child at Christmas presents.

"The arm lengths run from thirty-two to thirty-five inches, sir."

"All right. Now listen carefully. I want a representation of each of those lengths. It doesn't matter what neck sizes they're related to. Just be sure they're all accounted for."

"I don't quite understand . . ."

"All arm lengths. I want all arm lengths represented, and I don't care what neck sizes they're related to."

"Yes but . . ."

"Isn't that clear?"

"Why yes . . . yes sir . . . but may I . . ."

"And I don't care what colors the shirts come in either. Just give me a wide assortment. As for the cuffs, see to it that some are standard button, but most should be the French design for links. Select a dozen sets of cuff links too. And a dozen ties. Vary the tie lengths and shapes so they'll go well with the three collar styles. How long will this take?"

The clerk was almost delirious. He was writing quickly in the order pad he had hurried to the cash register to obtain. And all the while he was trying to maintain his proper Chasey decorum. "It shouldn't take too . . ."

"I'll be back in thirty minutes. Have it ready."

"Yes sir . . . yes *sir*."

"Now get me your manager."

"Would you care to see something else, sir?"

"Only your manager."

"Slacks? Sweaters? We have a . . ."

"I'll be back for other things later this week. I'll look for your help then. Your manager now."

"The manager . . . yes the manager . . . Mr. Bale . . . one moment, sir, I'll get him for you . . . Mr. Bale, oh Mr. Bale." He left humming.

He returned almost immediately with a debonair middle-aged man who was smiling warmly. Evidently the clerk had informed him of the size of this purchase.

"Mr. Bale, our manager," the clerk said.

"How do you do, sir," Mr. Bale grinned.

Victor ignored the amenities. He was writing. "I'm making this check out for seven hundred dollars, Mr. Bale. That should more than cover everything. Call the Equity National Bank and speak to Mr. Webber in New Accounts to clear it. I'll be back in thirty minutes. Have everything ready will you?"

"Yes, sir."

"Including the change."

"Certainly, sir."

He tore the check from the pad and left it on the counter. And without saying another word he departed.

There was a silence in the vacuum he left behind. The manager and the clerk were somewhat stunned as they watched him go. And when the spell was broken by the closing of the door, his presence was still strongly enough felt to cause them to jump.

"Thirty minutes," the manager said brightly. "I'll help you. Come on." They snapped to work.

For Victor Jordan there was much to do that day. From Chasey's he went to Mandy's Travel Agency and booked flight and boat reservations to Venezuela for two. Airplane to Miami, Florida, and the Caribbean pleasure ship *Carolina* from Miami to La Guaira ten miles or so from Caracas. In 1947, airline routes were not as plentiful or direct as they are today, and the big jets had not as yet revolutionized air travel. He would have to make Miami by way of Albuquerque, Oklahoma City, St. Louis and Atlanta. The entire trip to Caracas—boat included—would take seven days. However, he wasn't bothered by this. While there was another route he could have taken—air passage from Los Angeles—and while it would have been much more direct and far less time-consuming, it wouldn't have been as safe. There were very few Americans visiting Venezuela in those days. And those who were making the trip were conspicuous. Especially those going by air. A vacationing American with an attractive companion—two people who were merely part of a small boatload of summer funseekers and sightseers—was another matter. An all-important matter of relative anonymity. There would be time later to develop other routes. Besides, five days on a pleasure cruise with his present woman would be enjoyable in itself. A fringe benefit of caution.

He had first seen Chana Ramirez at a stag party in a private club two weeks after returning to Phoenix. She was one of the performers. An exquisitely proportioned singer-dancer. She had been the "party warmer," not one of the specialty acts. No community coitus. No tit tricks. No dildo demonstrations. All of that came later by others. She had just sung and danced. Naked. Using her entire body in an incredibly sensuous way. Writhing gently. Grinding slowly. Smooth, even, pelvic undulations. Tantalizing, as she spread her legs slightly, ever-so-invitingly, in those hypnotically rhythmic vulvar thrusts. She was in absolute control throughout the entire performance. Mistress of her body. Totally conscious of the allure of each part—the sleek olive skin, the firm swell of calves, smoothly curved buttocks, delicate arch of back, full quivering breasts, sensual shoulders, vital expressive mouth, glistening green eyes and abundant jet black hair worn like a mane. She was smoky. Fiery. Exotic. And she knew it. She could feel the heat she generated. There was no need to be flamboyant or excessive in her movements. Consequently, what she presented—while overtly sexual—was by no means gross. Just devastatingly provocative. Her job was to arouse. She did it splendidly.

There wasn't a man in the audience who didn't imagine the suggested paradise that lay between those lovely legs, Victor Jordan included. He looked about as she danced and saw the hunger in their eyes. The intense expressions. In her very femaleness, the sinuosity of her body, her grace, she had become something other than woman. She had become prime meat, estimated at twenty dollars a piece or seventeen cents a pound. Cheaper than hamburger. And the room was filled with eager shoppers. Their perspiration, their lip-licking intensity was almost cruel. Two cowboys in particular caught Victor's attention. One tapped the other on the arm. Without taking their eyes from her, they bent their heads together for whispered words. In a moment, they left, despite the fact that she had not finished her performance. Victor understood. They were getting ready to buy. The idea was offensive. In direct contravention to the realities of life. He had already decided that Chana Ramirez was going to be his woman. True, she wasn't aware of his existence as yet. But that was a minor point. The union was inevitable.

He excused himself with a sentence to his companions at the table and left the room as unobtrusively as possible. Outside the club, he glimpsed the two cowboys cutting around the corner to the rear door of the building. This was the club's "stage entrance," the way to its seedy dressing rooms. Victor followed. He stopped at the corner and peered around it. One of the men was unscrewing the lone bulb that illuminated the doorway. Suddenly, the area went semidark. Only a half-moon provided light. There were hoarse, whispered words. Urgent promptings. Then they hurried from the lot and down the street.

Victor waited. He considered their movements. Apparently they expected the dancer to leave after her performance. They seemed certain enough about her routine to have left the club when they did. They had plans. Apparently this was not going to be a simple, open proposition.

Soon there was the rumble of a car with a defective muffler. The macho sound. They pulled into the lot facing the back door. They cut the motor and turned off the headlights. He heard the click of both car doors opening. But the cowboys remained seated where they were. They were waiting now. They were ready.

Out of sight, Victor leaned against the building and calmly smoked a couple of cigarettes.

Approximately fifteen minutes passed before the rear door of the club swung outward. The light within was so faint—one blue bulb halfway down the hall—that only her outline could be seen by the men in the car.

"Hijo de una ramera!" she muttered. *"Donde está la luz?"* She turned and shouted down the hallway, "Hey, Charlie. You betta get this light fixed 'fore somebody breaks his ass." Part complaint—part request. She closed the door behind her and turned.

Suddenly, headlights snapped on, catching her in a blinding flood of brightness. Her arm came up to shield her eyes. The cowboys were out of the car and racing to her.

"Qué pasa . . . ?"

They were on her before she knew what was going on. One threw an arm around her neck. She tried to scream. He jammed a handkerchief into her mouth. The other fought furiously to get a grip around her waist. She kicked and smashed at him with her fists and arms.

"Hold the bitch for Chrissakes."

The arm snapped fiercely around her throat. She felt her eyes bulge. She couldn't breathe. She was gagging on the handkerchief.

"Oh sweet Jesus what a body! My God!"

"Get her legs! Get her in the car!"

"I felt her tits! Jesus what a pair of tits!"

There was an hysterical laugh.

"You gonna get fucked tonight baby. You gonna get fucked tonight."

She thrashed around furiously. Legs kicking. Arms flailing. There was no air. Dizziness. Darker. She was losing consciousness.

Victor watched everything. They lifted her. Dragged her. Swung her to the car. And as they fought to push her into the back seat, he made his move. Swiftly. Powerfully. He came charging down the lot as fast as his legs could pump. Their backs were to him. Three feet away, they heard his running over the sounds of their struggle. They

turned quickly. It was too late. He was in the air feet first,
legs snapping open like a switchblade. He caught his target
in the chest and on the side of the head. The momentum!
The drive! The force of his body and kick lifted the cowboy off the ground and slammed him against the edge of
the open door. Cracking bones could actually be heard. He
groaned like death and slumped to the ground. The other
had dropped the girl. He came charging. Victor had rolled
quickly to his feet to face him. A knife flashed. Victor went
in under it. Fast. Very low. And he came up driving hard,
his fist slamming mercilessly. Perfect timing. Perfect connection. He felt the soft, yielding squish of testicles. There
was an agonized scream, and the cowboy collapsed into the
dirt, writhing, clawing at his groin, making horrible, gagging sounds as he fought for air through the suffocating
pain.

The girl had torn the handkerchief from her mouth. She
slumped against the car, gasping. Nevertheless, she had
seen the smooth movements of Victor's attack.

He hadn't made a sound throughout the entire flawless
performance. And now, as he took her by the shoulders
and helped her to stand, he wasn't even breathing hard.

"You're all right," he said. "No damage."

She wanted no help, though. She broke away from him
and charged at the men who had tried to rape her.

"Perros! Puercos!" she screamed. And she kicked furiously at the forms on the ground. *"Animales!"*

Victor pulled her away. "Come on. They've had it."

But she struggled free for one final kick. *"Sus madres
son putas!"* And she punctuated the word for *whores* with
spit.

He drove to an all-night coffee shop on Central. At a
corner table she talked: she was grateful to him. . . . Not
many men would do that for a stranger. . . . Most men
were like those two pigs. . . . She knew men. . . . They were
her business . . . but don't get her wrong, man, she didn't
fuck for a living—she was a performer, no *puta*, but she
saw their expressions when they watched her body . . . and
rape and near-rape were not new to her. . . . That's the price
she had to pay for being in show business. . . . Someday
though it would be different. . . . Someday, Chana Ramirez. . . . Was that her real name? . . . Why did he want to
know? . . . it's not important. . . . Well, since he had helped

her tonight, she would tell him . . . Yñez Camarón. . . .
That was her real name but *Madre de Dios* she hated it.
You got an idea what that word means—*camarón?* No?
It means shrimp. You know shrimp—that little fish? That's
no name for a star—Yñez Shrimp. Chana Ramirez was
mejor, teatral—much better, theatrical. And someday . . .

They sat there for three hours. He told her nothing
about himself. But he treated her with noticeable regard
and respectful attention. At twenty-one, his philosophy concerning women was:

> Treat a whore like a lady.
> Treat a lady impolite.
> Tell a smart one that she's sexy
> And a sexy one she's bright . . .

She began to look at him differently. Her outspoken
contempt for men became self-conscious and finally disappeared altogether from her conversation. The showy
hardness of her manner softened perceptibly. This one is
maybe *especial*, she thought.

She looked at him with a becoming touch of shyness.
"Y'know, you very nice."

He smiled.

She grinned a lovely warm look and bent her head. It
was a moment of rare and charming embarrassment for
her. Suddenly she sat up and pulled her hair back blowing
air toward her eyes and along her arms. "Whoo! I don't
know what happen. Suddenly I get so *hot*—" She corrected
the impression quickly. "So *warm*, I mean. Y'know like—
oooo, man, that never happen t'me before." She pulled at
her blouse and fanned her face with a napkin. And they
both laughed. Finally, she leaned her arm on the table and
turned partially away so that he was looking at her profile.
She was picking at an imaginary imperfection in the table-
top. Her eyes were downcast. "Hey," she said softly,
"maybe you like me t'go home with you?"

"No."

"Whatsa matter, you don't gotta place? O.K., then you
come home with me, yes?"

"No."

She was thrown completely off-balance. She looked at
him with a bemused frown. "You don't like me?"

"I'll tell you what I'd like," he said, leaning forward on his elbows and looking directly into her eyes. "I'd like to take you straight home and see that you're absolutely safe. And then tomorrow I'd like to take you to dinner in a lovely restaurant, and after that, dancing in a beautiful lounge."

She brightened as though a beacon had been snapped on within. And she was speechless.

"Come." He stood and extended his hand.

She placed her hand in his.

And that was it. Two weeks later Chana Ramirez moved into his apartment. And she was certain that for the first time in her life she had fallen deeply, magnificently and truly in love.

Before meeting Victor, Chana had lived a life of sexual deprivation. Her associations had been many but fleeting. Her reactions almost consistently spurious. Like so many of her kind the real Chana Ramirez lived somewhere within a cake of ice. However, after that first hot orgasm of true love, her defenses evaporated like frost in a Santa Ana wind. And she became happier, more tender, more passionate than at any time in the past. Everything had suddenly turned beautiful.

But she was also afraid—afraid that it couldn't last. Somewhere, she knew, she would make a mistake. Somehow, she would lose all this newly discovered joy so easily. Naturally, then, she did everything she could think of to discourage that eventuality. And since her body had always been her chief means of expression, she offered it in every way imaginable.

In the course of the next six weeks, she more than fulfilled the promise he had fantasized the night of the rescue. She was a sex machine. Indefatigable. Ever-available. A wonder of imagination and control. There was nothing she couldn't do. Nothing she wouldn't do to make him happy. And although she never performed sexual stunts in public, she even demonstrated for him, and for him alone, dazzling skills that bordered on the miraculous.

Yes, as far as Victor was concerned, five days on a Caribbean cruise with Chana Ramirez would be a pleasant way, indeed, to while away the time. He couldn't think of going without her. Besides, he needed her. For one thing, he would be able to use her beauty. For another, he knew no Spanish. In Venezuela she would be the one person he could trust.

Two days before they were to leave Phoenix, he told her, "You're going to be very helpful to me. You'll see. And when we get back home, I'll buy you anything you like. As a matter of fact, we'll be doing this more than once. Make a list of everything you want. Eventually, you'll have it all."

She was ecstatic beyond belief.

"Don't you realize what this means?" she laughed, and her eyes flashed with excitement. She was quite beautiful. "I am twenny-three years old an' I don't have anything or go anywhere before this." She threw herself at him and kissed him fiercely. *"O mi hombre . . . mi vida . . . mi alma . . . te amo con toda la corazón."* She spoke her love as their mouths were locked.

The experience was not without its problems though: her passport distressed her deeply—she was certain she'd be known throughout Venezuela as Yñez "Shrimp"; the clothes he purchased for her were too subdued—she was afraid she looked like a candidate for a convent; the airplane hit turbulence over Oklahoma—she was sure it would disintegrate; the cruise ship was caught in a one-day squall—she was convinced the only remedy for seasickness was death.

However, Venezuela was worth it all. Even then, Caracas was becoming a surprisingly cosmopolitan city. There she was a queen. He took her almost everywhere he went. Her Spanish was quite good. Her vocabulary and grammar surprisingly accurate. The mistakes she made were attributed by the natives to the fact tha she was of Mexican origins and not Venezuelan. So, when she followed his instructions and conducted herself with decorum, speaking softly and slowly and only when she was addressed, she was treated with a deference that she found quite gratifying.

Victor had arranged with the travel agent in Phoenix for them to leave the tour in Venezuela and to catch another cruise ship for their return. This allowed him to remain in Caracas for ten days. He needed that much time to establish his cover operation—his reason for repeated visits to South America. He had plans even now that went far beyond the immediate purpose of this trip. Caracas would be only a start.

Before leaving Phoenix, he had obtained from the consul the name of an outstanding Venezuelan lawyer. A Señor Martín Verdadero. Even before making contact with the Colombian attaché—the emerald courier—he called upon Señor Verdadero and made an interesting proposal: if Señor Verdadero would see to it that all legal requirements were satisfied for the creation and continued operation of a manufacturing plant in Caracas, then Mr. Jordan would be pleased not only to retain him permanently at his customary fee but to give him a partnership in the operation as well. The product would be men's shirts. The importation of such a commodity was totally unnecessary. Venezuelan textiles, while admittedly in their infancy, were healthy enough to support such an undertaking. And a successful manufacturing operation would certainly contribute to their further growth and to the entire national economy. It would be started in a small way, of course, but enlarged steadily. This was an opportunity to establish an industry with far-reaching consequences. A responsible, knowledgeable and respected national was essential to its success. And since Señor Verdadero comes so highly recommended by a Venezuelan official to the United States, Mr. Jordan would be pleased if he would at least give some serious consideration to the offer.

Señor Verdadero didn't have to think too long. It was as though El Presidente were offering him a cabinet post. However, while obviously interested, he tried not to appear too eager. He would be very happy to manage the legal aspects of such a transaction. And he was flattered that his friend Francisco Vargas had remembered him so kindly. But as to the partnership which Mr. Jordan was so generously offering—well, he was somewhat overwhelmed . . . not quite sure how he should react. Would Mr. Jordan be terribly offended if he took a day or so to consider that aspect of his proposal?

Certainly not.

Mr. Jordan stood. He extended his hand. He looked forward to meeting with Señor Verdadero tomorrow at which time they would discuss the matter further.

The lawyer stood. He shook Victor's hand warmly.

"It's been a pleasure, sir," he said. "A most interesting

half hour." He looked at Chana and then back to Victor. He was beaming. "And I hope you will not misunderstand, Mr. Jordan, when I say that I have never met an interpreter as skilled and beautiful as Miss Ramirez." And still smiling he bowed slightly and kissed her hand.

This was Chana's first experience with Old-World gallantry. She loved it, and she responded perfectly. Glancing a bit sideways at him she smiled engagingly and murmured, "Why thank you, sir. You are very kind."

"Not at all, Miss Ramirez. Only truthful."

After they left the office Victor asked, "What were you two saying at the end?"

She was buoyant. "He thinks I am ve–ry beautiful."

Victor was pleased. The lawyer was in his pocket.

Step one had been taken easily.

From this meeting they went directly to Banca Primera de Caracas. It was necessary to establish his presence as the North American depositor from Phoenix, Arizona. He had been careful to mention his account to Señor Verdadero, and he expected correctly that the lawyer would be doing some checking.

A young clerk behind one of the desks was galvanized into action. "Ah yes, Señor Jordan," he grinned, "we have been looking forward to this visit."

Victor asked for and met the bank president. And gently let it be known that Martín Verdadero would be his legal representative in Caracas.

"We have a very exciting project being planned," he hinted mysteriously. "I hope you'll understand why I can't discuss it further at this moment. Actually I just wanted to meet my banker . . . the man with whom I will be doing so much business in the future."

They spoke for ten minutes.

Victor stood abruptly. He extended his hand. "I'd like you to know, Señor Gutierrez, I'm quite impressed. I see interesting and profitable days ahead for both of us."

They shook hands warmly.

Unlike Victor, the banker was genuinely impressed.

He smiled amiably at Victor. "Señor Jordan," he offered, "it has been a pleasure. And if I can be of any assistance to you at all I should be offended if you failed to make your wishes known."

"Well yes," Victor said as though remembering something. "The name of a skilled seamstress. Do you know of one?"

The banker was taken by surprise. "A seamstress? Well . . . no . . ." He couldn't allow his offer to seem empty. "But if you will tell me the name of your hotel, sir, I shall find one for you and have her there within the hour."

"That would be appreciated, señor."

Step two completed.

They returned to their hotel and waited.

The seamstress arrived within the hour as promised.

Having purchased forty-two shirts in Phoenix—two samples of each collar style and size—Victor now presented her with twenty-one of them. One full set. Her instructions were to disassemble all of them with great care.

She didn't question. If someone wanted things taken apart, it could be done as easily as putting them together. A job was a job. She would have them returned tomorrow afternoon. Everything would be to Señor Jordan's satisfaction.

Step three completed.

In the course of the morning, Chana became increasingly interested in Victor's activities. He had told her nothing in Phoenix. There she had believed the trip to be purely for pleasure. The only inkling of another purpose lay in his comment that she would be very useful to him and that he would buy her things on their return. Now, she began to see the outlines of an intriguing enterprise. Business represented respectable money to her. And lawyers, bank presidents, references to Venezuelan officials—! That could only mean *big* business. Enormous sums of respectable money. She was becoming excited. When the seamstress left, she made her feelings known.

There was a sudden burst of laughter. Pleasure. Her eyes flashed pride. "I don't understand everything that is happening, Victor," she said, "but you are *magnífico.*"

She ran on: he was a man of talents. Respected. *Un hombre de importancia.* Someday, he would be a *great* man. Oh, how she loved him, loved him!

She tried to question him. To learn more about what they had been doing, about how she could be of greater assistance.

It was the first time she had ever seen his face go dead. He looked at her for a long time without speaking.

She became flustered. She stammered. Obviously, she had done something to displease him. But she had no idea what it could have been.

"*Qué pasa, mi amor?*"

When he finally spoke, all he said was: "No questions. Never ask questions. And whatever you see—whatever you hear—must never be mentioned."

"*De seguro,*" she protested. "Of course."

But she was confused. Chilled by the sudden coldness of his manner. Why should her happiness, her pride, anger him? What had she done so wrong? She became silent immediately.

That night, he left her in the hotel and made his first contact with Luis Obregón—cousin to General Miguel de Ortega and Colombian attaché assigned to the embassy in Venezuela. In Phoenix, Victor had been told the attaché spoke English. He went to his home. He found him to be a distinguished-looking man in his forties. Anxious. Nervous. Involved in an undertaking that was clearly no longer to his liking. Decidedly a weak link.

Victor presented a coded letter of identification from Francisco Vargas, the Venezuelan consul. Luis Obregón read it eagerly. He could not have been more relieved. It opened the tap of his anxieties, and they flooded out. "I am in possession of one hundred eighteen finished gems," he ran. "Imagine. One hundred eighteen emeralds stolen by a mineowner from his own company and transported illegally by myself into a foreign country. Incredible, I tell you. Hideous. My career, my name, my life are in jeopardy. When I was carrying only three or four stones at a time there was no real danger . . . no great risk. But now— This last trip—a single trip and one hundred eighteen emeralds. No! I don't like this at all. And I will speak to my cousin General Ortega about this. Most assuredly I will."

Victor said nothing. He absorbed the particulars of the operation that were being revealed so carelessly. And he knew that something would have to be done about Señor Louis Obregón. For the time being though he merely said, "I'll relieve you of your burden in eight days. The consignment is safer where it is now than it would be in a hotel room."

"Please, Mr. Jordan," Obregón begged. "Take them now. I am sure you are more skilled in matters of concealment than I. If they should be discovered here it would be disastrous."

"I'll call you before I arrive," Victor answered, ignoring the plea. "You won't hear from me before then."

In the following days, he was quite busy. No time was wasted. He signed an agreement with Señor Verdadero. Fifty percent of the corporation was to be shared equally between Verdadero and another party who, as vice-president, would supervise overall production and sales activities. He wanted no trouble with the Venezuelan government. An operation, he felt, in which nationals held fifty percent of the corporation would satisfy all and keep him safely in the background.

With the help of his banker, he found a middle-aged haberdasher to manage the business: Señor Porfirio Lopez.

The man was ideally suited to Victor's needs: young enough to see opportunity and old enough to represent experience and mature judgment. He was overwhelmed by the prospects. Twenty-five percent of a promising business venture offered with no capital investment or risk at all on his own part! An association with Martín Verdadero. It was more than a person could dream of.

"Be assured, Señor Jordan," he said as they sealed the agreement with a toast of wine, "we shall have a manufacturing company that will be the envy of all of South America."

"I agree wholeheartedly," the lawyer added. And all four —Chana included—raised their glasses happily.

This was no empty venture to Victor. While he was in Venezuela to smuggle emeralds, he was determined as well to get full value from his investment money. If shirt manufacturing could become profitable, it should be treated with the same care as smuggling. Besides, a large, healthy, legitimate corporation would always be his safest cover.

Within a day, they found a small location where the business could be started. They estimated costs of renovation, machines, staff, office equipment and miscellaneous needs. From Porfirio Lopez, Victor received a list of items not easily obtainable in Caracas. He would have them shipped in from the United States.

The Wellsley shirts were to be the company's models.

And to his vice-president in charge of production and sales, Victor presented a full set of shirts with ties and cufflinks and the twenty-one samples that had been disassembled by the seamstress. Someone was put to work immediately to fashion templets from their parts.

The company's name was recorded officially.

"How do you say *fashionable* in Spanish?" Victor asked. Chana offered, *"Moda."*

"Is that fashion with . . . ?" And he closed one eye slightly and gently rubbed together the tips of his right thumb and index finger.

"Ohhh." She understood and smiled. "No. You want *elegante."*

And that's how Wellsley Shirts became *Los Elegantes* throughout South America. A multi-million-dollar corporation that did absolutely nothing for the Wellsley stockholders. But one that became the legitimate base of Victor Jordan's personal fortune.

It wasn't all business during the ten-day visit. He found time to take Chana to a number of points of interest. She loved the churches of Caracas. Their grandeur, style and age made her feel her religion as never before. She genuflected constantly. And lit her votary candles. And murmured Hail Marys. And entered confessionals on three separate occasions. And left money everywhere. And held Victor's arm tightly. And reflected on her life. And felt terrible gnawing guilt. And cried softly. And swore secretly to be a different person. Cleaner. Better. The churches of Caracas were a heavenly-hellish experience for her. But they didn't affect her sexual proclivities in the least. As soon as Victor kissed her she trembled with love. As soon as his fingers touched her body she heated with longing. She couldn't get enough of him, and she abandoned herself to their nightly rituals as fully as she gave herself to her morning Mass.

The young tourists did other things too. They ate well in fine restaurants. They danced in hotel lounges. They shopped and bought little things. For him, a silver key ring decorated with a Mayan profile in relief against an ebony background. For her, a purple *rebosa* that draped softly about her shoulders and a lace gold-and-white mantilla, which, when covering her head and lightly framing that lovely face, made her look exquisitely ethereal.

It was a good trip. Productive. Enjoyable. Satisfying.

Now to make it profitable.

Three days before they were to depart for Miami, Victor had the seamstress prepare two pouches for the emeralds. His instructions were quite explicit: they were to be made of a thin lightweight organdy fabric, one orange and one gold in color; the gold pouch was to be two inches in width and seven inches in length; the orange pouch was to be two-and-a-quarter inches wide and seven-and-a-quarter inches long; the gold was to have a three-inch flap at its open end; the orange was to have a thin double drawstring that would be four inches long after closing.

The pouches were delivered the next day. They met his specifications perfectly. He was satisfied.

Chana wondered what this was all about as she interpreted for him. But she remembered clearly his reaction when she had questioned him last. He had frightened her. This time she wondered to herself.

Her puzzlement was increased the evening before they were to depart. He told her to wait for him, and he left her alone in the hotel lobby. There was no preliminary statement. No effort to explain. "Wait here," was all he said. "I'll be back in an hour."

He returned in less than an hour.

Outside and one block away from the hotel he signaled a roving taxi. Presenting the driver with a slip of paper on which he had written an address he murmured a simple *por favor*. He was soon with Luis Obregón to claim his consignment of emeralds.

The attaché greeted him as though Victor were *El Gran Libertador*. Here was the long-awaited rescuer. The one who would ease him of his terrible burden. Luis Obregón's relief was almost palpable. But because he was a trained and cultured man, because he was after all a man of importance (and because Victor's presence in Caracas was in itself comforting) he tried to cover it in this second meeting with an air of charm and graciousness.

"Ah, Señor Jordan," he said beaming, "I must confess to having been a bit apprehensive these last few days. Not having heard from you at all until your telephone call last night . . . well, I was concerned that something might have happened to you . . . and quite naturally I would have wanted to assist you if that were the case. . . . After all, a stranger in a strange land . . . there are so many unpredictable possibilities . . . one never knows, does he?" He laughed lightly.

Victor understood. The fact that he was here to claim the emeralds made no difference; as long as they were in proximity the attaché would fear.

Nevertheless, Luis Obregón went through the formalities of hospitality. "Would you care for a glass of wine?"

"Just the emeralds," Victor answered. He wanted distance between himself and this rabbit.

"Of course, señor." He welcomed the response.

The attaché left the room and returned shortly with a small, black rectangular box. He offered it with his left hand. At the same time his right was extended for a handshake that would conclude the meeting. "It has been very good meeting you, Señor Jordan."

Victor took the gem box and ignored the proffered hand. He crossed to a small desk. There he sat and opened the box.

"You said one hundred eighteen."

And he dumped the contents across the large blotter pad. They formed two clutter-lines of little yellow envelopes. Methodically, Victor opened each one and extracted the soft tissue that protected its solitary green stone. He exposed them all. And counted them. One hundred eighteen. Lovely in color. Attractive in cut. Most around the size of his middle fingernail. This would be a profitable consignment.

The attaché stood behind him during all of this. Shielding him from imagined Peeping Toms. Fidgeting slightly. Trying to control his nervousness but jumping at little night noises. The actual appearance of all those stones lying exposed on his desk was almost more than he could endure. And as Victor slowly cut the soft tissues into smaller squares—about one quarter of their original size—with a pair of scissors he had brought with him expressly for this purpose, Luis Obregón was no longer able to contain himself. He had no idea what Victor intended at this point or how long this would take.

"Excuse me, señor." His voice was a hoarse whisper. "Wouldn't it be more convenient for you to do this in the privacy of your hotel room?"

Victor ignored him. Carefully he returned fifty-nine of the emeralds to the smaller space-conserving tissues. And then alternating the wrapped with the unwrapped he placed each one meticulously into his small gold pouch. In this way he allowed the wrapped emeralds to protect the unwrapped that lay between them. The process was tedious but when he had completed the packing of the gold pouch and folded the flap inside to prevent spilling, and when he had slipped the gold pouch into the orange one and closed its drawstring he held a beautifully packed smooth orange blackjack. His computations had been correct. The emeralds filled the pouches perfectly. He hefted his handiwork three of four times and permitted himself a small smile of satisfaction before placing it inside his shirt. Then he scooped together the remaining tissues and the envelopes and crammed them into the rectangular box. He stood. He turned. "You'll need this," he said presenting the attaché with the empty gem box. "I'll be back in a month." And he crossed to the door.

Luis Obregón followed him. He was sufficiently controlled now to protest a bit petulantly. "It was as I said Señor Jordan, was it not? One hundred eighteen."

Victor looked at him without responding.

"People should really learn to trust each other," the attaché answered the silence. But the voice quavered slightly, making the statement more request than demand.

Victor smiled without warmth. "Until next month, Señor Obregón."

The next morning, the emeralds were still in the pouches. Only now, they were taped to the inside of his thigh where they made a modest bulge as a natural part of his sex. (Later, aboard the ship, they would be transferred to his shaving kit.)

Victor was met in the hotel lobby by his two new partners. Each believed the idea to escort Señor Jordan and the lovely Señorita Ramirez to their ship at La Guaira had been his own. Actually it was Victor who had planted it. He wanted their assistance.

Everything went as expected. A few bolivars here. A few bolivars there. And thanks to the presence of his partners, the official treatment reflected respectful consideration of an obviously important American and his gorgeous female companion.

Soon, they were aboard the ship. Comfortably state-roomed. Pleasantly relaxed. It had been a very smooth departure.

The trip home was one continuous delight. The other passengers were convivial. The weather was excellent. The seas like butter. And Chana radiated.

She was bubbling. Ecstatic. Loving. Sexual. And the night before they were to arrive in Florida, she became Aphrodite incarnate.

They had just left a marvelous ship's party at which her vivacity had sustained the evening's fun and pleasure. Victor was locking the door of their stateroom. She came up behind him. Her arms slipped about his waist and she pressed her cheek to his back. Her mood shifted to something significantly deep and warm. The entire Venezuelan experience had suddenly swept over her. The lady like, respectful way in which she had been received everywhere. The pleasure and excitement of almost every incident, every scene. The marvelous feeling of value from having helped him with his new *Los Elegantes*.

"Do you know," she asked softly, "how ve–ry much I am in love with you?" Her voice was throaty, richly fervent.

He rubbed her arms.

"This trip has been . . ." She couldn't complete the sentence.

He tried to turn slowly.

She continued to hold him. Pressing. Squeezing. Making his movement difficult. He heard soft, stifled sobs. And when he was finally able to face her she would not look at him. Her head was bowed against his chest.

He took her face in his hands and lifted it.

Slowly her glance came up. And she tried to smile. It became a tremulous glow through tear-glistening eyes. The beauty of that look was pure, magnificent naked love.

"*O por Dios*," she whispered, "you are my life."

"And I make you cry?" It was asked softly with a gentle, teasing smile.

In answer she merely looked at him for a few moments, her eyes laying open her soul. And then she reached up slowly and placed her full mouth over his lower lip. Softly, gently she began to pull at it. She held it sweetly between her lips and ran the underside of her warm tongue over its tender interior.

He didn't move. He allowed himself to be loved. But her deep ardor, surfacing toward an open eruption of passion with each taste of his mouth, touched him instantly. He felt that single familiar twitch at the base of his penis. Deep inside the flesh within the scrotum. The floodgate opened. And the flow of hot blood forced a quick and steady tumescence.

She kissed the corner of his mouth.

He licked her lips lightly and heard a sudden catch in her breathing. And then with a sweet whimper she clamped her mouth fully over his and sucked hard until his tongue was drawn into soft rolling contact with her own.

Her body pressed firmly against him. He could feel the full sturdiness of her breasts. The pressure of her belly. The hard base under the pudenda as, instinctively, she began small flicking pelvic movements. He thrust forward to meet one of her rhythms. It was as though a nerve had been touched. She gasped and pulled him tighter to herself. There was a moment of grinding contact. Their breathing mingled. Became shorter. More audible. Husky. Stertorous.

He placed his hands on her shoulders and eased her away to look at her.

A concert of tiny movements was playing over her face. Minute quiverings of longing. In her eyebrows. Lips. Nostrils. Her fire was burning. Touching her nerve endings. Heating her insides. Glazing her eyes. She was building rapidly to a blaze.

Quickly he began to remove his clothes.

Quickly she did the same.

And when they were in bed together she spread herself eagerly and eased fully upon him. Taking all of him. Loving the fullness of him within herself. Feeling the oneness of her envelopment. She had her man. Her Victor. She was ecstatic.

They loved repeatedly that night. And each experience seemed to introduce them to newer facets of pleasure. Each one to richer textures of fulfillment. She even loved him in his sleep once—orally—and he awoke to tiny electric sensations that intensified rapidly and fused into crackling emotional charges.

The evening was like no other he had ever known. In later years he would remember it fondly as the most sexually gratifying night of his life.

The following morning she awoke first. She just lay there studying his features, thinking of her love and her good fortune. She couldn't resist touching him. Her fingertips brushed his lips. He awoke. And they were soon coupling one last time before leaving the bed to prepare for the ship's docking and their own disembarkation.

They showered afterwards. Dressed. Packed. And went to breakfast.

She was still glowing. Looking at him with flashing glances of pure love.

About twenty minutes before they were to leave the ship he took her by the hand and led her into the stateroom again.

"Lie on the bed," he said softly.

She laughed warmly. "Don't we do enough last night, *mi amor?*"

He smiled at the memory.

Quickly she stepped from her panties and lay upon the bed.

"This will be special," he said.

"Anything, *querido.*" It was a throaty, willing whisper. He handed her a pillow. She placed it beneath herself.

Then he removed the pouches of emeralds from his shaving kit. They were covered now by a tight-fitting condom.

She watched him daub the rubber with a yellow lubricant that he squeezed from a small silver tube. He returned the tube to the kit. She was bemused. Was this a new kind of game he was inventing? Minutes before leaving the ship? He had never before been strange in his sexual appetites. What did he want?

"What you want me t'do?" she asked softly. Her voice was troubled.

"Lie still."

And quite clinically he spread the labia of her vulva with thumb and forefinger until the vaginal orifice was exposed. Then slowly, gingerly, he worked the packet into the opening.

She lay without moving or making a sound. But her mind was a welter of distressing thoughts.

Soon the emeralds were entirely within her—except for the short drawstring of the orange pouch. That lay within the cleft of the vulva undetectable but easily accessible.

He asked, "How does that feel?"

"What is this we're doing?"

He looked directly at her. His voice dropped a note and became almost a monotone. "How does that feel, I asked."

"No tan bueno como tú," she murmured. "Not as good as you." She felt like crying.

"Can you walk?"

There was no answer.

"Can you walk?"

"Sí, yo creo."

"Good." he handed her the little red panties. "Let's go."

She held the flimsy garment. Her eyes were downcast. "Victor, I don't want t'keep this thing inside me."

When he didn't respond, she looked up pleadingly.

His expression was identical to the one she had seen when she questioned him. Only colder now. Deadlier.

She felt her insides begin to tremble. And then a pressure of anxiety in her throat. Her thoughts reeled. Was this her Victor? Her gentle considerate Victor? Her man? Her love? How could he look at her that way? Why was he doing this? What should she do?

His voice was barely a whisper. "That will stay with you until we are in our hotel room. This will take only one-and-a-half hours and you will do it without complaining."

For Victor Jordan there had never been the slightest possibility since he conceived the plan in Phoenix that Chana Ramirez would fail to comply. He knew himself well. He understood her. He knew clearly what he was capable of achieving and exactly how to accomplish it.

She heard his whispered words. She felt her stomach sink. Quietly she donned her panties again and followed him to customs.

There they were asked if they had anything to declare. Their luggage was checked carefully. They were required to empty their pockets. Chana had to dump the contents of her purse upon a counter where the items were examined individually as they were returned. And precisely as Francisco Vargas had stated, inspectors ran hands over their bodies in a quick but skillful search.

During all of this Chana remained perfectly silent.

"Why this close check?" Victor asked without seeming difficult.

"We're sorry, Mr. Jordan. We don't like it any more

than you do. But all returnees from South America are required to go through this kind of examination now."

"Why?"

"Drugs mainly. You'd be amazed at the lengths some characters'll go to bring in even a small quantity."

"Insanity."

"You're right. Trying to get rich quick. And for money there are people who would do anything. Thank you, sir. You and your lady friend are clear. Next please."

The trip proved to be agreeably profitable. Victor's share was appraised at $78,700. And although his friend Bob was paying the Venezuelan consul thirty percent and then selling the stones at fifty percent of appraisal, he paid Victor the full fifty percent and made no profit at all on his share. This was done at Victor's insistence. The jeweler was left no latitude for dissent. Victor had his $39,350 within two weeks.

On the second trip he made $40,275.

On the third, $55,000—and that introduced him to drug profits because three quarters of the packet consisted of the purest, highest grade of cocaine in Colombia. He disposed of the coke quickly in Los Angeles to a movie producer who actually secreted drug costs within the budgets of his films. This showed Victor something: profits in cocaine could easily exceed those of emeralds.

By the end of the fourth trip he had collected $184,625. He had used a little over $25,000 for immediate expenses and had invested an additional $30,000 in *Los Elegantes*. After repaying his brother-in-law Jorge Canto $11,000— the loan and interest—he was left with $128,525 net profit. Four months' work. Tax free. At that rate he would have his million in fewer than three years. Given additional investments, larger expenses, unforeseen costs—he would still make his four-year deadline. He was pleased. He would have been totally satisfied if changes had not taken place in Chana Ramirez.

After that first trip she was despondent. Confused. Disappointed. "Why you don't tell me this before?" she asked in their Miami hotel room as she handed him the packet.

"It doesn't matter."

"It matters to me." It was a sad whisper for herself.

She didn't dare ask him questions about the contents. She became quiet. But she wondered and fretted. And

when time approached for the second trip she resisted.
Weakly. But it was the start.

She began by objecting to the obviously disturbing elements of the trip. But she was careful not to express her distaste for her role as a mule, a carrier of contraband.

First, she complained about the kinds of clothes she was required to wear.

"I am not allowed to be myself."

He countered with a knowing smile, "And everyone in Caracas loves you."

"But that is not me," she persisted.

Then the airplane:

"It will fall apart." She made crumpling and explosive gestures with her hands.

He looked at her steadily.

"It will. It will," she cried.

And her career:

"I have a career. I am a ve—ry good singer and dancer. I am going to be a star."

In the end though she couldn't ignore that expression of his—with its unsettling implications—and she went with him again . . . and again and again and again. However, with each trip she felt increasingly cheapened by her role. Slowly her belief in him became shadowed with doubt. She began to conclude that he didn't love her after all. That she was only flesh to him too. True, he still bought her things. True he was still attentive. Still gentle. Considerate. Responsive to her sex. But she felt the loss of love. And that cheapened everything. Made her feel used. He was after all "*. . . un hombre como todos los otros hombres del mundo.*" A man like all the other men in the world. She was terribly unhappy. In little ways she became increasingly difficult.

He hardly responded to her outbursts. They made no difference; she was still accompanying him, still being useful. At this period of customs' practices, inspectors had not thought of conducting vaginal searches of women as stunning as Chana Ramirez. And the fact that she had become quieter during the trips—withdrawing more deeply into her pain and resentments—actually made her more helpful. Now so strikingly aloof, she was virtually untouchable.

Their sexual relationship was altered too. She offered

herself with less frequency. By the third trip he had to ini-
tiate all lovemaking. And during coitus she responded almost mechanically. Of course it had been more exciting,
more fulfilling when she tried to consume him in the blaze
of her passion, but he wasn't particularly disturbed by the
change. She was still there. Still functioning. Still doing
whatever he demanded.

What did disturb him though was her return to religion.
"I have been to confession," she said in Caracas, "and
the priest says not to do anymore what I am doing."

He was surprised. He hadn't considered that possibility.
He knew of confessional secrecy. He wasn't concerned
that his activities would go beyond the confessional box.
But the fact that she had spoken to someone—even if it
was only a priest—troubled him immediately. The first revelation he knew should have been the most difficult. A
priest had now made that difficulty meaningless. Who could
say to whom she would mention it next? He watched her
more closely.

Flying from Bogotá, Colombia, to Los Angeles on the
return of their fifth trip, Chana Ramirez's anxieties, con-
fusions and indignations finally coalesced. The result was
an overpowering curiosity and determination. Strong
enough to override the fears she experienced while being
airborne. Strong enough to produce a devastating act of
defiance.

Ordinarily when she was carrying Victor's delivery, she
was not permitted to leave his side. But she complained so
forcefully, so loudly, this time there was little he could do
to control her. She rose suddenly from her seat.

He grabbed her hand. "What are you doing?"

"I have to go."

"Sit down."

She glared at him. "Victor," she tried to whisper but
there was a distinctly emphatic tone to her voice, "when
we travel by the boat, I don't have this problem. On this
plane, I cannot sit for hours without going."

"Sit down."

She jerked her hand free and snapped angrily, *"Por Dios,
if I don't go to the bathroom this ve–ry minute, I am going
to shit right here!"* And she spun about and marched down
the aisle.

Her remark was heard throughout the section. Heads

turned. He wasn't about to run after her. He couldn't drag her back. He could only sit and wait.

In the lavatory, safely behind the locked door, she removed the pouches and opened them to examine their contents. She was carrying some cocaine this trip. It was a small amount that Victor wanted to use as a sample for two new contacts in Hollywood. The drug was in six small wax envelopes at the top of the gold pouch. Chana extracted three of the envelopes. She opened one. Seeing the white powder within, she believed the entire pouch to contain the same. It looked like sugar to her. She was puzzled. Wetting a finger with her tongue, she touched the powder and put it to her mouth. *"Madre de Dios!"* she gasped as she spat it out. *"Qué es este?* What is this?" And then a sudden horrifying thought struck her. *"Narcóticos."*

She felt weak instantly. Panicky. She imagined her body contaminated. Corrupted.

"Why has he done such a thing to me? What should I do?" She began to cry softly. She didn't want to return the pouches to her body. But Victor's eyes and voice kept exploding in her head. She cried and fretted and whimpered for a full two minutes. In the end she feared Victor more than a few more hours of contact with the cocaine. But she resolved that this was *el fin*. No more! She would never again do anything like this. And if Victor insisted she would leave him. Slip away. Never return.

Her vision was blurred by tears. Her fingers fumbled in anxiety and frustration. She began to replace the envelopes in the pouches. At that moment, Chana was sure, God was punishing her. The airplane lurched in a current and the coke packets slipped from her hands. Two fell into the sink over which she was standing. The third dropped to the floor. All three opened and their contents spilled. The sink was still wet from use by the previous occupant. The floor also. Quickly cocaine thickened in the moisture. Chana moaned in fear. Desperately she tried to scoop the wet powder back into the envelopes. But her tears and her anxieties confounded her efforts. The envelopes crumpled. Tore. It was impossible.

There was a light tapping on the lavatory door.

"Chana, are you all right?" It was Victor.

"Sí . . . sí . . . I am all right . . . *sí."*

"Come out of there."

"Un momento, Victor . . . one minute."

Frantically, she collected the crumpled wet envelopes and, not knowing what to do with them now, she flushed them down the toilet. She washed the sink. She wet a Kleenex and swept it over the floor. That went into the commode as well. Then she closed the pouches and covered them again with the slippery condom. And with great disgust and apprehension, she reinserted her loathesome package.

After drying her eyes and composing herself, she opened the door and rejoined Victor who had returned to his seat to wait for her.

"What happened?"

She didn't answer.

But she looked pale. Shaken.

They were both silent for the remainder of the flight.

In their suite at the Beverly Hills Hotel on Sunset Boulevard, she sat on the bed and bit her thumbnail anxiously. He went into the living room. She felt it was an hour before he returned. It was really only five minutes.

As soon as he started to open the delivery, he knew that his suspicions would be confirmed. Of course a check of the contents did exactly that. Victor felt a terrible flush of concern. He sighed. Oh, Lord, it was sad. Look at what fear and unhappiness could make a person do. He wasn't concerned over the loss of cocaine. There was more than enough remaining for his needs. And as to the loss of profit —he could survive that easily enough. But what a shame. Fear and unhappiness had twisted her to such an act. Fear and unhappiness—God, how destructive they could be! It was sad.

He taped the pouches to his side. Then he returned to the bedroom.

She was watching the door for his entrance. Her head was bowed. Her eyes looking upward. Her thumbnail still between her teeth. A lovely picture of touching anxiety.

He went directly to her. He sat at her side on the bed. He took her hand.

"It's all right," he said gently.

She couldn't believe her ears.

"You . . . you mean it's . . ."

"I know . . . I know," he repeated. "It's all right."

Emotions swept over her. Relief. Gratitude. Happiness. A hot rush of old love. Her eyes flooded with beautiful tears. Her arms flew around his neck. She hugged him fiercely. And she cried and laughed at the same time.

"Victor. Victor. You not angry."

He laughed warmly.

"I am sor–ry! I am sor–ry! I don't mean . . ."

"Shh," he comforted her. "I understand."

The words were flying from her. She was ecstatic. "I do anything you want . . . anything. I am yours." Her mood switched suddenly. A touch of pleading with the joy. "Only you don't make me do that no more . . . please . . . please, Victor . . ."

"Shhh . . . it's O.K. . . . it's O.K."

"You mean I don't have . . ."

"You won't ever have to do that again."

She clutched at him. She laughed and wept and covered his face with kisses.

And he laughed too and allowed her joyous relief to envelop him.

But he had already decided how she was to die.

It happened three days later in Phoenix. It was accomplished easily. A bit gruesomely. But quite easily.

She was totally unsuspecting.

He took her to dinner. To a new and out-of-the-way place.

She was dressed beautifully. She was radiant again. Her former belief in him had been restored. Her former love was as intense as ever.

After dinner he drove up past New River and into the desert to one of their old love-grounds. There was a full white moon turning the sky sapphire. And the air had its late fall bite. She didn't feel the chill, though. They lay upon a huge flat rock. Their rock. And without removing any of their clothes they made warming love. Afterwards he drew her into a gentle embrace. She snuggled, running her hand inside his shirt to caress his skin. And then in the middle of a sweet lover's kiss he sank a six-inch blade directly into her heart.

She didn't cry out. She felt only a brief clean line of pain. Something like a sudden and short internal screech. There was only one gasp, an instant of inner conflict as her body fought to hold her life. But life jerked itself away and flew swiftly through the top of her head. And she was dead.

Victor calmly laid the knife aside. Its blade was still exposed. He removed every article of clothing and jewelry she was wearing. He looked at the wound. There was very little blood coming from it. He folded her clothes and stacked them in a neat pile. And then he turned her on her back—arms and legs outstretched. Spread-eagled. He looked down at that magnificent body. Pity, he thought, so lovely . . . such waste.

The mutilations were done quickly. He cut each breast three times. He lacerated the nipples. He punctured the navel. And finally he slid the blade into the vagina and with one swift stroke joined it to the rectum. A brutal episiotomy.

As he cleaned the weapon on her dress he looked at his work and he was satisfied. When they'd find her it would look like a sex murder by some crazed rapist. He gathered her clothes—which he would later burn—and coolly drove home to his apartment.

He knew about the desert—it had many secrets and hid many bodies. But this one wasn't supposed to remain hidden. It was discovered after six weeks.

The young lieutenant in homicide who was placed in charge of this investigation was known as Taxman. Shortened inevitably to Taxi. He hated nicknames, and he objected constantly. Nevertheless, everyone continued to call him that.

In time he unearthed Chana Ramirez's relationship with Victor Jordan. But Victor was not present when Taxi visited his apartment. His absence led the detective eventually to locate Jorge Canto. He called upon the restaurateur.

"Where is your brother-in-law now, Mr. Canto?" Taxi asked.

Jorge Canto was quite proud of Victor's cleverness and accomplishments. He spoke readily. He told Taxi of the Venezuelan shirt manufacturing venture. Of Victor's regular visits to South America. But as for information concerning Chana Ramirez, Jorge could supply nothing.

"Yes, I've read of the murder. Terrible thing. She was really a beauty wasn't she? Are you suggesting my brother-

in-law . . . ? Lieutenant, please. Well of course he could
have known her, but if he did I don't know anything about
that. I'll tell you what I do know about my brother-in-law
though: someday he's going to be a fantastically successful
man. And soon too."

"When is he expected back, Mr. Canto?"

"Anytime now. He usually makes a trip a month. He's
away about two weeks each time."

"Thank you, Mr. Canto. You've been very helpful. And
I'm sorry if I've given you the wrong impression. I didn't
mean to imply in any way that your brother-in-law is involved in this killing. I'm just asking questions of anybody
and everybody who may have known the girl."

"I understand, Lieutenant. I'll tell him about your visit
as soon as he returns."

In time—a week—Victor did return. And the subse-
quent interrogations by Taxi left the detective with nothing.
Yes, he knew Chana Ramirez. They had been lovers. She
had been his companion to South America. But they had
argued about seven weeks ago. She was fiery. Explosive.
And she had demanded that he leave her alone. He had.
What was the argument about? Good God, with her it could
be over anything. This time it happened to be over the
clothes she wore. She liked to look flashy. He had insisted
she be more subdued. More subtle. And he had said he
wouldn't take her to South America anymore if she refused
to wear the things he had bought for her. Where did he
meet her? At a stag party. She was one of the performers.
A singer and dancer. Nude. They lived together for about
five months. Yes. Very nice. When she wasn't getting upset
about things. Oh, like her career . . . her fear of flying . . .
passport problems . . . her real name was Yñez Camarón. . . . It means shrimp . . . She hated it. Of course he was
surprised and troubled by the murder of a girl he used to
live with, but he was a businessman, Lieutenant, and his
feelings for her were never really that deep. . . . He could
never become meaningfully involved with a whore.

Taxi never did buy Victor's answers. Not even after two
cowboys were apprehended, placed on trial and found
guilty of the decade's most sensational sex murder—a
savage killing stemming from bitter revenge, revenge for a
beating they had suffered six months earlier when, ad-

mittedly, they had attempted to rape her. Their deaths in
the electric chair at the state penitentiary in Florence disturbed Taxi deeply. In his thinking, the mutilations of
Chana's body had been too clean. True, there was seminal
evidence of sexual activity. And numerous other particulars
—like the possession of a deadly knife by one of the cowboys—that led to their conviction. But he felt certain that
anyone insanely vengeful enough to nurse intense hatred
for six months and then to rape and brutalize would have
done so with a jagged, convulsive rush of violence. All of
Chana Ramirez's body wounds had been much too neat for
his liking. Too clean. Too calculated. And although he
was the arresting officer, he stated this belief repeatedly
enough to earn himself the impatience of his colleagues.
Especially when psychiatric testimony at the trial estab-
lished authoritatively that "cool and calculating demeanor
is often effected in times of extreme emotional stress." He
believed too that Victor's reactions to Chana's death had
been strange. Too unemotional. Too remote. The deeper
he got into Victor's habits, personality and psychology as
he investigated, the more convinced he became that the
wrong people were being executed. He continued to protest. And he continued to experience the sting of his colleagues' ridicule. In the end, Taxi could prove nothing.
However, he once stated his suspicions openly to Victor's
face, even making the theatrical and silly promise that one
day he would nail him for this one. Well, he never did
"nail" him for anything. And of course Victor Jordan went
freely about his business of amassing one million dollars
by the time he was twenty-five.

"Fasten your seat belts please. We'll be arriving at Sky
Harbor International in fifteen minutes."

Victor Jordan heard the stewardess's sweet soft voice and
opened his eyes. The memory had been relived in detail. It
left him strangely pensive. He had left Phoenix approximately three years after that episode in his life, $90,000
short of his goal. During those three years, Taxi had been
a frequent caller. A persistent investigator. A nuisance.
Nevertheless, Victor had admired his tenacity. It was something he could understand: Taxi, too, had been a man
dedicated to excellence; an unsettled score was something
with which he, too, could not live. Victor had liked that.

He sighed.

"Are you all right, sir?" the young, cool business-type at his left asked.

"Fine, Andrew. Just thinking." Then he offered uncharacteristically, "I haven't been in Phoenix in twenty-six years. It'll be good to see family again."

"And friends?"

Victor nodded. "There were people." He became silent. He wondered, what have the years done to them?

Well, Bob, the jeweler, was still in business. And flourishing.

The Venezuelan consul had long since returned to his country where he died peacefully in retirement in 1968.

And Taxi, the young detective, had remained with the department. Eventually, he became its chief. No one called him Taxi anymore. It was Matt Wheeler now. And he no longer thought of the nickname or of its originator—a Bible-selling murderer who had once called him the "Tax Man" because, like his namesake Matthew (who was a revenue collector before becoming a disciple of Christ), Matt Wheeler always hounded his subjects until full payment had been made.

Victor waited until the small man and his friend had left the plane. Then, between four bodyguards, he entered the magnificent lobby of Sky Harbor International Terminal.

13

It was nine o'clock when Sharon Kane left the Sorry Spike. There had been a brief shower. Clean October air now carried the crisp scents of desert life. But she was oblivious to them.

As she crossed the parking lot, she unwrapped her injured hand. The pale, pink fluid still ran from the wound. Since it contained no coagulants, it could be stanched only by a closing of the wound itself, only by a reconnection of the veins. She stopped. And covering the back of her hand with her good palm, she exerted a light pressure. The slickness spread into creases, between her fingers, under her nails. But very quickly, a remarkable transformation began to take place. Skin around the lesion puckered and pinched. Subcutaneous tissue roiled and drew itself into tiny, crawling ridges. And the entire wound began to close almost like a zipper. Then she stopped the healing process and held it where it was—advanced enough to halt the flow of fluid but short enough of completion to allow the hand still to appear cruelly mutilated. A flicker of self-satisfaction touched the corners of her mouth. It was a good idea. It would work well. She flipped the stained napkin into the air with a mirthless show of determination. It landed on the radio antenna of a parked car and hung there like a lifeless pennant. The symbolism did not escape her. She allowed herself a low grunt, and then, with long, quick strides, she continued her way toward the end of the lot.

The car parked farthest from the restaurant was a 1977 LTD. Its doors were locked. She merely gripped a handle and the locks snapped open. In the driver's seat, she touched the ignition switch lightly with the tip of a finger. The engine caught immediately, and she pulled the car away, tearing from the Sorry Spike's parking lot with resolute purpose.

Her destination was the First Evangelical Church of Christ.

14

The Reverend Paul Nelson was on the sixth day of his week-long Crusade for Jesus. It had all been prepared very carefully. He had been enthusiastic, certain of success from the start.

Today, however, the disappearance of Sharon Kane's body left him visibly shaken. Not from any special feeling for the girl. Actually, he had never met her. And he had seen her only once—when he looked quickly into the coffin shortly after arriving at the mortuary. She had been visiting her aunt when her fatal stroke occurred. And he was merely helping Mr. Demerest with the funeral service, something he did at a few funeral parlors in town when the deceased and relatives had no particular church affiliation. So, though there shouldn't have been such a strong reaction, there, nevertheless, was. It was just that something about her disappearance, something indefinably unusual—the police chief's manner, that man Revanint—was unaccountably unnerving.

Home from the mortuary, he closed himself in his office, answering his wife Clovis's pleas only with silence.

She was beside herself with worry. She didn't know what to do for him or about the evening's meeting, the starting time of which was getting near. Then, as she was about to dissolve into tearful helplessness, someone else appeared and succeeded in getting him to open his office door.

The "deliverer" arrived late in the afternoon after feeling an irresistible need to discuss the particulars of the scheduled service with him. She was a newcomer to

Phoenix, a very recent addition to the congregation, undertaking her first experience as his assistant. Her name was Geraldine Preston. She was deeply committed to her minister's interests. Composed, direct, delicately lovely, she had become the young pastor's extramarital bedmate only two days after having met him.

This was of no concern to Sharon Kane. What did interest her, though, was the fact that Ginny Preston was also a hopeful, young actress—the very one struggling with the role of Dandy Maynor's love interest in Weintraub's production of *The Trespasser*.

Sharon Kane left the car in the church's crowded parking lot.

The sounds of the revival meeting swelled from the church building and pulled her eagerly toward the front doors. "Who is it?" she heard the young minister's voice rushing and resounding in the great hall. "Who is it that pursues us through the days of our lives?"

And the congregation thundered, "Je–sus!"

"Who wants us? Loves us? Helps us? Makes us do the things we should an' gives us blessings when we're good?"

"Je–sus!"

Sharon stood at the rear of the sanctuary, looking down a long carpeted aisle toward a huge stage. The hall was immense. Jammed. People packed the rows like kernels on an ear of corn. And the electricity of fervent emotions crackled like the blaze of a forest fire. The meeting had been underway for an hour now and it was reaching its climactic moments.

"Who knows us? Knows us? Knows us?"

"Je–sus!"

"Loves us? Loves us? Loves us?"

"Je–sus!"

"Heals us? Heals us? Heals us?"

And the church rocked with an explosion of "Je–sus!"

"Hallelujah!" he screamed.

"A–men!"

"God be praised!" he shouted.

"A–men!"

He was magnificent. Strutting. Prancing. Rushing from one end of the wide stage to the other. Beaming. Sweating. Laughing. A spectacular religious cheerleader working his Christian fans into an orgy of spiritual hope.

A great pipe organ suddenly boomed. Perfectly cued. He tore into joyous song:

> You are my rock.
> You are my might.
> Oh, Jesus, be my God!
>
> You are my heart.
> You are my light.
> Sweet Jesus, be my God!

His hands swept the air invitingly over his head and twenty-five hundred voices sprang into a rapturous reprise. He was the Bouncing Ball of Salvation.

Sharon watched everything and felt the passions within the hall wash over her like great churning waves. "Perfect," she murmured.

"Sing for Jesus!" she heard him shout above it all. "Sing for Jesus, my friends, and while you raise your voices in sweet praise of the Almighty, come on up here. Come on up here, I say, and put yourself into the healing hands of Christ. 'Cause I feel the spirit of God upon me tonight!"

"Hallelujah!"

"And I know that God can heal you! Take away your pain. Give you hope. Make the lame to walk and the blind to see!"

They began to hurry toward the stage.

Sharon moved forward with them.

The huge organ still boomed the hymn, and the hall rang with the inspirationally mesmerizing swell of hundreds upon hundred of voices.

A line formed at the right of the stage.

Sharon became part of it.

On the great stage itself Ginny Preston moved efficiently back and forth, helping her minister-lover. She greeted each congregant. Inquired into the nature of his ailment. Led him to the center of the stage. Informed the Reverend Mr. Nelson of his needs. Helped him to kneel upon the large, purple pillow that was in readiness. And hurried to prepare the next supplicant for the coveted miracle. It was thrilling. She was onstage. This was theater.

Sharon waited for her to approach.

"Heal!" she heard the young minister implore in the background. "In the love of God the Father for his suffering children, heal. I say, Heal and be well again. Heal!"

"And what is your name?" The voice was soft and gentle.

"Sharon Kane."

"And what can the Lord do for you tonight?"

Sharon lifted her hand slowly.

Ginny's face paled. Her brows creased slightly in confusion and compassion. Lameness, yes. Pain, yes. Even blindness, yes. But a raw, gaping hole? No one could expect that to be healed at a touch. "I . . . I don't know . . ." She looked toward the minister but made no contact. He was praying fervently with closed eyes and uplifted face before an anxious mother and her tearful, frightened child.

"He'll help me," Sharon said evenly.

"Yes . . . yes, of course." Ginny turned the hand. "How did this happen?" It was a pained whisper.

Sharon only watched her steadily.

She looked up. Their eyes met. Sharon's gaze unsettled her terribly. She glanced nervously toward the young minister again. Still no contact. But now the woman before him was being assisted to her feet. This was Ginny's cue to bring the next sufferer forward. For an instant, she thought of leaving Sharon; Reverend Nelson should be informed of the unusual nature of this healing request. But something blew that idea away. Instead, she took Sharon's arm and said, "I think he's ready." And they started across the stage.

The minister had his back to them, dispensing final words of comfort and hope to the mother and her child.

"Reverend Nelson," Ginny whispered.

He started to turn.

"This is Sharon Kane . . ."

Sharon murmured, "I'm back."

The minister's eyes snapped wide in disbelief and fear. Blood squeezed from his brain. A roaring filled his ears.

"What . . . what . . . is this?" he choked.

"Heal me." And she extended her hand. "Heal me, Reverend Nelson." Her voice rose for everyone to hear. "Heal me, please, I beg you. In God's name, in His infinite kindness—"

He wanted to run. But she turned his feet to lead. He wanted to scream. But the chords in his throat went dead.

The mutilated hand hung before his face.

The congregation sang on. . . .

> You are my rock.
> You are my might.
> Oh, Jesus, be my God!

And prayed and watched. . . .

> You are my heart.
> You are my light.
> Sweet Jesus, be my God!

He stared at the hand.

Ginny Preston began to tremble. This was not like the others! Something different was happening here! She wanted to pull away but, instead, slowly, she began to raise her arms. And she took Sharon's wounded hand between her own hands. Held it. Squeezed it. Raised it to her lips in a prayerful attitude.

"Heal me, Reverend Nelson," Sharon pleaded. Her voice rang and filled the church. "For God's sake, heal me."

The minister felt his arms move. His hands came up. His palms encircled both of Ginny's hands, which still held Sharon's.

"Heal!" he heard himself shouting. "Heal in the name of the Father, the Son and the Holy Ghost!"

The organ boomed louder. The singing roared.

"It's working," Sharon cried ecstatically. "I can feel it. It's working!" She pulled her thoughts into a pin-point of concentration. "Oh, God, it's healing!"

"Hallelujah!" the congregation responded.

Suddenly, above the music, above the singing and the hallelujahs, above the prayers and the tears and the shouting that filled the great hall, a piercing scream rent the air. It came from Ginny Preston.

"My hands. My hands!"

She writhed in agony. She jerked. She screamed.

"My hands!"

But the Reverend Mr. Nelson continued to pray feverishly, holding her in a grip of steel as sweat poured down his face. And she couldn't escape. Her screams went on and on and weakened finally to moans.

A change came over the congregation. The singing staggered, dribbled, faded out. The prayers and chants slid into murmurs and then to a hush.

The organ hesitated to a stop.

The huge sanctuary was filled with an awed silence as all attention fastened upon the principal characters in this miraculous drama.

"Heal this child of God," the reverend's voice echoed in the stillness.

"It's healing!" Sharon cried through tears of joy.

And Ginny Preston moaned with their words in a near faint.

It was a perfectly structured moment. Inspirational. Awesome. And when she was certain of its maximum effect Sharon broke the rhythms and swung the proceedings into their final phase of glory.

The minister's arms went limp and dropped to his sides. He panted weakly as though drained by the ordeal. His eyes were vacant. His jaw hung slack.

Whimpering, Ginny Preston began to sink gracefully to her knees. Her head was tilted, her tearful face uplifted, her expression a mask of beatific suffering.

And Sharon Kane withdrew her once-wounded hand to study its unmarred condition with a mixture of disbelief and ecstasy. She whispered, "It's a miracle . . . a miracle. . . . My hand . . . it's well again. . . . It's well again!" And she held it up exultantly for all to see.

A murmur ran through the congregation. They had witnessed a mircle. It was an act of Divine presence.

But for Sharon, the act was not quite over.

Suddenly, Ginny Preston sobbed loudly, *"Eli, Eli, lama sabachthani?* My God, my God, why hast thou forsaken me?" And every person there watched in stunned fascination as she spread her arms slowly to resemble a cross. There were gasps. Cries. Tears. For clearly—very clearly—everyone could see the bloody holes that ran completely through both of her palms.

The minister was transfixed.

A woman cried, "HER HEAD. HER HEAD."

A series of small scratches and cuts began to etch across

her brow, releasing wisps of blood that trickled toward her eyes.

"Our minister . . ." Sharon announced with a twisted grin, ". . . our minister has been touched by God. . . . God has been here tonight . . . within this church . . . within this hall!"

The effect was spectacular. People dropped to their knees, hands clasped, sobbing in fervent prayer. Some sat speechless, overwhelmed by the events. And others—hundreds of others—surged forward to touch and to be touched by the good, the pious, the divinely blessed Reverend Paul Nelson.

To the whimpering young actress still on her knees, Sharon whispered quickly, "It had to be done, young lady. You were in my way." And, exposing the minister to the rush of his parishioners, she eased herself upstage.

She was pleased with herself. This time she had executed everything with consummate skill.

15

After Sharon Kane had left the Sorry Spike, Dandy Maynor turned on Howard Demerest again. "How could you stick that knife in her hand?"

But before Howard could explain anything and create even greater problems, Matt Wheeler got him out of the restaurant—fast.

Soon, the others left, too. They didn't want to remain. They would never forget this night's events, and each person preferred now to consider the evening over. Still, without their realizing it, they were connected now—another condition from which Sharon Kane was sure she would benefit.

However, there was one consequence of that meeting she did not expect—something that was definitely not in her interest:

Wheeler and Demerest were in the parking lot out of Margaret's hearing. Matt was furious; he asked Dandy's question: "How could you have done that, Howard?"

"I didn't, Matt. I'd never do anything so violent."

"Then what . . . ?"

"It was as if she were inside me, compelling me."

Her remark about Victor Jordan sprang to Matt's mind. The recollection made his insides quiver. "Howard," he said more gently, "go on home and get some rest now. I've got a lot of thinking to do about this. I'll call you in the morning."

But Demerest grabbed his arm. "Wait," he insisted. "Matt, I know how she can be stopped."

Wheeler sighed, "Howard, go on home . . ."

"Her heart's beating."

The Chief looked at him suspiciously. "So?"

"But she's dead . . ."

"Jesus, Howard, I don't want to talk about this now."

"Matt, she's dead," the mortician insisted. "Why should her heart have to beat?"

The Chief exploded, "Because obviously, even *if* she's dead, she must need a beating heart."

"Exactly."

Matt Wheeler stopped.

"She needs that circulation, Matt."

"But you clamped off a main artery and vein." Understanding was coming. Something exciting.

"That's right."

"Then, somehow, they must have unsnapped."

"That happens sometimes. They're still in her neck, though. They have to be."

"So, if she needs that circulation and something or someone should snap those clamps shut again and keep them shut . . ."

Demerest was excited. "It would take only some pressure, Matt." He wrapped his fingers around his friend's neck. The choking position. Thumbs near the windpipe. "Here and . . . here." He pressed sharply once and dropped his hands. "I've done it before. That's all it takes. That would close them, I know it."

Wheeler touched his throat. He spoke softly, thinking aloud. "The flow would stop—unless, of course," he added a terrible thought, "it was she who opened them in the first place; in which case, she could do it over again and who-knows-what to any person who'd try to close them."

"But you've got to do something and this may be all there is!" Demerest cried desperately. "My god, Matt, who can tell what she's up to?"

The unmistakable suggestion of calamity in Sharon Kane's final words flashed in remembrance. "You're right, Howard," Matt Wheeler murmured after a pause, "you're absolutely right. Something's got to be done." However, he didn't care one bit for that conclusion.

16

Ben Canto was both exhausted and agitated by what had happened. Sitting in his office for a couple of hours after the others had left and failing miserably in his efforts to concentrate on the papers that lay before him, he reasoned that he'd be of no value to the restaurant for the remainder of the night.

"Watch the cleanup," he told his manager. "If you need me for anything, I'll be home."

He didn't see her when he entered the apartment. She was in the dark. The wall switch controlled only one lamp. And its bulb threw a faint glow that reached only slightly beyond the table on which it stood. She was on the couch, facing him.

"Hello, Ben," she said.

His skin prickled in the stinging electric shock of surprise. Immediately, he threw the two other light switches on the wallplate; the room leaped into brightness.

"How the hell did you get in here?"

"I turned the knob and the door opened."

"That's impossible. Did you get the manager to let you in?"

"No." She stood and crossed to the door. "Look." She turned the knob.

There was no disputing the lock's action, but his resentment was not to be dispelled so quickly. "Well, you can let yourself out of here just as easily as you got in. Good-bye, Sharon Kane." And he cut to where she was standing at the door with the intention of forcing her out.

"Please, Ben."

"Good-*bye*."

141

She didn't want to control his mind. There were just so many things she could hold onto at once. And she was sure that she would have to stretch herself very thin as she went on. Everything would be better for her and her plans if his reactions were purely his own. And although she had some regrets about using him this way, she had to win him. He was an important link. Through him she could incite others. And from their anger would come her success. This meeting was vital. Her eyes filled with tears. Her voice broke with unhappiness. A very skillful act.

"Please, Ben," she repeated softly, "just five minutes."

"Sharon, there's nothing to say," he snapped. But he couldn't push her from the apartment. He couldn't use physical force against tears.

"I want to explain . . ."

"You shouldn't be here."

"I felt you, Ben. I felt you when I touched you in the restaurant."

Actually, she was right. Just seeing her in the restaurant, hearing her voice, feeling her touch again had caused buried desires to surface, while, simultaneously, the old angers were fired to a consuming intensity. Ambivalence tore at him then and continued to tear at him now. And he wanted her both to remain and to get out of his life.

"Sharon, you're wasting your time," he insisted.

"Five minutes . . . please." Seemingly so sincere, so plaintively in need.

He wavered but fought instantly to recover. "I thought you said you were going to the hospital. That's where you should be. You ought to take care of that hand." It was said grudgingly, but she caught the subliminal tremolo of concern. The hand-stabbing was serving another of its purposes.

"I have to talk to you first . . ."

"Take care of it. Go on."

"Later." She had kept the hand behind her all this while. He had noticed only that it was not bandaged. There was a pause.

"Can you use it?"

"Uh huh."

Another beat. Then he waggled his fingers. "Let me see it."

A warning sign flashed in her thoughts. *Careful.*

"Come on," he snapped, "show me the hand."

She brought the healed member up slowly but at the same time, transmitted a clear suggestion. "It's stopped bleeding," she said.

What he thought he saw was the mutilation as it had appeared to Ginny Preston. "That crazy old man," he mumbled as he took the hand and studied it. "Ought to put him away. I think you should prefer charges. Does it hurt?"

"No."

He looked into her eyes and fought for a moment to make a decision. Then he said, "Get into the bathroom. I'll bandage it until you see a doctor."

She followed him and watched with a satisfied smile as he rummaged through the medicine cabinet and an assortment of drawers under the sink. She had settled to the edge of the bathtub.

"Why'd you come back?" he mumbled gruffly as he searched.

"I never left. You did." No reproach. And said so regretfully.

He stopped unscrewing the top of a bottle of antiseptic and shot a look directly into her eyes. "There are many ways of leaving, Sharon," he corrected her emphatically.

She made the brief electric silence that followed communicate volumes. But nothing came through so eloquently as the capitulation in her slow nod of agreement. He shook his head. A slight smirk pulled at a corner of his mouth. There was a one-snort laugh. "Oh, Sharon," he murmured, "Sharon . . . Sharon . . ." On one knee before her, he went back to his doctoring.

As he held her hand and studied its imagined wound, she reached with her good hand and tentatively—oh, so gently—touched his hair. One stroke. Something she knew he would have to take as a silent statement of apprehensiveness and love.

He didn't look up. However, his voice caught slightly as he murmured, "This'll probably hurt . . ." He poured the antiseptic on both sides of the hand.

She winced convincingly at the non existent pain.

"Sorry . . . sorry . . ." he stammered helplessly.

She reassured him. "It's all right . . . all right."

As he placed gauze pads gingerly over the "wound openings" and bandaged the hand with near-professional skill, she heard him mumble throatily as though the words were struggling through against his will, "You loved me . . . you know you did."

"I did . . . and still do." She was very good at this.

He looked up quickly. Was she mocking him? No. No, it didn't seem that way. Her eyes were steady. Her expression a convincingly honest display of tenderness and regret. He became slightly flustered. Felt a familiar flush of desire. Returning to his bandaging, he tried to cover this feeling by snapping strips of adhesive tape into place with more than necessary vigor, while offering a flat, blunt concession that matched his movements: "And there's . . . no . . . sense . . . denying it . . . I . . . loved you."

"And still do," she added quietly.

He looked up quickly and rejected that possibility with a sharp grunt.

But she countered with such sad simplicity, "We all try so hard to stop loving. Life would be much easier if we understood that love goes on."

"It can be killed," he disagreed tersely, completing his final check of the bandaging.

"No," she answered, "only isolated . . . walled-in by pain and resentment."

Again he looked at her. Something was peculiar. Different. He pulled her to her feet. And while he returned everything to the cabinet and drawers, he said matter-of-factly, "I'd have been good for you . . . and *to* you. I was hoping we'd get married, Sharon."

Her response chipped even further at his resentment. "I know . . . I was wrong."

That was not what he wanted. He wanted to fight; pride was pushing him. "Then why?" he snapped with evident contempt. "Explain why you lied to me."

She offered a generalized confession: "Because we're all a little crazy, Ben, and we do crazy things as we struggle through to our sanity."

"And now you're supposed to be telling me you're sane, is that it?"

"Well, maybe not sane yet," she grinned charmingly, "but san*er*."

The candor was so engaging. He couldn't help smiling.

Then something clicked, and they shared a little chuckle. But he checked himself. The laugh faded. He couldn't allow this. He had been injured deeply by this woman. Still—she seemed so different now, so much more . . . together . . . that's it, together. Even her flippancy had greater substance. The walls of his resentment and anger were tumbling. He tried one last time to be brusque. "Go on inside and sit down," he ordered. "I'll make us some coffee." However, it didn't come out entirely ungentle.

Turning obediently, she went into the living room.

They sat facing each other. They talked. First hesitantly, touching removed but near-related subjects.

He asked about Marlee, her year-old daughter.

"Beautiful as ever," she beamed. "My Aunt Ada is watching her."

He mentioned her husband as she sipped her hot coffee; she waved a short gesture that spoke finality to that relationship.

He wanted to know about Dandy, about his obscene friends, about her connection with the chief of police, about her strange statements in the restaurant, about everything that had taken place so recently. She answered every question. And her answers were always sensible and satisfactory. In time, their words became less self-conscious, and they were engaged in the free give-and-take of personal and meaningful conversation.

By the time they were finished, it was 2:00 A.M. And if he had been challenged on the point, he would have been forced to admit that he had really enjoyed himself. This was a new Sharon Kane. True, he had loved the old Sharon very deeply, but the differences he now detected made her more exciting. Now, she was even fascinating, as well as lovely and sexy.

He stood and looked at his watch.

She rose.

"I'm wiped out," he said. "It's been one helluva day."

"Thank you for talking to me, Ben." She let her appreciation eddy between them like a warm current. "I didn't come here to start things between us again—although I'd welcome a second chance and know just what to do with it this time. I just wanted you to understand me. You're too good to be hurt, too important to be scarred with bitter and painful memories, Ben. Thank you. You've made me feel better." She offered her bandaged hand.

He took it. He studied her, still trying to quell that last flurry of conflict within himself. "Are you staying with your aunt?"

Her gaze matched his. "No," she murmured, "somewhere else."

"Where?"

"Bethany and Twenty-first Avenue."

He didn't know the location of Calvary Chapel.

"I've moved to Phoenix."

He was still holding her bandaged hand, still looking steadily into her lovely blue eyes. "Big move . . ."

"A lot's been happening to me," she whispered.

"One more move and you're mated."

A game. But more than a game. A soul decision on his part.

She waited. Everything had been developing perfectly. But this was the moment she had been playing toward. The critical moment.

Suddenly, he turned with a rough sigh. "You'll stay here tonight," he growled. "I'll get some things for you. You'll sleep on the couch. And tomorrow, I'll take you to the doctor for that hand." He hurried from the room, uncertain about, and not entirely pleased with, the wisdom of that decision.

Soon he returned and dropped sheets, pillow and a blanket on the couch. He started to prepare the couch, claiming that her hand made it necessary for him to do this for her.

Nothing was said throughout the preparation.

After a few last touches to the bedding, he straightened and looked at her. Silence. Self-consciousness. Then he finally grunted, "Good night" and went into his room and closed the door.

He tossed on his bed. Sleep couldn't claim him despite his weariness. Her presence, her nearness were almost unbearable.

She lay on the couch, thinking, waiting.

At four in the morning, her waiting was rewarded. She opened her eyes to see him looking down at her. He was outlined against the faint light that glowed in his room.

Excellent, she thought. After a moment, his hand went out slowly. And she took it.

Through the next thirty minutes, she loved him as lost lovers reunited are supposed to love. At first, cautiously, letting him test the currents of his feelings, easing his body gingerly into the flow of contact. And then, with fake tenderness, pulling him deeper into tiny whorls of ardor, moving him from one to the next easily, gently, lifting him on endless eddies of sensation. She made him play in all of them and gasped and quivered convincingly in his mounting intensities. Try as he did to remain in these shallows, he was forced inexorably into the running undertow of passion. They clung to each other as he was being swept away, legs entwining, rubbing, wrapping, fingers caressing, squeezing, mouths searching. The river raced. He tumbled in it, submerged, and reached for the light, the air, that glorious suspension of Being. He felt her lifting into him . . . felt her . . . lifting. She felt him spurting into her . . . felt him . . . spurting. And he was in light, in air, in ecstasy.

He had never experienced her this way. Later, as he lay in the calm, silky languor of encroaching sleep, the twilight lake of fulfillment, he smiled dreamily and murmured, "Sharon . . . Sharon . . . Sharon . . ."

Propped on her side and touching his face with infinite delicacy, she whispered, "Yes?"

"You're a mystery, you are . . ."

No answer.

"I swear, I don't know you . . ."

"Shhhhh."

"Who are you . . . who are you . . ."

And he was asleep before he could hear the answer come in that throaty voice again, the one that was neither masculine nor feminine, the one that could have been either or both:

"Revenant . . . Revenant."

17

It was 11:00 A.M., Saturday.

"Tell Mr. Canto his brother-in-law is here to see him."

"His brother-in-law? Certainly, sir. That's Mr. . . ."

"He'll know the name."

"Of course . . . how stupid of me . . . I'm . . . I'm very sorry, sir."

His response was only the faintest of smiles and a steady, half-lidded gaze.

She became even more flustered, laughed embarrassedly, rose quickly from behind her reception desk and hurried into the main dining room of the Golden Spike, landmark restaurant of the great Southwest.

He looked about. Except for some enlargement, the place was the same. No dramatic changes over the years. The same ambience. Marvelously kept. He liked that.

In moments, a whirlwind of exuberance came blowing from the kitchen, through the restaurant and into the foyer. Jorge Canto. He was exploding with happiness. "Victor. Victor . . . Victor!" Arms were outstretched. Words were pouring from him. "Is it really you? Yes, it is, it's you! Why didn't you tell us you were coming? We'd have picked you up at the airport. What a surprise. What a wonderful surprise!" He laughed and swept his brother-in-law into a heartfelt embrace.

Victor responded warmly.

Jorge Canto bubbled on. "Have you called the house? You're staying with us of course. Does Marta know you're here?"

"No . . . no." The answer was part of a soft chuckle.

"She'll faint. She'll absolutely faint with joy. Cathy, tell

Steve I'm leaving. I don't know when I'll be back. Tell him to have Emilio call me when he gets in. I'll be home. Victor—I can't tell you how happy I am to see you!" He held Jordan by the shoulders. Pleasure radiated from him. Everyone was affected—receptionist, early luncheon guests, background busboys. Even Victor's bodyguards hovering nearby smiled. It was a new experience for them to see their employer being so emotional, allowing himself to be physically touched, actually responding.

Jorge put a hand on Victor's back. "Come. It's not far. We'll be there in ten minutes."

Jordan moved with him but as they turned, he murmured, "Follow us" to the cool, young business-type who was obviously in charge of the group.

Jorge finally noticed them. "Are you . . . ?" He turned to Victor. "Are these gentlemen with you?"

Victor nodded.

"I'm sorry. I've been so rude. . . . Please forgive me, it's just that we haven't seen each other in . . ."

"It's all right, Jorge," Victor smiled. "They understand." And he turned and led the way to the street.

At the house, it was the same thing. Marta screeched and laughed and kissed him and cried and bubbled and fluttered about like someone rediscovering a presumedly lost and glorious treasure.

Eventually, though, the mood became one of warmth and gentleness, and all three settled into that amiable exchange of information that tries to bridge the time gap between long-separated and loving relatives. They brought each other up to date. And each was pleased with the other's success. But then the glow of their mutual pleasure was suddenly dimmed.

"How's Ben?" Victor asked quietly. "You haven't mentioned him once."

Jorge rose abruptly and crossed to a humidor of cigars.

Victor caught the nervous flicker of Marta's glance. "What is it?"

"A misunderstanding," she whispered.

But Jorge had heard her, and he turned quickly and snapped, "It's no misunderstanding, Marta. He's a fool! My own son is a fool."

"Please, Jorge . . ."

"He is, Marta." He turned to Victor. "Got himself mixed-up with a little whore."

Victor could understand that. He smiled. "He's still young, Jorge."

"Not too young to marry."

That was different. Victor's voice dropped. "Are they married?"

"If her divorce has been finalized."

Victor shook his head a little sadly. "A married woman . . ." he murmured.

"A married whore!" Jorge corrected.

"Why do you say that? Why do you call her a whore?" A simple question, it was the final wedge in the levee of Jorge's control. The story gushed in a flood of anger and despair.

Half-way through, Marta began to sob. And when Jorge had concluded, he sat heavily beside her on the couch and awkwardly took her hand. His own trembled. The wounds, obviously, were still raw. The anguish palpable.

Victor was dismayed. This family, though he had not seen its members in years, was still dear to him. It was family. And family was the only unit of value in the marketplace of human relations that held any significance for him at all. The pain would have to be erased. He could not allow them to suffer this way. The problem would have to be solved.

There was a last question. "Is his restaurant succeeding?"

"I hear it is and I'm glad. I was wrong about the expansion, and I'd admit that publicly."

Victor was relieved. The absence of rancor in Jorge's response made reconciliation on that point very possible. All that remained was the girl. He smiled gently at them. "Everything will be all right," he said reassuringly.

That had an interesting effect upon them. They sighed as though a weight had been removed from their hearts. As far as they were concerned, Victor's great worldly success was proof that his desires and promises were always satisfied and kept.

Victor stood. "I have to go now. There's some business. If you want to contact me I'm staying at the Hyatt Regency." They protested but he overrode them gently. "No, no . . . if I were alone I'd stay here, but it's better this way now."

"But how long will you be in Phoenix?" Marta worried. "Will we get a chance to see you again?"

"Certainly," he said with a grin.

"I'll make you dinner."

"That will be nice."

"When?"

"I'll call and let you know, all right?"

She beamed. "Oh, Victor, it's so good to see you again." She kissed him on the cheek and embraced him.

He held her close for a moment. As he stepped away he touched her face lightly. "And don't you worry about Ben," he said. "Everything will be all right."

In the lush comfort of the rented Mark VI Continental, Victor Jordan turned to the cool young business-type sitting beside him. "Andrew," he explained casually, "there is a young woman. Her name is Sharon Kane. When we complete our business in Phoenix, I want you to find her. She may be in Los Angeles. Convince her to stay away from my nephew."

Andrew nodded. "Yes, sir."

"Do whatever is necessary."

Andrew understood the full implications of that order. "Yes, sir."

They rode in silence the rest of the way to the Sunset Playhouse where Victor Jordan would have no difficulty at all in locating the object of his concern.

18

It was 11:00 A.M. Saturday.

Felicia Ohrman was just stirring from a disquieting dream. She and Alex had discussed the incidents at the Sorry Spike far into the night, and she hadn't fallen asleep until three o'clock. She tossed as daylight filtered through and chased a disturbing fragment of thought into the recesses of her mind.

And then the telephone jangled.

She started and strained against the jarring intrusion. But on the third ring she reached over and lifted the receiver.

"Felicia," a familiar voice barked urgently. "Felicia, this is Mike Ross."

She bolted up. "My god, what time is it?"

"You're not late; don't worry, it's O.K. Is Alex there?"

"Yes . . . yes . . . why, what's wrong?"

"Put him on please; it's important."

Alex had awakened with the ringing of the telephone and raised himself to his elbow as he heard the concern in her voice. "What is it?"

She handed him the receiver. "It's Michael."

He sat up quickly, instantly alert. "Yes, Mike."

"We have trouble, Alex."

"What is it?"

"Ginny Preston's in the hospital."

"What happened?"

"I don't know. I don't understand it. Something crazy in a church."

Alex moved off the bed quickly and began dressing even as he spoke. "Which hospital is she in?"

152

"Good Samaritan."

"O.K. I'll find out what happened. Where are you now?"

"At the theater."

"Get her understudy ready . . ."

"She's in Hollywood. Just called to give me notice. She's up for a film."

"Oh, no! Well, let's pray Ginny's not seriously . . ."

"They won't let you in to see her, Alex."

"What?"

"No visitors . . . and they won't explain."

"They'll explain . . . they'll explain," Alex mumbled as he tightened his belt. "Listen, if a Mr. Victor Jordan comes to the theater while I'm gone, put him in my office with Dandy and tell him I'll be there as soon as I can."

"O.K."

"And Mike . . ."

"Yeah?"

"Not a word of this to anyone, hear?"

"You're so right."

"I'll see you soon."

He handed the receiver back to Felicia. "If it isn't one thing it's another in this crazy business!"

19

It was 11:00 A.M. Saturday.

Sharon Kane was sitting in the last row of the Sunset Playhouse. She had left Ben Canto while he was still asleep, placing a one-sentence note on her pillow: "You are love." Now she waited for the next performer in her strange scenario. She didn't have to wait long.

As the heavy fire-door on the upstage wall slid open, brilliant sunlight cut a shaft down the acting area and framed the entrant in silhouette. He turned and forced the door closed again before crossing from shadows into the full working lights of the stage. It was Elliot Dark. Looking about as though he hoped to find someone, he called out, "Hello . . . ? Anybody . . . ? Am I the first today?"

"*I'm* here," Sharon responded playfully from the orchestra's darkness.

Elliot walked to the edge of the apron and peered into the house. "That you, Ginny?"

No answer.

"Ginny?"

Still no answer.

"Ginny, your games can be a pain-in-the-ass at this hour of the day." And he started to turn away.

"Hey, don't get angry . . . please don't." She drifted almost ethereally into view. "I didn't answer because you wouldn't have known me anyway. I'm sorry. Really." She came down the aisle. Right up to the stage.

He looked down at her. "Who are you?"

"Kane's the name and *theater's* my game." She smiled beautifully, turning his earlier "game" accusation back upon him. "Hi." She offered her bandaged hand. "Ooops,

154

forgot about that." A perky apology. And she raised her left hand instead.

He thawed in the easy-going charm of her manner. "An actress, huh?"

"Isn't everyone?"

He took her hand. "Hello I'm . . ."

"Elliot Dark," she bubbled, *"Once Upon a Love, Always an Albatross, Morning After Blues, The Jokester, Turnabout, Proteus Grant, Song of Tomorrow, Don't Spit in the Wind . . ."*

"Whoa," he laughed, delighted.

"I love that last title," she laughed with him, *"Don't Spit in the Wind . . ."*

"Easy to remember."

"Good advice."

"It was a fine show too."

"They were all fine shows. You're a fine actor."

"Why thank you." He sat at the edge of the stage, and they grinned at each other now like old friends.

"You didn't give me your first name."

"Sharon," she replied warmly. "Sharon Kane."

"Well, Sharon Kane, it's a pleasure to meet someone so full of life at this hour of the day." It was said with the faintest touch of sadness as though a personal shadow yearned for at least a sliver of sunlight.

"Well, Elliot Dark," she mimicked, "that's the sound of a man who could use a friend."

He rolled his eyes. "That's the sound of a man who could use a *vacation.*"

They both chuckled at the correction, but the distress had been bared. There was no recalling it.

She comforted him. "Hey, if it's the play don't worry. All rehearsal periods are monsters. You know that."

He studied her a moment. Felt a powerful urge to talk. She was looking at him with such interest, such friendly concern. He wanted to tell her what was distressing him. Did he dare though? Better not. He wouldn't like his self-doubts to get back to Mike Ross—or for that matter to anyone else in the production. No. Too risky. Better to suffer in silence. But oh those gentle, blue eyes looking up at him. And oh that lovely faint frown of solicitude. "It's not rehearsals; it's me," he heard himself admitting. "I can't even get my lines down."

"Oh, come on. You probably know them better than you believe."

"In my apartment," he sighed, "but when I get here . . ."

"Your problem is, you don't have anyone helping you."

He leered comically. "How do you know that, Miss Kane?" And they laughed together at the innuendo.

Riding the rapport she had effected, Sharon raced up the four working steps that led to the stage. "Show you what I mean. Give me your script. C'mon. Sometimes we need a little help to show us how great we really are. Give me your script."

He hesitated.

"C'mon," she insisted.

"O.K.," he grinned. "Page seventy-three." Then he whispered *sotto voce*, with a playful confidentiality, "It's the scene that got me into an argument with the director yesterday."

Sharon took the script from him. She inhaled sharply as a charge of excitement ran through her. "Page seventy-three . . ." It was murmured as though she were remembering something of special significance. "Let's sit on the bench," she suggested strongly. "More light there."

He followed her.

Elliot Dark was slouching on his spine not expecting anything unusual. Her first sentence, though, snapped him to attention. It was said softly. But with a shading of honesty that he had never heard from Ginny Preston.

JAN: *Why are you blinding yourself, Leonard? If you let him do this we may lose him.*

Though he had intended merely to throw lines, Elliot found himself responding immediately in character.

LEN: *We won't lose him.*
JAN: *But . . .*
LEN: *Janice, listen. It was only a few years ago that people were saying the same thing about astronauts.*
JAN: *It was different . . .*
LEN: *No. Honestly. The exploration of the unknown always scares us.*
JAN: *It was different . . .*

LEN: *The same thing. Risk contains uncertainty and un-certainty produces fear . . .*

JAN: *Are you crazy? Are you comparing the entire NASA space effort with Mrs. Oze?*

LEN: *Of course not . . .*

JAN: *She hasn't the faintest idea where the things go or how to bring them back.*

LEN: *I know, I know—but in a very real way this is easier . . .*

JAN: *How do you know?*

LEN: *It doesn't require anything—no gantries, compli-cated missiles, tracking stations, computers, armies of people . . . just Mrs. Oze and Kris.*

JAN: *But that's what makes it so dangerous . . .*

LEN: *Only if you underestimate your boyfriend's intelli-gence. It's a trip, Janice. That's all. Just a trip. The destination is unknown, but the mind in question isn't. Kris is very resourceful. If he can succeed in going one way, that mind of his is quite capable of bringing him back. And he's proved it countless times with those mind-bending drug trips he loves so much.*

JAN: *Wait a minute . . . wait a minute; it's something else, isn't it, Leonard? It's something else.*

LEN: *What do you mean?*

JAN: *I heard something just then, a little ring of some-thing . . . Leonard, he's your brother . . .*

LEN: *I don't know what you're talking about . . . but, Janice, even if he were my son I'd let him do this. Do you have any idea what it means? Where he'll be? What he'll see? It's the most incredible oppor-tunity in the whole sweep of existence. It turns moonlandings into backyard adventures, Voyager explorations into neighborhood tours. Any man should be willing to give five years of his life for a chance like this.*

JAN: *Then you go, Leonard.*

LEN: *What? . . .*

JAN: *Let Mrs. Oze try it with you.*

LEN: *I . . . I . . .*

JAN: *Do it, Leonard.*

LEN: *I . . . would love to . . . of course . . . but I can't*

> *. . . I . . . I have my family . . . my job . . . my . . .*
> *my . . .*

JAN: *It's something else, isn't it, Leonard? I heard it a*
moment ago . . . a little ring of something. . . . It's
something else.

KRIS: *Hey, Jan—man, what're ya doin' here?*

It was Dandy Maynor. He had entered the theater in the middle of the scene. Hearing Sharon's voice, he had felt a flood of emotions simultaneously: pleasure at the sound of her voice; concern about her hand; anger at the memory of Demerest's insanity; regret that he and she had not spent the night together—and *excitement,* an excitement that transcended everything else and held all the other emotions in check. It was the first time he had heard the play's lines delivered with so clear a note of reality, the first time two principals had ever relaxed enough to allow true meanings to emerge. And there were other suggestions in the tones now, too, suggestions that piqued interest and made one want to learn more about their hidden meanings. He was amazed at the degree of pleasure this could bring. He wanted to join. Felt a need to participate. He stepped on-stage now exactly on cue and was accepted into the scene by Elliot and Sharon as though the entire thing had been planned.

JAN: *Hello, Kris.*

LEN: *Kris.*

KRIS: *What's goin' on?*

JAN: *I came over to say hello to Leonard.*

LEN: *She doesn't want you to try this thing with Mrs.*
Oze.

JAN: *Leonard!*

LEN: *She thinks it's too dangerous. She wants me to stop*
you, and she's accused me of ulterior motives in
supporting the whole idea.

KRIS: *Oh c'mon, baby . . . there ain't no more t'this*
thing than there is in one freak-out acid trip.

JAN: *Get Leonard to go.*

KRIS: *Len? Lenny? That's wild.*

JAN: *Why?*

KRIS: *Because the on'y trip Lenny c'n handle is a fast run*

> *to the john. An' sometimes he can't even make that without trouble.*

JAN: *I'm glad you think it's funny . . .*

KRIS: *The worst that c'n happen is I'll ball some chic wherever I end up an' finally get a piece-of-ass that's out of this world.*

JAN: *Very clever.*

KRIS: *Look . . . you're my lady . . . an' I dig you 'cause nobody's ever heard before. It's like I feel it in me do what I have t'do, an' you don' try t'fuck-up my head . . .*

LEN: *Jan, think of the music he may bring back.*

KRIS: *Lenny's right . . . there's gotta be sound out there nobody's ever heard before. It's Like I feel it in me now—just screamin' t'get out—an' I can't put a note to it, I can't touch it. But if I hear it while I'm gone, if I c'n just see the shape of it once, then I'll have it. Oh, baby, I'll have it.*

LEN: *Can you think of a new color, Janice? A new form? No. Very few of us can. But he can almost do it. He's like an artist on the verge of creating new shapes and colors. This experience will be the greatest thing that'll ever happen to him.*

JAN: *I'd feel safer if some authorities knew about it.*

LEN: *Out of the question.*

JAN: *Why?*

LEN: *Because this is a scientific and technological age. And what can't be detected by the senses and thoroughly tested and measured by machines is considered the province of the kook.*

JAN: *There it is again, Leonard.*

LEN: *What?*

JAN: *That little ring of something.*

LEN: *You're . . . you're crazy, Janice . . .*

KRIS: *I didn't hear nothin'.*

JAN: *Well, I did.*

A silence hung over the stage after she uttered the last line. The spell was almost physical. Something very special had taken place. They felt it. Slowly they slipped back into actuality. Saw each other again as Sharon, Elliot and Dandy. Allowed the buds of satisfaction that tickled their insides to bloom into expressions of wonderment and joy.

And as they looked at each other with this new breathless appreciation, the word *"Fantastic!"* exploded and echoed from the rear of the house. It was Mike Ross. He came rushing toward the stage. "That was it. That was it! My god, that was it."

No one had ever seen him so thrilled, and such overt enthusiasm was immediately infectious, adding to the already evident pleasure. They all laughed. They glowed. They erupted in overlapping exclamations, evaluations, compliments.

"Elliot," Ross offered his hand, "you . . . you leave me speechless." They shook warmly. He turned to Maynor, "Dandy . . . *perfect!"* He squeezed his shoulder meaningfully. "And you, Miss—whoever you are, you're a dream come true." He leaned over impulsively and kissed her on her cheek. "What's your name?"

"Sharon Kane," Elliot and Dandy chimed.

Ross laughed. "Come on, let's sit down," he said briskly. "We have some talking to do."

Ross and Sharon sat on a rehearsal love seat. Dandy and Elliot drew up chairs and faced them.

"All right," Ross began, "the chemistry happened. . . . I don't know exactly why, but I'm pleased to death it did."

"Felt good," Elliot agreed warmly.

Dandy bobbed his head and grinned.

"And you, Miss Sharon Kane—in some way you seem to be responsible for it."

"She is!" Elliot exclaimed. "I never got that kind of reality from Ginny. Playing off it was simple. Everything flowed."

"Man, she could make me even like this play!" Dandy added.

"O.K., O.K.—let's see where we go. You're an actress, obviously."

She smiled.

"What have you done?"

"Nothing you'd know."

"Like what?"

"A religious thing recently," she offered cryptically.

"Saint Joan? The Lark?"

She shook her head. "An original."

"O. K. No difference. You're a natural."

Dandy and Elliot agreed readily.

"Now listen," Mike Ross continued, "what we've just had here was a performance—and from a cold reading, no less. That's incredible. I don't have to see more. I couldn't see more in a formal audition. So what I want to know now is if you'd be willing to do the part of Janice in this production?"

Dandy and Elliot whooped their pleasure.

Sharon only smiled.

"But what about Ginny?" Elliott remembered suddenly.

"Ginny's in the hospital. Had an accident. It may be serious."

"That's marvelous," Elliot erupted ecstatically. He checked himself. "I mean, that's terrible." He was mortified. "That's really terrible."

Dandy fell off his chair laughing.

Elliot tried awkwardly to explain.

"We understand, we understand," Ross chuckled and turned to Sharon again. "Of course she may be able to rejoin us soon, but if she can't would you be willing to try the part?"

"You've forgotten the understudy . . ."

And Dandy, still laughing, couldn't resist with: "She's probably dead, Elliot. Things are getting better all the time." He rolled on the stage.

"Come on, Dandy," Mike Ross reproved. But he grinned as he said it. "Annie's out. She's in L.A. trying for a film, Elliot." Then back to Sharon. "Well how about it, Sharon? You want to take over?"

Even Dandy watched her now, chattering his head in silent encouragement.

There was just one charged, pendant moment before she accepted quietly with: "Nothing would please me more." And all four of them joined in one happy outburst.

The voice that called and cut through this clamor was strong and controlled. "Dandy . . . *Dandy*." It stopped the jabbering on the stage and pulled everyone's attention toward it's imposing owner, a tall sturdily-built man in his early fifties, standing in the aisle near the first row.

He made a striking appearance but in a uniquely subdued way. Pale-gray suit of evidently expensive gabardine. Azure shirt. Complementary silk tie. Shoes of dark gray suede. His posture relaxed, with one hand slightly hidden behind his back while the other barely touched the back-

rest of the seat. And *fire*—the fire of a perfect emerald
flashing from the ring on his little finger even in the light
weakly spilling from the stage. A large ring, exquisitely
designed but decidedly not ostentatious—the only jewelry
he wore and seemingly a natural and appropriate part of
his being. He had short, carefully barbered graying hair,
a strong set-jawed face and stunningly piercing blue eyes.
And at this moment he was smiling faintly—though to per-
ceptive Michael Ross now approaching, it was unmistakably
and clearly with the reservation of a man who rarely, if
ever, responded freely to the merriment of others.

Dandy brushed past the director and reached the apron
first. "Mr. Jordan? That you? Hey, how're y'doin'?" He
jumped from the stage. "Good t'see ya. Good t'see ya." He
grinned. Fidgeted with nervous amiability. And very self-
consciously didn't know what to do with his hands, jamming them finally into the rear pockets of his jeans. "I
didn't know you were gonna be here. Great! Great!"

Victor Jordan hadn't moved a fraction of an inch. His
expression never wavered. "Do you know why I'm here?"

"No. Should I? Why? What's it about?"

"Introduce me to your friends, Dandy."

The others were descending the four worksteps to the
orchestra.

"Oh yeah . . . I'm sorry. . . . Hey, everybody, this is Mr.
Jordan. He's my . . . uh . . ." He hesitated. Looked uneasily
at Victor. ". . . business manager, right?"

"Guardian."

"Yeah . . . right . . . my guardian. Well, this is the director of the show, Mike Ross . . . one of the actors, Elliot
Dark . . . an' another actor, Sharon Kane—she just joined
us an' that's what all the screamin' was about."

Victor acknowledged each introduction with a short
movement of his head, but he stopped abruptly in the
middle of the last motion as he heard her name. "Miss
Kane?" he asked.

She had stepped before the others, and she was looking
directly into his eyes now with a boldness that bordered on
insolence. "*Sharon* Kane." The emphasis was calm and
soft, reinforcing the impression.

He could hardly believe his good fortune. "Do you know
Ben Canto, Miss Kane?"

She smiled. "Yes, Victor."

His own smile broadened. It didn't even matter that she was being so patently familiar. He could permit such transgressions when things were going his way. "He's my nephew."

She watched him steadily. "I know all about you," she said, "and I can't tell you how much I've been looking forward to this meeting." It was little more than a whisper.

They were in the theater's office, sitting in armchairs facing each other; except for Andrew, who stood inconspicuously at a distance, they were alone.

"I'm impressed by the obvious influence you have over two people who are very important to me, Miss Kane," Victor was saying. "My nephew's abandoned his family, and Dandy's just assured me that now with your participation in this production, it will no longer be necessary for me to neglect other interests in my effort to keep him aware of his responsibility. That's very impressive. Very. But in respect to Dandy, that assurance isn't important. He can be controlled without your help, you understand. What does trouble me—and it's something I need another kind of assurance about—is your relationshhip with Ben."

"How much?"

"Am I troubled?"

"How much are you offering, Victor?"

Now, the use of his first name nettled him. He studied her. Who was this snip? What made her so confident? She sat there before him with the subtle arrogance of a professional bridge player holding a seven-no-trump hand, seemingly directing the game her way. At another time, under other circumstances, she might have intrigued him. But now he was vexed. She was not going to make the rules to this game, not this sweet-faced little trollop. His expression flattened. He ignored her question. "Are you and Ben still seeing each other?"

"We slept together all last night."

"And are you married?"

"Not yet."

"Good."

"But that doesn't change a thing, Victor. I want to know what you're offering."

He eased back into his chair and settled both hands on

the armrests. "I'm going to offer you some very good advice, young lady. . . ." His voice was cold.

"You're a disappointment," she interrupted.

His head leveled. His eyes narrowed.

"I was sure you'd offer money," she continued. "Victor Jordan believes in money. It buys things. Jades. Paintings. Sculpture. *People.* You are a collector, aren't you, Victor? Artists. Athletes. Andrew over there. Dandy. All are things to you. And the more you own, the safer you believe you are. So be safe, Victor. Be very safe. Try to buy *me*. Try."

It was all delivered so easily, a naked evaluation, an effortless provocation.

Victor felt another flush of anger. His voice began to go dead. "There will be no money . . ."

She interrupted, matching his tone. "Good. You couldn't have offered enough anyway."

"You're going to leave this city. . . ."

"I like it here."

"I want you out of my nephew's life. . . ."

Her eyes didn't leave his. She leaned forward, and slowly, deliberately, she intoned, "You can't have everything you want, young man."

Though he didn't reveal it, Victor Jordan was taken aback by this. *Young man?* And the conviction with which she had pronounced that last sentence. For an instant he had felt almost childlike in it. The impudence. Wait—what was that sensation? It was new to him. A mild cold prickling. He couldn't identify it. No matter—it was gone almost before it had occurred. In its place, though, was something he recognized easily enough: resentment, a deep and burning resentment toward this smiling, insulting little—

He stood and looked down at her. "We'll see, Miss Kane," he said.

He left the office and the theater without another word. However, settled again in the plush rear seat of the Lincoln Continental and looking straight ahead, he murmured to Andrew, "She needs instruction. Give this to Domitro. He's to teach her a lesson—a good one."

20

Though coming from opposite directions, they arrived at the theater simultaneously, just as Victor Jordan had turned into Sixteenth Street—Alex and Felicia in one car and Anthony Krozier in another.

"Mr. Weintraub," he called, jumping out and slamming the door of his Toyota. "Hold on a minute. You and I are going to have a talk."

Alex recognized the signals immediately. "Dammit," he muttered. Evidently, the day was going to be an unbroken series of problems. He had come directly from the hospital where he was informed of Ginny's condition by the chief of orthopedics. It had been necessary to raise holy hell before he was given that information ("You understand, Mr. Weintraub, the curious nature of this injury is something the hospital does not want unduly publicized."), but he was finally told everything. And he was aghast. Mangled. Her hands were mangled. As though a hot poker had been driven through them. Flesh scorched. Bones smashed. Nerves, tendons, muscles ripped, crushed. She had no use of her fingers at all. However, a mystifying incongruity in all of this caused the doctors to enjoy some hope of recovery: she was experiencing no physical discomfort whatsoever; there was a complete absence of pain. It wasn't shock either. The hands themselves still retained their full capacity to feel sensations—the tickle of a feather, the prick of a pin. Perplexing but encouraging also. As for the period of hospitalization, there was no telling how long she would be incapacitated.

Alex had been allowed to see her for five minutes. This

too, was unnerving. For although she was calm and coherent, she saw every detail of her experience with traumatic clarity. She wept softly as she described the episode to him. He wished only that he knew some way to comfort her. The poor kid. The poor kid. Why should this insane religious aberration have happened to her? And then he gasped in a breathtaking stab of surprise. She had mentioned a name. *Sharon Kane.* He stopped her. He questioned her. He had her describe the young supplicant. Her face. Her clothes. Her hand. It *was* Sharon Kane.

As he left the room, his mind was a turmoil of questions. Why was she at that church? Why there and not the hospital? Was it because Ginny was there? Was she in any way responsible for Ginny's mutilation? And if so, how? And why was she with Dandy? Because he's in the play, too? Did she know about *The Trespasser?* What-in-the-hell was going on? Jesus Christ!

"Mr. Weintraub," Anthony Krozier was saying quite forcefully. "I've just been looking over our contract—"

Alex turned quickly to Felicia. "Leesh, do me a favor and tell Mike I'm here."

She nodded understanding and hurried to the stage door.

Alex turned back to Anthony Krozier. Experience had taught him that any time a playwright started a conversation with a reference to his contract, it meant trouble. Well, he was in no mood for nonsense today. The only way to control this moment was to move boldly. "What's eating you?"

Krozier's resentment burned across the space between them. "I seem to have rights I've never been given a chance to exercise."

"Like what?" Alex snapped.

"I have author's right-of-approval in casting."

"So?"

"I was never told that."

"It was there for you to read."

"Well, I've never exercised that right, and I'm doing it now. Dandy Maynor is out of my play."

"Too late. Right-of-approval holds only during casting. Read your contract again. Paragraph six; section *a*— Dandy stays."

Anthony Krozier felt the weeks of anger peak. "He's laughing at the whole damned thing," he hissed. "He's so contemptuous, he doesn't even show now for rehearsals. He's killing it, man, and you don't care what's going on!"

Alex stepped closer. "Don't you ever say anything like that to me again, mister," he spat. "I care about everything. Do you hear that, everything! And nobody's going to kill this play. *Nobody.* Not Dandy. Not a hospitalized actress. And not even *you!*"

The attack startled Krozier.

"Don't tell me about production," Alex followed through. "It's been my life. And I don't start any play I don't care deep in my soul about!"

Something had reached home. Krozier seemed unsure.

There was a significant shift of tempo as Alex sucked in his breath and pulled back his vehemence. His voice sounded only gruff now. "So, don't tell me about Dandy Maynor. I know all about him, and he's the least of our troubles now. Do you want to worry? Think of Ginny. She's what we should be concerned about."

"Ginny? What's the matter with Ginny?"

"She's in the hospital."

Krozier was crushed. First Dandy, now this. The steam was gone. "Is she serious?" he asked with concern.

"Enough," Alex answered with a sigh. "And I've got to find somebody to replace her fast because her understudy was a mistake." He smiled roguishly at Krozier. "You'll get your chance to exercise that right-of-approval now."

They both grinned. The quiet of mutual self-consciousness prevailed now.

Alex relaxed perceptibly. "Let me tell you something, Tony," he added, his voice gentle with understanding. "I know what you're going through. Believe me, I do. The hunger related to a first play—the terror of failure. Success would be so sweet. But a play is a toboggan ride. It starts the second we spend our first investor-dollar. There are all kinds of trees and boulders in the course, and we can crack-up at any moment. As the previews approach, we pick up a lot of speed. It gets scary. Riders panic sometimes. They want to jump off, or they do something crazy that turns the ride into a disaster. And that way everybody gets hurt. So we try to stay calm, keep our eyes open for all the obstacles and steer the toboggan through a safe run. Then it's one of the most exhilarating rides a person can have. I'm not being patronizing. I know what you're feeling because it makes no difference whether it's your first play or my thirty-eighth—the feelings are the same for both of us."

Rich silence.

"Alex," Krozier started to say something, obviously tinged with embarrassment. He looked up suddenly, though, with a new thought. "Oh, by the way, I hope you don't mind if I call you Alex."

Alex Weintraub grinned with genuine warmth. "I was wondering when you'd get around to that."

Krozier responded with a matching grin. "Alex," he began again, "I don't mean to add to the problems. I'm sorry."

"No apologies. I admire your commitment. You've got a mighty temper there, but you're obviously a man who's willing to put himself on the line for what he believes is vital. And that's as good as a person can be."

He offered his hand, and they shook with a newfound understanding and affection.

"Come on," Alex concluded, "let's get inside and see how we're going to handle our replacement for Ginny."

Felicia Ohrman met Alex at the stage door. Conflicting emotions quivered over her face. "Alex . . ." she started. She was clearly nervous, slightly breathless. "Alex . . ."

He was immediately concerned, but even before he could ask "What?", Mike Ross brushed past Felicia to grab his arm.

"Alex," he was saying with unexpected enthusiasm, "Alex, you're right on time. Felicia's told me about Ginny's condition." He was urging him forward and maintaining a running explanation of what was certainly a blessing from heaven. "It's terrible about Ginny, but something's happened here that is so good, so fortunate, I don't even want to believe it. But I have to. Because I saw it. I saw it with my own eyes, Alex. It was like watching a good piece of the jigsaw puzzle fall marvelously and unexpectedly into place."

"Slowly, Mike, slowly." He turned and looked back at Felicia. She was biting her lip. "What is it? What's happened, Mike?"

And Elliot Dark hurried over, beaming. "I think it's going to work, Mr. Weintraub. She gives, y'know what I mean? She doesn't just—"

"No, I don't know what you mean, Elliot." He turned to Ross. "What's going on, Michael?"

The director looked at him momentously. "I think we have a replacement for Ginny. She came in cold and blew my mind. Name's Sharon Kane, and she put a scene together with Elliot and Dandy that you just wouldn't believe."

Everything after her name became muted. There she was again, the ubiquitous Sharon Kane. More questions leaped. What was she doing here at this time? What connection did her presence here have with Ginny's hospitalization? He became tense. All right. O.K., she's here. He felt ambivalent. On the one hand he was apprehensive about the possible answers to those questions. And on the other, he was peculiarly excited about Ross's endorsement of her potential. "Where is she?" he asked.

Meanwhile, Anthony Krozier had heard the director's words. Caught his hope. It was the first brightness he had witnessed in almost four weeks of rehearsals. And it was infectious. He followed eagerly as Alex, Ross and Elliot hurried to the stage.

Only Felicia held back.

She was standing stage center with Dandy, who was asking why Wheeler had been so interested in her, and she suggested obliquely that it was about that five-car accident she had caused. Dandy grinned. "Good thing he didn't get you into a patrol car, lady; you'd have probably destroyed the whole fuckin' police force on the way downtown." She laughed delightfully, "Thanks a lot, you shit." And she swiped playfully at him with her bandaged hand. He took the slap on his shoulder, hunching and hee-heeing happily. Then he caught himself. Quickly concerned. "Hey, hey, watch the hand." He held it gently. "I was gonna kill that crazy bastard. Might even do it yet. I know you told me it's O.K. but are you sure?" She nodded and kissed him on the cheek.

It was then that Mike Ross called as he approached. "Sharon, this is Mr. Weintraub."

"Hi," she said brightly. "We've met."

"What makes you think you can fit into this play?" Alex challenged immediately. He was determined to get her alone, and that kind of challenge would prepare the way.

"Mike seems to feel I could work out." Still unperturbed. Still bright.

"She's good, Alex," Ross affirmed.

And Dandy added, "No trouble with lines when she's around."

"That's true," Elliot acknowledged.

Anthony Krozier, on the perimeter of the group, listened with undisguised interest. His animosity toward Maynor had not diminished. It was almost revulsion. But apparently something must have happened earlier. The director couldn't have imagined this. Elliot Dark couldn't be lying. And even though he disliked Dandy Maynor intensely he had to allow—however grudgingly—that The Freak and Elliot, too, had somehow come through finally. The play. The play. That was the important thing. And if everyone could be so quickly excited by this young lady's talents, then he, Krozier, wanted very much to see a demonstration of them. Who knows? Maybe some miracle could still steer this toboggan to a successful finish. He'd welcome help from wherever it came. "Let's see what she can do," he suggested.

Alex stepped closer to her. "What are you doing here?" he asked.

She raised her eyebrows and looked around with charming confusion.

"Let's hear her read," Krozier insisted.

Alex threw a look at him as though he were about to spear him with an impatient comment.

But the playwright said flatly, "Paragraph six; section *a*."

And Weintraub held himself in check. Shafted by his own words. Well, he couldn't say no to Krozier's request now. And actually he wasn't entirely sure he wanted to. If she was as good as Ross said, he'd have to hear her read. O.K., so he wouldn't say no—but he'd damn well get some answers from her before he'd say yes.

They were in Felicia's dressing room. Alex Weintraub and Sharon Kane, alone.

All at once his mouth went dry. His viscera quivered. He had the oddest feeling that he was about to experience something momentous. What was it Ross had said at Chez Gerard's about the actors? *It's as though we're being forced to step up to a mirror from which different faces are liable to stare back.* Why, though? he thought. Why should I feel this way? She's probably only one more smart-assed contemporary kid, so cocksure of herself in every situation she'd unnerve even God. No, it's more than that. There are questions. All right, Miss Mirror, let's see what kind of faces you've got to throw back at me.

She turned. She looked at him. This time, she wasn't smiling. "I'm telling you," she breathed, "don't do anything that will jeopardize this." It was an order—softly spoken but, nevertheless, an implicit threat.

"I have questions . . ."

"I know."

"You want into this show for some reason but if I . . ."

"I could force you."

"That'll be the day."

Her voice whispered instantly within his head: *See the phone—pick it up—dial it fast—feel the burn—drop it— watch it die.*

He comprehended immediately her connection with that unaccountable experience of yesterday. It jolted him, but he didn't have time to dwell on it. He found himself lifting a clothes hanger and urgently "dialing" Victor Jordan's New York number. Resistance proved impossible. He was actually seeing the telephone again. Seeing the dial! But at the same time, he knew it was a hanger; he was fully conscious of an illusion that he was being compelled to accept. He felt it burn again. Dropped it. Saw the hanger fall, twitch, stand on its end for a moment. And then it was over. The entire re-creation. It had lasted only moments but it left him breathless. He sank to a folding chair and looked at his palm. This time, though, there was no mark. He glanced up quickly at Sharon.

Her expression was set. Serious. "I could force you," she repeated, "but it is time for you to understand some things."

"How did you do that?" he whispered.

"It wasn't difficult. Your hypnotists do it every day."

He had caught something. "I don't have hypnotists," he parried, trying to lead her.

She understood. She smiled. She followed. "Not yours personally."

"Then that *your* puts me into a category from which you exclude yourself."

"That's very good," she approved, and she sat down opposite him.

"What is it? What's that category?"

She paused for a moment, not entirely certain that he was ready for this. Finally, she murmured, "Humanity."

His pulse quickened. "What are you talking about?" he pressed deeper. "How can you separate yourself from humanity?"

She studied him a full fifteen seconds before responding. "You'll have to wait a while for that answer, Alex."

He wasn't deterred. He swung quickly to another tack. "Were you responsible for what happened to Ginny?"

"If you cooperate, she'll be all right."

"Were you responsible?"

"Yes."

"Why?"

"I must be in this play."

"Why?"

"The play's important, Alex, very important."

"I don't need you to tell me that; I'm producing it."

She leaned forward and spelled out her answer with shattering intensity: "This play, Alex . . . this play must be an instrument of retribution as well as my legacy."

It stunned him. "Retribution? Your legacy?"

Her response was an unwavering stare.

"Wait a minute," he recovered on a thought, "I don't understand—are you suggesting the play is *yours?*"

"Not suggesting, saying."

"But Krozier wrote it."

"For me."

"He says it's his."

"True."

"You mean, he stole it?"

"No."

"Then, how . . . ?"

"The way you were compelled to hold a hanger and see a telephone."

Again, he was speechless. And again, in his surprise, he saw glimmers of ramifications. "Then . . . then you've been arranging other aspects of this production as well?"

"Yes."

"With me, too?"

"Yes."

"When?"

Suddenly, his fingers began to tingle, his heart started to pound and, for an instant, he caught an image of a throbbing blue light over her face. He recognized it instantly. It had been there in his first reading of the play. Then the light was gone.

"You understand as much as you're ready for, Alex," she said evenly.

"Who are you?" he whispered.

For an agonizing moment, she did nothing more than stare at him. Then, without another word, she turned and left the dressing room.

The rehearsal that afternoon was utterly soul shaking.

When Alex emerged from the dressing room after Sharon Kane, he went directly to Felicia.

"What happened?" she asked tensely as he approached.

"Give her a workout."

"I'd rather not."

"Right now, we have no choice." He was obviously troubled.

"Are you all right?" she asked.

He exhaled loudly and touched her chin. "Make her work." It was almost an order.

Despite her apprehensions, Felicia moved to her stage position. There was something in Alex's manner that cancelled objection immediately. All right, young lady, she thought as she inhaled deeply to quell her remaining doubts, let's see what you can do.

Since the dawn of theater there had never been an audition like it. Instead of selecting a particular scene, Mike Ross decided to start at the top and to run the play until they had seen enough. But from the opening lines, there wasn't enough. And since the show was written with no intermission, they ran it to the end. It was pure, naked, supercharged electricity. All they needed were the costumes, makeup, lights and audience, and they would have made theatrical history.

For the first time, Felicia felt her fears dissolve completely. For the first time, she was able to stretch into her moments, to swing open the doors of her deeper creativity, to soar. She found herself relaxed as never before. Freed of a compulsion to try. Everything simply flowed from her.

The bewilderment. The anguish. The joy. The despair. The love. The relief. The power. This was not acting. She *was* Mrs. Oze. And her approaches to the climactic scenes captured each nuance with a clarity that generated excitement so explosive it was positively less effective.

And the others were only slightly less effective.

Dandy and Elliot repeated what they had done earlier with Sharon. Now, though, it was expanded to embrace the whole play. Cues were picked up perfectly. Emotions were clear and pure, voices exciting and interesting to hear, lines miraculously remembered.

Even the three minor characters in the play rose to levels of performance that were exhilaratingly new.

And flowing through it all, Sharon Kane projected the unifying character of Janice as perfectly as a highly detailed portrait come to life.

In one afternoon, their gasping, moribund play had been transformed into a vital entity, with each organ functioning healthily and in perfect harmony with the others. A golden theatrical moment!

The effect upon Ross and Krozier was marvelous to behold. They were euphoric. Their "baby" might live after all. Might grow. Prosper. There was hope now. They felt it in every cell of their beings.

And as for Alex—there were almost no words. All he could do when it was over was sit there and exhale the words, "Absolutely unbelievable."

Mike Ross gripped Krozier's arm hard. "You should be very proud of yourself, Tony," he beamed.

The playwright could hardly contain himself. With a grin that seemed ready to split his face, he turned to Alex and said flatly, "Paragraph six; section *a*."

And Alex responded, pleased and troubled, "No need for that. We agree. She's in."

All three went to the stage where everyone was milling excitedly, congratulating each other and complimenting Sharon. Before they reached it, though, Alex stopped Mike Ross with a sudden thought: "Hasn't there been a call for me?"

"I forgot. That guy Jordan was here."

"He was? When?"

"Just before you arrived."

"Why wasn't I told?"

"We all got caught up in this excitement and . . ."

"Dandy. Dandy!" Alex called and cut him off.

"Yeah?"

"Did Mr. Jordan speak with you?"

"Oh, hey, nothin' t'worry about. No more foolin' around." He put his arm around Sharon's shoulder.

She smiled strangely at Alex. "You'll find him at the Hyatt Regency," she said.

And the insane incongruity of this situation suddenly struck Alex Weintraub like a demolition ball: here he was accepting this girl just as he would any other person . . . any *ordinary* person. Here he was ignoring an absolutely improbable discussion that had actually taken place less than two hours ago. How could he ignore her behavior of last night or her connection with Ginny? Am I so hard-up for a successful production that I'm completely willing to forget the implications of what that girl has already told me? He had shocked himself off-balance. Severely. And he couldn't face the consequences of these thoughts just now. He had to get away from her.

"Felicia," he turned from Dandy and Sharon, "I'm going to the Hyatt. Come with me. There's a lot I have to tell you."

But even as he said the words, he somehow sensed that he would not be telling her everything. He threw a quick glance in Sharon's direction, expecting to see her watching him. But she wasn't. Instead, she was looking happily into Dandy's eyes.

"Gotta celebrate tonight," Dandy was saying. "This was out-o'-sight today . . . gotta celebrate."

"Great. Take me to a concert," she said.

"Where?"

"Lovejoy's in town."

"Really?" He was delightfully surprised. "I didn't know that. Wild! They're friends. We'll get Goose, Josh an' the girls."

"And after, we'll all go back to the ranch."

"Lovejoy, too," he added.

"Right," she agreed.

"An' we'll have us one wild brawl."

"Fan—tastic!" she exclaimed.

And he laughed marvelously and swung her in a bear hug.

"Look, I'll meet you at the concert," she offered when he had put her down.

He protested. "Hey, you did that last night . . ." .

"Clearing things away," she cut in. "It'll let me spend more time with you." It was a shaded promise of sexual paradise.

He grinned as he held her close. "All night tonight?"

"We'll see," she murmured.

He was satisfied. Then a sudden thought occurred to him. "Wait a second, you won't be able to find us at the concert."

"I'll find you," she intoned. "Don't you worry about that. I'll find you, all right."

The stage emptied. First, Alex and Felicia. Then, Dandy Maynor. Mike Ross. The others. Sharon Kane.

Anthony Krozier was the last. He had withdrawn to the orchestra again after the initial heady swirl of enthusiasm. There he lingered with elbows resting on armrests, and fingers cathedraled in self-satisfaction, savoring the glory. The anguish was gone. Even his dislike of Dandy Maynor had been mitigated. His play. *His* play. It was working. And just this morning, he didn't believe it would happen. How could that be? *She* did it. Somehow, her presence made it all come together. He owed her . . . something—if only thanks. He had already congratulated her but, yes, he owed her, and he would have to tell her so.

Domitro Londos had come from Greece two years earlier. In Athens, he had been a small-time drug pusher and pimp. A nuisance to the Greek constabulary, which was then trying to close some doors to the Turkish heroin traffic. Never important enough for the big bust, Londos managed to get in their way often enough to make them wish something would happen to him. Something did happen.

Through a friendly intermediary, he was given a job to do for Victor Jordan. Nothing difficult. Merely the breaking of enough bones to ensure the hospitalization of a minor official whose obstinacy was creating problems in one of Victor's shipping operations. It was accomplished so neatly that Victor had Andrew offer the Greek a position with his company. Specialized work. Good pay. Chance for advancement. Protection from the law. He took it. And he never regretted the move. Various assignments followed. And no matter what they were, Londos completed them with an efficiency that became inspiring. Shortly, he was made one of Victor's personal bodyguards. A totally reliable man. A man devoted not only to his employer's safety but to the satisfaction of his slightest whim.

He waited now for Sharon Kane.

This be very special, he thought behind tall oleanders not too far from the stage door. Ribs . . . legs . . . high so she be in cast long time. . . . No . . . no good . . . she don't be able t'go 'way then. He reached absently into his jacket and deftly adjusted the holster of a .44 Magnum almost like a woman arranging a breast in her brassiere cup. Break nose, cut face good. . . . Pretty gorl don' like faces busted. . . . Where she be? He had watched the others depart. She don' leave by other door does she? The thought made him angry with her.

Then the stage door opened.

He recognized her immediately from Andrew's careful description. He moved quickly. Stepped into the open and approached her.

She walked directly toward him.

He stopped before her "Mr. Jordan say you be very foolish gorl." And his huge fist suddenly lashed at her head with the force of a sledgehammer. It didn't miss. It didn't stop. It just didn't connect. Before he could complete the swing he found himself hurtling through space as though some giant hand had flung him aside like a despised insect. And there was a sound. A turbulent, whooshing blast of air. He smashed against a wall of the building. The thud was sickening. Sand, debris, loose paper swirled with him in the rush of the wind. He rolled over. Fought to regain his senses. His body screamed with the pain of a dozen broken bones. Blood filled his mouth. His mind was a blur of survival fears. She has done this! She has done this? What! What? How? How?

Just then, the stage door opened again.

"Sharon," she heard a voice call. It was Anthony Krozier. "Wait a minute, I want to tell you how much I . . ."

She had turned at the sound of her name, surprised. Her concentration slipped.

Londos was on his feet. Reeling. His face swollen with pain, confusion, rage. The .44 Magnum was in his hand. He had it raised.

"No!" Krozier screamed as he saw it. "Watch out! WATCH OUT!" What was it that moved him? The threat to his play? The life of a girl? He never knew. He threw her aside just as the gun roared. He felt the first shot crash into his chest. Felt it tear through him. Ripping. Pulling. Felt everything instantly gush. Falter. Collapse. He didn't feel the second take away half his head. He was dead before it struck.

Sharon saw every detail in the moment. Saw his chest and face disintegrating. "Don't!" she cried out. And she spun wildly around and hammered Londos with a terrible command: *"FREEZE!"*

Instantly, it was as though ice had filled every pore of his body. He couldn't move. A statue of truncated violence.

She whipped back to Krozier. Scurried on her knees. Took his face in her hands and pressed and squeezed it like someone kneading clay. But she was doing it desperately. She pulled at his chest. Scooped at it. A frenzied effort to put everything right again. And she commanded, all the while, "Don't die. Don't die."

She looked into the air above her. "Come back, come back, Krozier, this wasn't supposed to happen."

Her actions had created a nightmarish head. She couldn't shape flesh where there was none. Couldn't recapture blasted brains. Soon, she realized it was hopeless. And anger was born in that moment. Anger toward Domitro Londos. It lifted her to her feet. She turned sharply in his direction and fixed him with a fierce stare.

He was totally conscious of everything that was happening. But he was unable to move a nerve. He saw her approaching now, a set, deadly look on her face. His insides came alive all at once. He felt a hideous twisting of fear.

She stopped before him. Quickly, her hands came up and cupped his head.

He felt them. Felt her fingers around his head. Cupping

it. Squeezing it. But that was all he felt. In that split second of time, he was dead. His head was gone. It had simply disappeared! Incredibly, instantly, vanished! The torso dropped to the ground, twitching, flopping grotesquely for a time before it lay there, still.

PART IV

The Challenge

LADY

When I wake up,
    I know
That our breakup
    is so
Like a dream—
A terrible dream.
Something's bitter,
    A kind
Of a taste in
    My mind,
Like I'm mad!
It's gettin' so bad.

    I'm cryin' . . .
        Lady, Lady, Lady—
    Come on back t'me.
        Lady, Lady, Lady—
        Ain't it plain t'see,
    My Lady, Lady, Lady—
        What I'm singin's true:
    Oh Lady, Lady, Lady—
        There's no livin', girl,
            No livin' without you.

I can see it
    So clear:
Every moment
    Was dear,
Like a dream—
A beautiful dream.

An' that's all my
    Life is:
Either nightmare
    Or bliss—
An' the key
Is your love for me!

    I'm cryin' . . .
        Lady, Lady, Lady—
        Come on back t'me.
        Lady, Lady, Lady—
        Ain't it plain t'see,
    My Lady, Lady, Lady—
        What I'm singin's true:
    Oh Lady, Lady, Lady—
        There's no livin', girl,
            No livin' without you.

Music and Lyrics by Dandy Maynor
Abelard Music Publishing, Inc.
    Copyright 1976
From the LP Album: "Maynor Moods"
Eagle Records—Album #2792ADJ

21

Things were steaming at police headquarters. The wires were burning with information about Victor Jordan.

"This one's just come in, Chief," Sergeant Clemmens stated crisply, hurrying into Matt Wheeler's office and laying a fresh report on his desk. "Your man's got some hard muscle around him."

"That's only three. I need the other one." A thought. "Get me Captain Garvey in New York again."

Matt ran through the information once more. The folder before him was getting fatter. Items had been accumulating steadily since his arrival at the office at 7:00 A.M.

From the moment they left the Sorry Spike, Margaret had sustained an endless and heated monologue about that poor girl whom Howard had brutalized so insanely that she, Margaret, would never be able to look him in the face again.

Matt had listened only fitfully. His own thoughts had been much more disturbing: Victor Jordan, coming to Phoenix. Was it true? If so, for what? And the way it popped into my mind—in that girl's voice. That girl. Howard was right, she's dead. I've seen enough blood to know blood—and that was something else coming from her hand. She should be in her grave. And then he thought of his conversation with Demerest outside the Sorry Spike. A simple, quick pressure on her throat. But could he do it? Would he actually try? Sleep had been impossible.

Saturday was usually his day at home with Margaret. This Saturday, though, he couldn't stay away from the office.

As soon as he arrived, he set gears meshing. First, he

185

called Howard Demerest, as early as it was, to find out how he was feeling after last night's wild experience. And he was relieved to learn that Howard was "staying home all day and taking something for my nerves." Even over the phone, the mortician had to be reassured that his suggestion for stopping Sharon Kane was not being ignored. His distress only intensified Matt's feelings of helplessness and frustration.

After this call, he did exactly what the scene at the Sorry Spike had been designed to accomplish: he canceled the A.P.B. on Sharon Kane. Better let her make the contact, he thought. He'd see her again. She had said that. Well, he'd wait. That way, nobody would get hurt needlessly trying to bring her in.

Then he started on Victor Jordan. He checked the passenger lists of all incoming flights and found his man quickly; he sent a surveillance team to Sky Harbor to spot his arrival; had a photographer go along to snap pictures covertly; checked every major hotel in the city to find out where Jordan might be staying; called his friend, Tom McGowan, with the National Crime Information Center in Washington, D.C.; contacted another friend, Wallace Garvey, with the New York City police department.

His buzzer rang.

"Captain Garvey, Chief."

"Thanks, Clemmens." He heard Clemmens click out.

"What's happening, Matt?"

"Wish I knew, Wally. Just trying to put together everything I can on this man. Can't for the life of me figure why he's back here in Phoenix after all these years."

"Victor Jordan." There was a low whistle. "That's big, my friend. He's insulated. If there's anything there, you're gonna have to peel away lots of protection to get at him."

"Tom McGowan in D.C. said the same thing. That's why I want everything you can give me on those four men with him."

"Well, tell your photographer he did a great job at the airport. Came over the telecopier like life, and we skimmed them out of our files like cream. Wait a second. Hold it. . . . Something's just come in: this one's foreign so I was holding back until I heard from Interpol. Name's Domitro Londos . . . sonofabitch! He's got a record. . . . Now, how could we have given him a permit for a .44 Magnum with this kind of sheet?"

"Big men have a way of getting what they want, Wally."

"Goddamnit. Well, I'll get this on the wire to you right away."

"Thanks, Wally."

"And Matt—"

"Yeah?"

"I don't like it when someone's strong enough to get a permit from my department for a recognized hood. If there's anything there, my friend, get him."

"Oh I will, Wally. I will."

He hung up. "Clemmens!"

The sergeant sprang into the doorway.

"There's something coming over right now on a Domitro Londos. Get it for me and . . ."

"Londos? Domitro? Hold it, Chief." He disappeared and was back in a second with papers in his hand. He referred to the report. "Dead. Double killing at the Sunset Playhouse."

Matt leaped to his feet. *"What?"*

"Weird. Decapitation. Can't find the head, but the I.D. was made from wallet information."

"When did this happen?"

"Still happening. The bodies were discovered only minutes ago by a Richard Skolar, the theater's gofer. What's a gofer, Chief?"

"And the other body?" He was ramming things into his pocket.

"Anthony Krozier, author of the play."

"My God! Who's on this?"

"Murray. Doug Murray. He's still there."

"Tell him not to move a thing. I'll be there in five minutes." And he was on his way even as he spat the words.

"O.K. Hey, Chief, what's a gofer?"

22

At the very moment Matt Wheeler's driver was switching on his siren, Alex Weintraub was turning his car over to a sprightly young man for valet parking at the Hyatt Regency Hotel.

On the way from the theater Felicia had been rapturous about the recently concluded rehearsal.

"Alex, Alex, Alex—" She vibrated with enthusiasm. "That was the most exciting rehearsal I've ever experienced!"

"You were good."

"Good? I was magnificent. We were all magnificent. And that Kane girl—what a find! Don't you let her get away. Whatever you do, don't let her get away!"

"I thought you said she's weird."

"I did. She is. I mean—I don't know. What happened in my dressing room?"

He tried to tell her. But not everything could be framed. Whenever he attempted to indicate that there was something unnatural about her, he found the words jamming his throat and his thoughts veering to another point.

In the end, Felicia knew only what Sharon Kane wanted her to know. And her feelings were exactly what Sharon had structured. It all seemed only intriguing now. Mysterious, yes—but really innocuous. Everything seemed so different. Ginny's travail, not entirely forgotten. Just momentarily minimized. The madness at the Sorry Spike? Neatly repressed. At the moment, Felicia was the pure, successful artist. "Personally, Alex," she glowed, "I wouldn't care now if she were the Devil himself, so long as we can continue to deliver the way we did today." She laughed marvelously.

He bit his lip and nodded a kind of troubled agreement.

They entered the lobby and checked at the desk.

Yes, Mr. Jordan was occupying the Grand Canyon Suite. The clerk called ahead to announce their visit.

Even before Alex could tap on the door, it was opened by Andrew.

"Come in, Mr. Weintraub. Mr. Jordan is expecting you." He stepped aside to let them pass.

They were shown into an enormous, tastefully furnished living room.

Victor Jordan was standing in the center of the room. Quite relaxed. A glass of white wine in his hand.

What struck Felicia Ohrman immediately about the man was the quick, cool way he undressed her with a glance. Naked. For only an instant, though. She was fully clothed again as he turned toward Alex. A woman lover, she thought.

"Mr. Weintraub," he said in an odd mixture of formality and warmth, "it's good to see you again." But he didn't offer his hand.

"Victor," Alex matched his tone, "may I present Miss Felicia Ohrman?"

She offered a radiant smile and extended her hand. "Mr. Jordan."

He took it. Smiled in return. His eyes held hers approvingly. "Miss Ohrman. Please be seated." He indicated the couch. "Would you care to join me in some wine?"

"I'd love to."

"Mr. Weintraub?"

"No, thank you."

Andrew had a glass before her even as she was settling comfortably into position.

"I've been an ardent admirer since your Academy Award performance in *Angelus*," Victor stated.

Felicia nodded and smiled a gracious, "Thank you."

"If that pleased you," Alex spoke from an opposite armchair, "you'll be overwhelmed by *The Trespasser*."

Jordan looked at him. "I wasn't pleased by the film, Mr. Weintraub," he smiled faintly. "I was pleased by Miss Ohrman *in* the film."

Alex parried the rebuff nimbly. "Then you may not enjoy *The Trespasser* at all, Victor," he conceded, "but you'll surely be overwhelmed by Miss Ohrman *in* the play."

"I'm sure," Victor said. He turned toward Felicia. "I'd appreciate Miss Ohrman in anything."

And out of everything, she thought accurately, remembering the approving interest of that first denuding glance.

"Well," Victor breathed, "I'm glad everything is suddenly going so well with the play. I've spoken to Dandy. He'll be no more trouble."

"He was excellent today," Felicia admitted.

"Good. I want this experience to be very special for him."

"Why?"

Alex was immediately intrigued. Felicia's directness was always unsettling in social encounters. Apparently, she had decided to take on Mr. Victor Jordan. He watched with quiet delight. This would prove interesting.

"Why do you want this experience to be important to him? It can't be the money. He'd make a thousand times more, truly a *thousand* times more, in his own field of music."

Victor sipped his wine. Yes, he had gauged her accurately. A woman with spine. Lovely. He smiled. "Your tone suggests disapproval of Dandy, Miss Ohrman."

"To be frank, Mr. Jordan, until today, I loathed him. But this afternoon's rehearsal has modified my feelings to a controlled contempt."

Victor nodded. "He's not the most polished of personalities," he conceded amiably.

"You've avoided my question."

Yes. Spine. Tenacity. Lovely. Victor closed his eyes for a moment and saw her naked on his bed. When he opened them, he asked, "Will you have dinner with me some evening?"

"Perhaps. If you'll be candid with me now."

Alex said nothing. He was enjoying the contest.

Victor grinned. "It's in the nature of women to be curious, isn't it?"

"It's in the nature of women to be enlightened," she countered.

"Good. Now, your question: Why do I want this experience to be important to Dandy Maynor? And your answer: because there's a plan for him. It's really very simple. Dandy is required to win a significant award in *all* areas of popular entertainment."

Alex and Felicia looked at each other with a slight eyebrow and lip movement that said, "Well, there's nothing like a little ambition, is there?"

"I can assure you, he'll do it," Victor Jordan stated with quiet conviction as he read their glances. He sipped his wine.

"And who requires this?" Alex finally joined the discussion.

"I do."

"Suppose Dandy doesn't agree."

"That's unimportant. There's a principle at stake."

"May I ask what it is?" Felicia prompted.

Victor paused for a moment. He considered whether it was wise to answer that question. After awhile, his wine glass was placed on the exquisite copper-crafted table before him. He stood. Crossed to a spot behind his armchair. He turned. He looked at Felicia and saw her on his bed again. The picture was sufficiently enticing to encourage the requested answer. "Do you have any idea how wealthy I am, Miss Ohrman?" he asked by way of introducing the point.

"You're not trying to impress me, are you, Mr. Jordan?" she smiled.

"Not at all," he grinned crookedly in return. "Merely establishing a foundation for the candor that you require before accepting my dinner invitation. I'm reputed to be one of the fifteen wealthiest men on this earth. The fact is common knowledge within my sphere of influence, but it's one that I've discouraged publicizing indiscriminately. You see, extreme wealth is a peculiar creature: it thrives in a rather isolated habitat. It's private. And gawking by the curious always makes it nervous. However, the most peculiar aspect of what one of my associates once called "this Golden Beast" is the nature of its self-awareness. What it understands about itself. You see, wealth knows it is not important in-and-of itself. Once it has grown great, becoming bigger stops being its singular passion. I once heard a comedian joke: 'Money can't bring happiness. The man with two billion dollars is no happier than the man with one billion nine hundred million.' And strangely, from my position that's true. What becomes important, then, is what the creature can do. The games it can be made to play. The games, Miss Ohrman, the games. I saw Dandy Maynor for the first time eight years ago while a friend and I were driving down Forty-fifth Street in New York. We were discussing this very point as we passed Dandy. And a game was begun. Dandy was sitting on a building fire hydrant with his back against the wall—shirtless in the summer heat, watching the passing traffic. An attractive young man of no apparent virtue or accomplishment. My friend wondered if the Golden Beast could shape a star from such mud. Miss Ohrman, I believe great wealth can do everything. 'Not just a star,' my friend stipulated, 'but a *super*-star.' So the game calls for Dandy to win a significant award in every area of popular entertainment. I've bet a very cherished possession—an emerald mine—against a shipping concern on this. So you see, Dandy must do it."

"You mean—" She was about to add: *or else.*

"Yes," he anticipated her.

"But what if Dandy decides that he doesn't like the game?"

"He's already in it, Mr. Weintraub."

"And if he should decide to quit?"

"He can't."

"Why?"

"Those are the rules."

"So winning has become the Golden Beast's nourishment," Felicia murmured her conclusion.

He heard her. "It's all that's left, Miss Ohrman. Now you owe me one dinner engagement."

Andrew hurried into the room.

Victor read the concern on his face. "Excuse me a moment," he said. He crossed to his aide and received the whispered message as Felicia threw Alex a glance that said, "He's something all right."

Victor returned. "We have a guest."

"Oh, then, we'll leave." They started to rise.

"No," he stopped them. "He knows you're here, and he wants you to remain."

Matt Wheeler entered on those words. He walked directly toward Victor Jordan, his expression one of cold, professional pleasure. "Mr. Jordan," was all he said.

Victor acknowledged the greeting with an equally crisp, "Chief Wheeler."

Alex and Felicia were both surprised by Matt's arrival. Alex stood. "Chief?"

"Mr. Weintraub, Miss Ohrman. Richard Skolar told me you were here. There's no pretty way to say this: Your playwright's just been killed . . ."

The shock knocked Alex back into his chair.

Felicia gasped incredulously.

". . . and your bodyguard did the killing." He ended facing Victor. It had been one sentence, without a hitch, without emotion. Clean. Swift. Factual. And Matt Wheeler watched for a reaction on Victor Jordan's face.

There was none. Not so much as a twitch of a muscle.

Amazing, Matt thought. Hasn't changed at all. Still cold. Still dead.

"It was a double killing. Londos is dead, too. Decapitated. And we can't find the head."

Ahhhhh! There it was. A passing of something over those blue, blue eyes.

"What happened?" Victor asked calmly.

"Apparently Londos shot Krozier—that's the playwright —and was killed as well."

"You said decapitation."

"Yes."

"Horrible."

"Tell me, Mr. Jordan, what was your bodyguard doing at the stage door of the Sunset Playhouse?"

"I have no idea."

"Did you know Anthony Krozier?"

"No."

"Did Londos?"

"Not to my knowledge."

"Well, we'll find out. Meanwhile, Mr. Jordan, I want you to remain in Phoenix."

"I'm leaving in two days."

"No you're not. You and your three other bodyguards are material witnesses. There's a court order being signed right now to hold all of you in custody if you should try to leave town. You'd better call your lawyer."

Felicia and Alex had been silent through this entire rapid exchange. But they had listened avidly to every word that was said. And Alex easily detected the satisfaction that had surfaced through the ice of Chief Wheeler's professional manner.

The producer stood quickly. He wanted to get away to think. "Do you need us now?" he asked.

"Yes. Will you wait for me in the lobby, please?"

"The lobby? Well . . . O.K. Come on, Leesh."

She stood. "Alex, what does this mean?" she whispered as they hurried out without so much as a good-bye to Victor Jordan.

Matt Wheeler watched them go. When they were out of sight, he turned again toward Victor. He was smiling now. The thoughtful smile of a hunter close to his prey. "Do you remember me, Mr. Jordan?" The tone portended trouble.

Victor folded his arms across his chest and gazed at an obviously implacable enemy with measureless calm. "Very clearly, Taxi," he answered softly.

"Good," Matt muttered. "You're looking well."

"The years haven't been unkind to you either, Chief."

Nothing more was said. They just watched each other for a full ten seconds. The only movement was a faint speculative nodding of Matt Wheeler's head. But the silence screamed. And when it had communicated the full substance of his contention, the police chief turned and walked out slowly, leaving a clear promise of imminent confrontation hanging in the air.

Victor Jordan was decidedly affected. What could have gone wrong to bring this man down upon him? A simple little assignment—the "instruction" of a snot-nosed little girl. So easy! But it had soured. And *decapitation*. Good lord. What had happened at that theater?

He settled into the soft, white armchair again.

At the side of the room Andrew waited patiently. He recognized the pensive and set stare of those cold blue eyes. He knew he would be needed soon.

It soured, Victor thought again, and I can't believe Domitro failed to even see the girl. She may know what happened. And now the prospect of trouble with the police. No, not the police. Matt Wheeler—adamant, persistent, the memory of a computer tape. Why did Londos murder that playwright? No matter—Wheeler will want to connect me to it. Unbearable! A simple three-day visit to my home city, and he'll try to turn it into a permanent nightmare. His look said it clearly. And I must be in Lisbon in four days. Damn him! He was difficult twenty-six years ago as a lieutenant; his position as police chief now will make him impossible. Very well.

He raised a finger. "Andrew."

Andrew was at his side in an instant. "Sir?"

"Send Mussum and Jaddis to find the girl. Dandy may know where she is. Bring her to me as soon as possible. Lord. What had happened at that theater?

"Yes, sir."

"Then call my attorney Laurence Stoneman and apprise him of these developments."

"Shall I cancel your Lisbon plans?"

"Certainly not."

"Anything else, sir?"

"Yes, I want you to kill the chief of police." It was said so matter-of-factly. So casually. No more than an instruction to a gardener to trim a hedge.

"His death may create special problems, sir."

"Alive, he'll create more. I know him. Do it today. There's a line in Shakespeare's *Julius Caesar*: '. . . think him as a serpent's egg, which, hatch'd, would as his kind grow mischievous, and kill him in the shell.' Anticipation, Andrew. Anticipation is the primary element of survival and success in this life. Just make his death look like an accident."

"Yes, sir."

23

After Sharon Kane had killed Domitro Londos, she turned her attention away from the headless body. She had told Dandy she was "clearing things away." That was true. But there was still much to be done and so little time. She'd have to get on with it now. She exhaled sharply and addressed herself to the next item of business on her agenda.

Smiling in the middle of a warm observation about his brother-in-law, Jorge Canto opened the front door of his house to find Sharon Kane standing there with her finger on the chime button.

She said, "I thought it was time you and I spoke." And she brushed past him into the foyer before he had an opportunity to recover from the shock.

When he did react, it was with smoldering anger.

By then, however, she had entered the living room and settled on the sofa.

"What do you think you're doing?" he seethed through clenched teeth. "Who do you think you are barging into my house this way? You're not wanted here, young lady. Get yourself out. Immediately. Do you hear me?"

"First, I have something to say . . ."

"Who is it, Jorge?" Marta called from the kitchen.

"I thought we should talk because Ben is important to both of us," she continued.

"Jorge?"

"Don't come in here, Marta," he shouted, charging across the room to grab Sharon by her arm. "Out this minute. Do you hear me?" And he yanked her to her feet.

"Just a minute," she snapped. "I didn't come here for this—"

"Out! Out!" He was pulling her toward the door.

"Jorge, what's happen—" Marta Canto stopped in the middle of her words when she saw them.

"Don't do that." Sharon was twisting herself free. "You're going to hear how wrong you are to . . ."

"Get out before I pick you up bodily and throw you out."

"Jorge, what *is* it?" Marta begged.

"This is your son's *girlfriend*." He twisted the word with contempt.

Marta had never met Sharon Kane, and though she often read the obituaries, she had missed the one covering her death. She was totally dismayed by this scene.

"I want you to understand me now," Sharon was saying flatly, "because things are going so well between Ben and . . ."

"You listen to me, you little slut . . ."

"Don't you call me that. You don't know me at all."

"I know you too well."

"You're a closed-minded little man, Mr. Canto. You're like a spoiled brat who won't listen to reason."

It was totally unexpected. A verbal punch in the face. He stopped short in his fury. His final words were barely audible. "I want you out of this house . . . *now,* miss, or I won't be responsible for what happens next."

She stared at him for awhile. Finally, she said, "O.K. I'm going." She crossed to the door. She stopped. "I didn't want it to turn out this way," she lied. "But I tried. O.K. Let me tell you something, though—Ben and I are good for each other, and nothing you or your brother-in-law Victor Jordan can say or do will change a thing between us. Oh yes, don't look so surprised. We've met already, and he made *his* little threats, too. But you just remember this— and it'll help to tell him the same thing: threats can easily turn back upon the one making them. So the best thing all of you can do is to leave Ben and me alone before some- one really does get hurt, because if that happens, I'm sure I won't be the one."

She left.

Outside, she nodded her head. Yes, she had created the

exact degree of distress. There would be linkage, from
Ben's love to his father's anger to . . .

Twenty minutes later, Jorge Canto telephoned his brother-in-law at the Hyatt Regency Hotel and told him every
detail of her visit, stressing in utter amazement the tacit
threat of her departing words.

24

They saw each other in the same moment.

Alex and Felicia were sitting in the spacious lobby, and Matt Wheeler was coming from the elevators. Alex stood quickly; Matt strode directly to him.

"Thanks for waiting. There are things we have to talk about," Matt began straightaway.

"Certainly," Alex responded. "It's terrible about Tony. I'll help any way I can."

"Miss Ohrman," the Chief asked, "are you all right?"

"Yes, fine, Chief Wheeler. The shock of it is staggering, of course, but I'll be all right."

"I'm going to have my driver take you home. Mr. Weintraub and I will be talking for some time, and there's no need for you to be subjected to this additional strain."

"I'm all right, Chief."

"It's better this way."

Alex caught a subtle shift of the police chief's eyes. It was a request for his assistance. He stepped in quickly. "I'll be there as soon as we're through, Leesh. You relax. We'll have dinner later, O.K.?"

One of the last things Felicia Ohrman could ever be accused of was insensitivity. She understood by the way things were being said that she would be in the way. Standing, she quipped her acceptance of the situation: "Well, being driven home in a police chief's car is a first for me anyway." And she leaned forward to kiss Alex lightly on the mouth as Matt Wheeler told his driver to go directly to headquarters after taking her to her apartment.

"You have a car." It was a statement-question.

"Yes," Alex said.

199

"Good. You won't mind driving me to my office when we're through, will you?"

"Not at all."

They watched Felicia depart with Sergeant Finley. When she was out of view, Matt turned and explained, "What I want to tell you might have been too much for her at this time. Besides, I'm really looking for some feedback from you that may help me to put some things in order. And since these new events bear upon both of us, your thinking may be of some value right now."

"Whatever I can do, Chief."

They sat on one of the long, comfortable sofas that dotted the lobby.

Matt began without preliminaries: "There's something creepy about each of the bodies. Krozier was shot twice with a .44 Magnum. That should have blown huge chunks out of the man, but his face and chest are only caved in. Horribly misshapen. As if he'd been patched frantically by some insane plastic surgeon. And in addition to this, Londos's decapitation is bloodless. The neck is sealed, covered with skin as though the torso had matured that way, headless."

The police chief stopped and watched Alex, wondering just how much of what he was going to say would be accepted.

At the description of the bodies, Alex felt his breathing catch for a moment in apprehension. But his expression revealed only troubled interest. "Go on," he urged.

"Well, that's very unnatural, to say the least. Do you notice the word I've used—unnatural? Store it away in your mind. We'll get back to it in a moment. Let me jump to last night now, to the girl we met in the restaurant, Sharon Kane. Mr. Weintraub, I'm going to tell you something that's absolutely insane. I don't have an explanation for it and I don't know that there *is* an explanation for it, but that girl is—"

"Unnatural," Alex cut in.

Chief Wheeler jerked his head in surprise.

But Alex Weintraub was even more affected. Amazed would be more accurate. Why should he now be able to reveal this to the chief of police when the thought couldn't even be framed while he was explaining Sharon to Felicia? Apparently, that strange girl wanted a communion to occur at this time. Apparently, it was time for Wheeler and Weintraub to cooperate toward some undisclosed end. He felt relieved. It was good not to have to bear the onus of such eerie information alone.

"How did you know that?" Chief Wheeler asked.

"I'll tell you everything later. Go on."

Encouraged by the prospect, Wheeler continued eagerly. "Well, here's my thinking so far: Sharon Kane knows Dandy Maynor; I've learned that Dandy Maynor knows Victor Jordan, and Victor Jordan brings along Domitro Londos; Domitro Londos and Anthony Krozier both die, and both deaths are very unnatural. *Sharon Kane* is very unnatural. Do you understand what I'm suggesting, Mr. Weintraub?"

"I think so, Chief. *Unnatural* becomes a link between her and those deaths."

"Exactly. And since she knows Dandy, and Dandy knows Jordan, and Jordan brought along Londos—I have to conclude that somehow she may be involved in these two killings."

The possibility troubled Alex terribly. "I've just signed her to be in my play," he heard himself say.

Matt leaped at the information. "Then she was at the theater, too?"

Alex nodded his head.

"Come on," Chief Wheeler said, jumping to his feet. "I have an appointment; I'd like you to go with me and on the way, I want you to tell me every little thing you know about Miss Sharon Kane."

"Where are we going, Chief?" Alex asked, standing.

"Mr. Weintraub, I'm going to tell you something else now, something that, professionally, I shouldn't be revealing but that, intuitively, I feel you should know: that girl who was at the Sorry Spike, the girl you've just hired to be in your play, was declared dead four days ago, embalmed and prepared for burial. And yesterday, that same girl got up and walked out of Howard Demerest's mortuary."

A chilling shock exploded throughout Alex's body.

"And to be perfectly honest with you," the chief continued, "she scares the life out of me. Now, I don't have the faintest idea *how* it could happen, what she wants or what she may be capable of doing next. But there may be someone who can tell me something, and that's the person we're going to see right now."

Matt Wheeler was no fool. He knew the answers to these questions could never come from the usual scientific and medical communities. Those directions would have to be dead ends. And he wasn't about to enlist the aid of kooks and weirdos either. They would only make the bizarre more untenable. But perhaps someone else could help. Someone acquainted with the more abstract disciplines. A respected intelligence. Someone not limited by the dictates of laboratory methodology but who, nevertheless, would be a source of valid information.

They were on their way to the home of Dr. Philip Townsend. Dr. Townsend was not only the closest friend of Anthony Krozier on the faculty of Canyon State College, but he was also Chairman of the Department of Philosophy. A man with national credentials. An authority in the field of thanatology, the study of death.

Dr. Philip Townsend was a man in his late forties with long, auburn hair and a full but neatly cropped, graying beard. Conservative, steel-rimmed glasses went well with his slightly florid complexion, giving him the appearance of a controlled and yet intense man.

"I called Dr. Alice Pritchard," Matt was explaining as they sat in the kitchen, coffee before them. "She's chairperson of the English department at your school."

"Yes. How did she take it?" Dr. Townsend asked.

"Shocked almost speechless."

"Yes." He nodded his head understandingly.

"And she said you were his closest friend on campus."

"True."

That puzzled Matt. "Do you mind if I ask you a personal question, Dr. Townsend?"

"Not at all."

"Since he was such a close friend of yours, why haven't you been affected at least as much as she or myself or anyone else?"

Philip Townsend appreciated that kind of forthrightness. He smiled faintly. "A person's behavior, Chief Wheeler, is the expression of what he believes. I'm a philosopher. My area of special interest for the past seven years, the study of death, has shaped my beliefs. Death no longer shocks me."

"Not even that of a close friend?"

"Not even that of my child. I'm saddened, of course. The loss of people dear to us is always sorrowful. They leave gaps in our lives. But Death is no demon; he's only the misunderstood black sheep of the family. How a person has lived is much more important than the time or the means by which he died."

"And how did Anthony Krozier live?" Chief Wheeler asked.

"A good life. He harmed no one."

"What else?"

"A full life. He was intellectually and physically vigorous."

"A good teacher?"

"Excellent. Very demanding, but the students loved him for it because he made them achieve. He had an uncanny ability to see the minds of authors in their works. I used to tell him he was as much a philosopher as he was a teacher of literature. And, as a matter of fact, he said this play of his would probably prove me right."

"What do you think of the play?" Alex asked quickly and eagerly.

"I don't know what it's about."

That surprised his guests.

"I know that sounds odd," he explained, "but Tony wanted everyone to be surprised on opening night, and I wouldn't dream of destroying that pleasure by probing."

Alex was incredulous. "You mean he never talked about it?"

"He talked about how it was written but never about the story line or theme."

Alex glanced quickly at Chief Wheeler. "What do you mean, 'how it was written'?" he asked Townsend.

"It took only six days. It was an explosion of creativity."

"Those things happen," Alex said.

"Yes," Dr. Townsend agreed with a smile.

"But you're still surprised by how quickly it was accomplished, aren't you?" Matt asked.

"Chief Wheeler, inspiration lives behind locked doors, and discipline is the only key that can free it. Tony had no control in that respect. Oh, he talked a lot about what he'd write someday, but it's really a struggle to find the right key to open those doors. Can be very painful too. True, there are times when inspiration forces itself out, and those moments are glorious. But when that happens to a *non*-writer like Tony—well to answer your question: Yes, it is surprising. . . ." Then slowly he added the words, ". . . and very interesting."

"Why did you say that?" Matt asked quickly.

Dr. Philip Townsend looked through his eyebrows from one guest to the other. He smiled. "I don't know how you'll take this, gentlemen."

They watched him with anticipation.

"Tony may not have written that play," he said simply.

Alex and Matt threw startled glances at each other. Good lord, some kind of confirmation! They were getting closer to something.

"Explain that please," Alex insisted.

"Well, Richard Bach, the author of the best-selling *Jonathan Livingston Seagull*, claims to have been guided by another intelligence. A woman named Jane Roberts in Elmira, New York, insists a nonphysical entity called Seth has been writing her books for years. And countless other examples exist of the same nature."

"But . . . but how is that possible?" Matt Wheeler stammered.

Dr. Townsend paused. "This gets a little deep," he cautioned pleasantly.

"Go ahead," Matt answered. "We can stand the pressure."

"O.K., let's look at it this way: you've been around death a lot, Chief, but what do you actually know of it?"

"What does anyone know?"

"Oh, quite a bit, quite a bit," he interrupted with a smile. "Not as much as we'd like to know but a great deal more than we knew only six or seven years ago. And we're learning more all the time. For example, Dr. Elisabeth Kübler-Ross and Dr. Raymond A. Moody, Jr., doing separate studies, reached the same conclusions recently concerning postdeath experiences."

Alex was fascinated. "*Post*death experiences?"

"Exactly. They interviewed hundreds of people who had been declared dead medically and who were returned to life. And the reports of their discoveries are remarkably consistent."

"Like what?"

"Well, like the separation of self from one's body. Apparently death is not as final as many fear. The findings indicate that a dead person, or spirit, if you prefer, experiences a period of reflection in the company of a guide; that it is completely aware of activities going on in the presence of the body; that it enjoys a sense of well-being, serenity and hope; that it reaches a moment of decision—whether it should go on with the guide or return to the body—and a few other particulars. And interestingly, it made no difference at all what the convictions of the subjects were; atheists, agnostics, and the religiously devout all reported similar experiences."

"Maybe they weren't dead to start with," Matt suggested.

"All right," Dr. Townsend agreed, "let's call them 'near-death' experiences. It doesn't change a thing. You see, even if that were the case, why should they all have told such uniform stories? They weren't acquainted with each other. No one knew what the others had said."

"Fascinating," Alex murmured.

"Yes."

"But not scientific," Chief Wheeler objected.

"That's not entirely true," Dr. Townsend said quickly. "Dr. Kübler-Ross is attempting to support her findings scientifically. And there are numerous other scientific investigations into death going on right now. But unfortunately if we need pure scientific confirmation of these points then we're in trouble because the problem becomes science itself."

"How so?"

"Well, science is concerned with things physical and what we're learning is in the realm—"

"Of the spiritual," Alex concluded.

"Right, but we don't use words like that anymore. *Supernatural, occult, mystical, psychic, metaphysical:* they all have too many medieval and unfortunate associations. You know, like sorcery, demons, charlatanism. No. Today we believe these negative connotations have made death a nightmare so terrifying it has distorted our view of life and weakened our chances of enjoying a richer happiness. Today we are starting to understand that death may not be a monster. It may only be another side of a cube. So we call our studies either 'thanatology' or 'investigations into multi-dimensional reality.' "

"Let's apply this to Anthony Krozier," Alex suggested quickly, onto something. "If someone else wrote his play, where does this . . ." He groped for the appropriate term.

"Other entity exist?" Dr. Townsend helped.

"Exactly."

"Well, let me see if I can explain it to you this way, and this, incidentally, is the most acceptable of contemporary concepts on the matter: if you have a dog, you know he'll hear things beyond your own range of perception. We even have dog whistles that seem to be making no sound at all to the human ear. That's because they work on a frequency level beyond our aural capacities. But blow one and the dog comes running, or does whatever dogs are trained to do when they hear it. Well, since this is true for hearing, it may be true for other senses as well. Let's take seeing as an example. Light travels approximately 186,000 miles per second. Since we can see only when there's light, that speed represents the boundaries of sight. It was only a while ago that scientists believed nothing could exceed the speed of light. That was the *ultimate speed*. However, today we know there are speeds beyond that. We're looking into them. The investigation, incidentally, is known as *Tachyon*. And, gentlemen, its implications are amazing. Because if we can see only up to the speed of light, then whatever may exist beyond that speed would be just as much outside our range of vision as the sound of that dog whistle is to our range of hearing."

"And you're saying there may be intelligences living in environments where these speeds are normal?"

"You should be in my class, Chief," Dr. Townsend grinned approvingly.

Alex sensed things getting closer to Sharon Kane. "Go on, please," he urged.

"All right," Dr. Townsend continued. "Imagine yourself in a room in which all the walls as well as the ceiling and floor are made of mirrors. Can you do that?"

"Yes. Go ahead," they said.

"As you look about, you'll see yourself *ad infinitum*, correct?"

"Endlessly," Alex agreed.

"Now, imagine that each of your images is a different person, different from all the others as well."

"O.K.," Matt followed.

"Now place a real wall between each one."

"Got it."

"Let's say that that wall is the inhibiting speed of light for each of those environments. Each one has its own speed, and the residents of each one are stopped in their perceptions by that speed. But all together, they're still in that one small room in which *you* are standing. They all occupy the same space, so to speak. Of course, if a person isn't knowledgeable about what we're discussing now, he won't even suspect their existence."

Matt was startled. "Then you're saying, in this very room, this kitchen, right here with us at this very moment, there may be other intelligences that I can't see?"

"That's the logic of it, Chief."

"All right, if I can't see them, why can't I *feel* them? Why don't I bump into them?"

"Because the sense of touch may be just like the others. There may be things outside our range of feeling just as there are things outside the ranges of hearing and seeing. And, furthermore, they may all be tied together."

Alex murmured slowly, his voice a blend of awe and amazement, "Then in respect to Tony Krozier and his play, you're saying that some other intelligence knew how to get through the wall and how to make itself heard." It was not a question, it was a staccato of growing understanding.

Dr. Townsend nodded his head. "And from the standpoint of my studies, gentlemen, that's really what death may be all about—merely the shuttling within and between different environments, through different invisible walls, from one to another and another *et cetera, et cetera.*"

"Jesus Christ!" Matt exploded.

"Yes, even for him too," Dr. Townsend smiled.

Alex could hardly sit still. A few more points and he would have it. He leaned forward excitedly. "Let's frame a hypothetical question, Doctor," he raced ahead.

"Certainly."

"Suppose someone in one of these—" He didn't know exactly what to call the environments and he waggled his fingers frustratedly in the air.

"We call them *parallel realities*," Townsend said.

"Thank you. Suppose someone in one of these parallel realities had been here in this dimension before and decided to return."

"That's the basis of rebirth or reincarnation."

"It's possible then?"

"Some of the greatest thinkers in history have believed it's not only possible but inevitable."

Chief Wheeler saw where Alex was going. The excitement caught him too. He jumped in. "All right, let's take this one step further. Suppose someone in one of those other realities decided to return to this one but chose instead to use the body of a girl already *here*. Could that be done?"

"Logic suggests the possibility. Although most people don't like to contemplate that because it means possession by spirits and makes them think of Hollywood films and books like *The Exorcist*."

Alex wanted to get right to the point now. "What if the girl's body were dead?" he asked.

"Well, in light of what I've already said—and I'm going way out on a limb in extending it because there's nothing but logical extrapolation to support this conclusion—I personally think he could, if he understood enough about the nature of existence and how to handle it."

The sensations upon hearing these words were as intense as the anticipation that had preceded them. Chief Wheeler and Alex Weintraub looked at each other with open-mouthed astonishment. With awe. And with an exciting desire to put the rest of this Sharon Kane puzzle together as quickly as possible. However, it was all so impossible to believe! Like fantasy. Madness. They had the explanation they wanted, and yet they were finding it almost impossible to accept.

"Tell me, please," Matt requested soberly, "how much of this is actually believed?"

Dr. Townsend understood. "It is tough to swallow, isn't it, Chief?" he sighed. "But let me assure you, it's not science fiction. Formal study into the nature of death and multi-dimensional realities is in its infancy, of course. But in one aspect or another, it's attracting the attention of respected and responsible philosophers and scientists the world over—those I've already named and many others."

"And obviously *you* believe it," Alex observed quietly.

"Let me put it this way," Dr. Townsend concluded. "At this stage of our investigations, we face a new question every time we reach a conclusion. But in the words of Dr. Jerome Gans of the Research Institute of California, 'I am willing to face the questions,' and to keep on probing."

Outside and in their car again, they were silent. And they remained silent most of the way back to police headquarters, each digesting the overwhelming import of what he had just learned. Finally, Chief Wheeler grunted, "So, Sharon Kane, that's where you're from—well, now I want to know why you're here."

He looked at Alex Weintraub.

The producer was nodding his head slowly but emphatically in agreement.

"And I'll tell you what I think," the police chief added. "That play of yours may have the answer to that question. Let me have a copy to read, O.K.?"

"Of course," Alex agreed. And through the rest of the drive, he ran the script through his mind scene by scene, looking for some clue, some hint of why Sharon Kane was using him and all the others in her puppet-game of death.

He could find nothing.

But Police Chief Matt Wheeler would.

25

Concert time.

Sharon Kane, Dandy Maynor, Goose, Josh, Nancy, and Lorna all were there, standing in the wings, feeling the heat of a fiery performance.

The arena was jammed to overflowing. Twelve thousand screaming lovers of Lovejoy were being treated to the ultimate in visual and aural rock entertainment. One end of the giant arena had been converted into an enormous stage. Super-quadraphonic speakers, stacked high on both sides like great black pyramids, blared the unrelenting power of the five tireless musicians. Compelling. Gut-wrenching. The energy level was enough to power an aircraft carrier.

And the sight of it all! Overhead in huge jagged electric letters the name *Lovejoy* cut like lightning through explosions of vividly colored smoke. Under it an enormous television screen raced a profusion of frenzied images. A paroxysm of disjointed experiences. There was flash everywhere. Gilded geometric shapes loomed like gargoyles in a musical inferno; laser beams ricocheted off two multi-colored, endlessly rotating, eight foot-tall plastic cubes.

And there was Lovejoy—in green alligator cowboy boots. Skin-tight red lamé pants. Stripped to the waist. Faces and bodies painted with the signs of the zodiac. Eyes, mouths made up in ghoulish exaggeration. Their voices hoarse with their fevered messages of life.

The crowd was wild, jumping, roaring, rushing the security guards that ringed the stage. Throwing tokens of their adulation: amulets, bracelets, panties.

A night to remember.

Sharon took it all in. The sounds, the sight, the raw sexuality. It was a hot, sentient bath. And she wallowed in it for a long time before turning it off for private thoughts. She looked at Dandy standing beside her.

He was watching intently, strangely calm. Eyes aglow about something, but not exactly about the music coming from the stage. All the others—Josh, Nancy, Goose, Lorna —were pounding their palms, shuffling feet, humping the air to those repetitious, driving rhythms. But not Dandy.

She sneaked into his mind. Oh, the thoughts! Good. Ahhh, good. She sucked in her breath. Yes. Dandy would work out fine.

Now it was time. She closed her eyes and pulled her own thinking into a pinprick of purpose. It pierced the walls of the giant auditorium. It went into the night. Over the houses, the traffic, the trees.

She saw long lines of cars snaking up and down the Black Canyon Freeway. She seemed to race against them. Over them. Lower. Lower. Then, she found the one she was seeking.

Inside the rented Chevy Camaro, two of Victor Jordan's bodyguards, Earl Mussum and Frank Jaddis, were deeply concerned about their inability to locate the object of their assignment.

"We better find that broad tonight or I won't wanna be in the same hotel with the ol' man," Jaddis fretted.

"Man, I've never seen him so pissed," Mussum agreed. "He wanted her, yeah, but then that call came from his brother-in-law and did you see how white he went?"

"That's what I mean."

"Then it was: 'I want her even if you have to break her arms and legs to get her here.' Man, those words came out like they were burning."

Jaddis nodded his head in anxious agreement.

There was another thought that was bothering them as well. Both men were thinking about Domitro Londos and wondering if the girl was connected in any way with his scary death. Neither one, though, would dare to voice that concern.

Earlier, they had gone to the ranch to see if Dandy could help them. They had been circumspect, and they made it appear like a harmless request: Mister Jordan merely wanted to talk to her about the play or something.

For a moment, Dandy was going to tell them about his agreement to meet her later at the concert. But then he thought: No. They'll take her away and screw up the whole night. Mr. Jordan can wait. Won't hurt him to see her in the morning.

And he denied any knowledge of her whereabouts. It was a rare moment of defiance toward his "guardian." An important step for Sharon Kane and her plans.

By now, Mussum and Jaddis had exhausted all ideas on how to find her. They had called Alex Weintraub, Mike Ross, and all the members of the cast. Nothing. No one could or would help. Even their check of the telephone directory proved, of course, to be fruitless.

They were on their way back to the Hyatt Regency to discuss their search with Andrew. Perhaps he would have some ideas on how to proceed.

Jaddis turned the Camaro into the ramp.

"Hey, wrong exit," Mussum noted. "You got off too soon. We go to Van Buren. This is McDowell."

"Aw, shit. My mind is somewhere else."

"O.K., wait. Make a left at the light and go down McDowell to Second Street. Then you hang a right, and that'll get us to the hotel."

"O.K."

However, McDowell Road would first take them to the rock concert.

She opened her eyes and smirked with satisfaction.

Eric Gena, the pianist and lead singer of Lovejoy, was trying to make himself heard above the bedlam that punctuated the end of the number.

Shrieking, whistling, leaping fans. They created a din of approval so palpable he could barely be heard despite the super-amplification used by his group.

"Hey, you're wild," he laughed appreciatively and shouted into the microphone. "Great, great. We've had one far-out night tonight, ain't we?"

And though they couldn't really hear what he was saying, they responded quickly to his obvious pleasure and drowned him out entirely.

In time, he managed to subdue them enough to engage in the pleasant badinage at which he was so skilled. A word. A phrase. Some suggestive comment to a young girl stage-side. There were calls from the audience and lewd retorts. Excellent rapport.

"Hey," he said warmly, "you guys are so great I could bust my ass forever for you. But we gotta wrap this gig now."

Cries of protest and regret.

"No, wait. Wait. You're not gonna be sorry 'cause we got a far-out surprise for you that'll pucker your brains . . . no shit . . . got some friends with us tonight an' they're gonna come out now—that way we get a chance to take five an' you get a special treat—an' then after that they're gonna join us for the last number an' we'll all tear the roof off this fuckin' joint. Hey, people—DANDY MAYNOR AND FIRE AND AIR!"

The effect was spectacular. The surprise caused a momentary vacuum. But then recognition struck and the entire arena exploded with renewed excitement and acceptance.

Sharon Kane watched Dandy. She heard his name being screamed repeatedly as he and the others walked onstage. She remembered his thoughts yesterday as they were driving to the ranch: the concert in Chicago, the terrible longing to be into music again, the emptiness from not having written a word or a note in months. She saw him beaming as he said some words of thanks to Eric Gena in passing and took his place at the mike. She waited in the wings and watched.

Josh went to the drums. Goose hooked up his guitar. The girls flanked another mike at stage right, for vocal backup. And Dandy greeted the crowd.

"Wanna tell ya how happy we are t'be with ya," he said simply with an engaging, shy smile.

A girl's voice squealed, "You can be with me all night!"

There was laughter. Agreement from other females.

Dandy grinned approval. "Leave your name an' telephone number at the box office. All contributions gratefully accepted. Glad to see you tryin' t'help the sexually poor an' needy."

More laughter.

"Hey," he got down to business, "I wrote a song today. First song in months . . . an' it's because of this chic I met yesterday."

A male voice piped, "Lend her to me, *I'm* poor an' needy."

Dandy laughed and sang back a line from one of his early hit records: "Ain't no beggars 'lowed 'roun' my house."

The crowd whooped appreciatively.

"Anyway," he continued, "we're gonna try this new one now. Unfortunately, three guys from our group ain't with us, but we're gonna do it without them. The song's for Sharon, an' I call it 'Someone'."

Sharon Kane nodded. Pleased. And for a moment, she even forgot how vital all of this was to her plans.

He hurried to the piano and synthesizer as the others started the intro. The beat was solid. Clean. Direct. He ran his fingers over the keys like a blind man caressing braille script. Then he leaned over into the piano mike, and his voice came out strong and sure—

> Looking at life
> Through glasses dark with
>   Longing and regret
>   Can make a soul forget
> How good it all can be.
>
> Walking in rain
> That burns with drops of
>   Bitterness and doubt
>   Can make a person shout:
> "There is no sunshine!"
>
> But glasses fall apart,
> And raindrops disappear,
> And sunshine settles on your heart,
> And happiness is here
>
> When there's . . .
>
> Someone to make you whole again,
> Someone to chase away sighs,
> Someone with laughter on golden lips,
> And hope like a dream in her eyes.

It was a golden moment for Dandy, like the one in the theater; a kind of purity, a collaborative expression of honesty and excellence.

Sharon felt his joy pouring from the stage. She was satisfied with the way things were going. Now to pull the moment together. She directed her thoughts again to Mussum and Jaddis who were at that instant passing the electric marquee outside the building.

"Why're you stopping?" Mussum asked.

"I don't know. The sign says there's a rock concert in there now."

"So?"

"Well I just happened to think—Maynor's a rock singer, and he might be in there, and what if he's lying to us about the girl and she's in there with him?"

"What if my grandmother had balls? Come on, will ya? There are ten million other places that broad could be—why there?"

Jaddis drove into the parking lot. "I got a feeling," he murmured.

Dandy and his group were running the number, repeating it again and again. Driving the beat, but never losing the lovely melody, never garbling the lyric. And the song sang its way into the reaches of the arena, lifting, touching everyone. When it was nearly over, even while the final chords were drifting toward silence, it began to be overlapped by a swelling enthusiasm that soon detonated into pandemonium. Dandy Maynor and his group were obviously on top of another great success!

Jaddis and Mussum entered the huge hall on that wild ovation. It made them look around in some bewilderment before they directed their attention to the stage. But when they did . . .

"Look a' that!" Jaddis cried when he saw him.

Dandy was bowing and waving joyously and signaling the crowd to let him be heard. Finally things became quieter. "Glad you liked it," he beamed and thanked them. "Truthfully I kinda like it too."

More applause.

"I think you oughtta meet this chic I mentioned earlier.

Just knowin' her has made me wanna get to work again. Sharon, baby, come on out here for a minute, will ya?"

She came from the wing and joined him at the mike.

The audience clapped and whistled and shouted.

Mussum and Jaddis recognized her description immediately. The hair. The coloring. The bandaged hand. "C'mon," Jaddis ordered. And they ran to find their way to the stage.

Lovejoy appeared again.

Eric Gena joined Dandy and Sharon. "Cool lady," he acknowledged to the crowd. "And now," he said to her while he continued to use the mike, "if you'll just go over there and stand with the girls, Lovejoy and Fire and Air are gonna join up to wrap this gig with—" and he screamed the song's title into the microphone—" 'MAGIC MAN'!"

Everything erupted at once: the stage in sound and lights, the house in frenzied approval. It was their big number. Their feast of showmanship and gimmickry. Visualmania. Lasers slashed. Smoke swirled. Pictures raced. And the two huge, multicolored cubes on either side of the stage whirled dizzyingly.

Mussum and Jaddis pushed their way to the wings.

"MAGIC MAN! MAGIC MAN! MAGIC MAN!"

It was about a wizard who turned people into giant butterflies, which he then mounted on the walls of his castle.

Jordan's men split up. They were taking no chances on her getting away. Mussum went stage left. Jaddis, right.

The audience was screaming. Stomping. Dancing in the aisles.

Sharon looked to her right and left. Her eyes met theirs. And they felt themselves being drawn onstage.

You're Victor Jordan's, she was saying to herself. Victor's. Butterflies for Victor Jordan.

They resisted. Tried to turn and run away. It was useless. The pull was inexorable. Like an all-pervasive suction drawing them into the vortex of theatrical madness. The activity onstage had reached a crescendo of abandonment. They went spinning into it. Sweeping across the stage. Arms and legs spread wide. Their jackets open, flapping like wings.

And the audience thought it was all part of the act. Brilliant! Butterflies. Butterflies. Human butterflies!

Sharon went suddenly weak. Something was happening.

She felt them slipping from her. What is it? What is it? She closed her eyes as though in pain. Concentrate. Concentrate. She pulled her thoughts once more into that pinprick of purpose.

And Mussum and Jaddis went flying against the huge whirling cubes. The lights danced off them. Sharp, colored travel spots ballyhooed their spinning. Each had his own cube. Spread-eagled upon the face of it. Stuck there against all centrifugal law. And then smoke began to billow. The giant plastic surface upon which each was pinned began to bubble. Sizzle. Began to melt. And Mussum and Jaddis felt themselves being pressed into the plastic. They were like hot metal on ice, melting their way deeper, deeper, deeper. And the faces of the cubes began to seal over them. They cried out. They screamed. But there was so much sound, so much noise, no one heard them. The cubes whirled. The music thundered. The audience roared. Their screams died under the smooth surfaces that covered them. They were encased, confined within solid plastic blocks. A highlight of the Lovejoy performance. *Butterflies.*

26

They were partying at the ranch.

And they were high. God, were they high! If laughter were dynamite, they would have blown themselves away. Not a minute of the concert was forgotten. They relived it all. The audience. The music. The effects. Again and again they shouted things they remembered. Wallowing in them. Loving them. And whenever that final number—"Magic Man"—was mentioned it was always with astonishment and jubilation. How did it happen? Who were those guys? Who gives a shit anyway? It was out-of-sight. Wild. Crazy. Out-of-goddamned-sight!

They had been so involved in their music, so immersed in their individual efforts no one had actually seen Jaddis or Mussum clearly. And the features of the entombed men now appeared as distorted and difficult to discern as objects frozen deep within huge blocks of ice. It would take a full day to cut through that plastic. A full day to free the buried bodies. Until then their identities would remain unknown, and the fact that they were almost certainly dead didn't trouble Lovejoy at all.

"Man, if I could figure out how it happened I'd do that every night an' use up every bum on skid row," Eric Gena cackled, and everyone laughed agreement.

Now the coke was working. Now the grass was high. Colombia was in Arizona. And all was right with the world.

Lovejoy had brought their girls with them. Groupies. Strange birds with wild plumages. They chirped incessantly. Did marvelous tricks on command. And tried to survive by impaling themselves upon erections of the fa-

218

mous. They all had nonnames: The Princess, The Countess, The Box, The Witch. And now they were laughing and dancing and singing with growing abandon.

But something was wrong with Dandy tonight. He wasn't finding much of anything happening at the ranch particularly exciting. Oh, he was high all right—happier than anyone else. But his pleasure came from the experience of the concert and not the drugs or sex beginning to dominate the party. And this was different for him. New. Ordinarily, he would have been among the first to freak out on something. Now, though, his mood was quieter. His pleasure ran deep.

Sharon found him outside the house, lying on a torn vinyl couch that took up a corner of the flagstone patio. "Everything all right?" she asked.

He grinned and continued to stare at the stars. "Couldn't be better."

She sat on the arm of the couch and watched him. After awhile she whispered, "Thanks for the song."

There was a long silence during which he only nodded his head almost imperceptibly. Then it began, slowly at first, coming from somewhere deep inside his being, and then more rapidly, more enthusiastically, as it broke through the barriers of articulation. "I know what music is now. Really, not what I used to think. I was close, but I didn't really understand. I thought it was the crowds and their loving me and the action. The music part of it was important, sure, but I didn't actually see how important until today. When I finished writing that song this afternoon, I felt so good I could have died just then and been happy. I felt like my skin had been opened and I'd finally flown out of myself. Free. You know what I mean? Really free. And that's what it is—everybody has to have a knife that opens the skin and lets him be free. With me, it's music. And when that happened today—God, I'd have taken on the world to stay outside like that. Nothing on this earth could have scared me back inside myself again."

"And now?" she asked.

He stood. "That concert tonight reinforced everything."

"What about Mr. Jordan?"

He reached his arms out and stretched and seemed to expand. "I think it's time he and I split," he said.

She tested him. "Are you strong enough to do that?"

Again he nodded his head. "Now I am."

Good. That was exactly what she needed. Now, just one more thing: "Will you stay with *The Trespasser?*" she asked carefully.

"Hey . . . I wouldn't split from *you.*"

"I mean, even if I'm not in it."

"Why, where are you going?"

She didn't answer.

He looked hard at her, trying to see into something her silence was suggesting. "Do you want me to stay with it?" he asked.

She held him with a steady gaze.

"If that's what you want," he agreed, reading her look correctly.

She smiled appreciation. She stood. Reached up. Slipped her hands behind his head. "Dandy Maynor," she murmured, "would you mind if I kissed you?"

He grinned most engagingly. "I certainly do like your ideas, lady," he said.

"I mean, kiss you for real."

And their mouths met in a lingering, searching kiss that linked one soul to another in a rare moment of purity. It was not the kind of kiss to be followed with sexual interplay—especially with that kind of party going on behind them—and for the first time in his life, Dandy Maynor was satisfied to let it stop there. It was its own highpoint. Its own fulfillment.

He touched her face lightly. "Yes, indeed, you are something else, lady," he breathed. Then he turned to go back inside again.

"Dandy."

He stopped. He looked at her.

"The way you spoke to me tonight. The words you used. Thank you."

He understood. The pose was gone. Even verbally. And he knew, he'd never need it or resort to it again.

"Hey," he said with a contented smile, "why do I feel so good?"

He didn't need an answer.

Inside the house, he passed through the living room, stepping over and around bodies in various stages of stupor. He went to the hallway that led to his room.

Music was blaring from the stereo in the F.J.R. (Funky

Junky Room), and he looked in to see Eric Gena and The Witch on the bed, copulating to its frenetic rhythms, while Joe Maresco, the Lovejoy drummer, was rutting The Princess on the sofa.

"Come on in, man," Maresco grunted, "you're next."

"I pass," Dandy said.

"Get it . . . while . . . you can . . ." Gena advised, working so very hard.

"Got something else to do," Dandy answered.

"You're crazy . . . Dand–o . . . fuckin', suckin' an' truckin' . . . man—there . . . ain't . . . *nothin'* else."

They didn't hear Dandy Maynor murmur "Shi-i-i-t" as he entered his room and closed the door.

Outside on the patio, Sharon Kane felt particularly good about what had taken place tonight. The deaths of Mussum and Jaddis, Dandy's newfound sense of freedom. Everything was going so well.

Suddenly, her legs buckled. She collapsed to the flagstone pavement. She felt a strange pressure in every part of her body. A compelling force. Pressing. Pushing her.

She was not entirely surprised by it. She knew its appearance was inevitable. She had even experienced something like it on the stage of the arena while she was controlling Jordan's men. But then it had come and gone so quickly and she had been so intensely centered upon her purpose, she had been unable to examine it. Now she studied it. Yes. It was as she had expected. But it was so severe! *And so soon.* Too soon. Much too soon. She fought. Struggled with it pointedly. And it passed. In a little while, she was able to pull herself to her feet again.

Her surroundings came back to her. She heard the electric piano in Dandy's room running some arpeggios.

She breathed deeply, in full control of herself again. However, a new sense of urgency influenced her movements now. There was a true danger, she realized, that her mission would fail.

She was dying.

27

It was a thin, vibrating, high-pitched sound. A single needlelike note. Persistent and painless. He was dreaming of a light as slender as a thread—a glowing sliver that was cutting a free-form contour through a black wall, the way acetylene torches burn through metal but faster, much faster. And the sound seemed to be another manifestation of that light. Only it became louder as the light ran its course to the starting point. At that moment, the cutout collapsed inward. The sound screeched. Light flooded. And he jumped up dazed.

Sharon Kane was standing at his bed.

"Who—who's there?"

Unaided, lamps flashed everywhere in rapid succession. He saw her.

"I want you to do something," she stated. It was not a request.

Alex Weintraub tried to pull his wits together. "What . . . what are you . . ."

"Preview the play tonight."

"Why don't you get back to where you came from?"

"I'm dying."

It was ice on his cortex. His mind imploded, and he was instantly alert. Dr. Townsend would love this, he thought. Here's a dead girl telling me she's dying! "How's that possible?" he demanded. "You brought the body back to life; are you telling me you're leaving it?"

"I'm being repulsed. I don't know how long I can hold on. I want that preview tomorrow."

"You're not getting any help from me, you understand

222

that? You're dangerous, miss, mister—whateverthehell you are!"

"You can be free, Alex."

"Free? From what?"

"Fear. Victor Jordan has you tied in it."

He stopped. How did she . . . He'd only begun to consider it last night at the Sorry Spike when Felicia's observation had caused him to face the ugliness of that possibility.

"Don't miss your chance, Alex," she warned.

Victor Jordan. Victor Jordan. Everything always seemed to come back to Victor Jordan. A light of insight suddenly blazed: she had concocted this entire project. Victor Jordan was obviously connected with it. Then she wasn't out only to help him wrench free of Victor, no matter how she put it. Oh, no! She was probably interested in Jordan herself. "You want him, don't you? This business of freedom for me is secondary. You want him," he challenged, "and I want to know why."

"Set yourself free, Alex."

"I want some information!"

"You know what he is, you fool. You see what he does —to you, to Dandy. He's at the top of the tallest ladder, Alex, and he's climbed over everyone to get there! That's been his life. A history of pain and death. A girl here in Phoenix, an attaché in Venezuela, a general in Colombia, a businessman in France, two priests in Argentina, a storekeeper in England—the list is endless—and no one has touched him."

It struck Alex suddenly. And he pronounced it with deliberate calm. "You sound like the Avenging Angel."

She stopped. That strange, enigmatic smile touched her lips again. "Now you understand." Her voice was almost a whisper. "He thrives on life's lies. Only he matters, and terror is the touchstone of his reality. It has brought him respectability . . . admiration. He is timelessly evil, and he owes a debt. I am here to collect it."

Alex's tone was touched with wonderment. "Do you have a name?"

"Names are unimportant. Such identifications become meaningless even before the end of one's lifetime."

"Your name."

"Call me Revenant."

"Revenant," he whispered, looking steadily into her eyes.

"You're in Sharon's body but are you male or female?"

"I've been both—as you have. It's part of the game we all play with living, Alex."

The air in the room had become still.

Alex Weintraub relaxed his opposition to test the boundaries of what she was willing to reveal.

"Did you kill Tony Krozier?" he asked.

"Londos did that."

"But you killed Londos."

She nodded.

"Where's his head?"

"You're a disappointment, Alex," she snapped. "Don't you understand the play you're doing?"

Jesus, the play was real. Everything Dr. Townsend had told him was true. There *were* other realities—other *places*, other *intelligences*. Death was only the shifting from one place to another. And with enough understanding, we actually *can* control that shifting.

"How did you do it?" he demanded. "How did you transfer his head to your world?"

"Consciousness controls matter, Alex. Your investigators are discovering that now."

"And yours is so strong . . ."

"No stronger than yours," she interrupted. "Only clearer. One day—when you die again—release will free you from the inhibiting concepts of your physical existence. You'll see more clearly; you'll understand then."

"And that understanding is control?"

"Even to the point of passing from one material world to another to use it."

"Then—"

"Living and dying are our teachers, Alex, living and dying." There was such finality in the way she said that.

Alex swung suspiciously to a different tack. "I received a call tonight from another one of Victor's men. He and his buddy were looking for you."

"They found me."

The implications of her tone were unmistakable. "My God," he erupted. "You condemn Jordan like a righteous judge, and you're guilty of doing the exact same thing."

There was a long pause. Her eyes clouded. "There *is* a difference, Alex," she finally said. "That you don't know it now is another disappointment." Her voice was flat, expressionless, but distinctly emphatic. "You'll learn, though. You'll learn." Then, she added with the same directness that had characterized her initial greeting, "We're near the end. You're going to help me, or everything will have been a waste."

All they had said to each other raced through his mind in that instant. And oddly, through everything, and quite inexplicably, the words concerning Victor Jordan stood out in boldest relief. "Are you controlling me now?" he asked.

"No." It was a truthful answer.

But he challenged it. "How do I know that?"

"You must want to do this. I need my strength now for other things."

Yes, she was being truthful. He sensed the honesty in the words. All right then, he told himself, if Jordan activates that much concern in you, there's only one thing to do and that's face it. Face him. Help her and help yourself. "What do you want?" he gave in. But he wasn't sure at all that this was the right thing to do.

"An eight o'clock curtain tomorrow night."

"You realize, of course," he added quickly, "it may all be a waste anyway. After you leave . . ."

"Ginny will be fine," she cut in.

He flustered, "Are . . . are you sure?"

"Except for sudden violent death, whatever takes place in this life, Alex, happens because we either want it to happen or because we don't understand enough to prevent it from happening."

It was just too early in the morning for that particular profundity; he only grunted.

As soon as she had left, he dialed two numbers and started things in motion.

The first: "Hello, Mike . . . Alex . . . Sorry to wake you at this hour. . . . We're pushing up the preview date. . . . Tomorrow night." He looked at the digital clock on his dresser and corrected himself. "No, it's one o'clock now— I mean, tonight. . . . That's right, Sunday. . . . Mike, please . . . *please*. . . . I'll tell you why at another time. . . . Mike, I didn't hire you as director to fight with me. . . . O.K. . . . We'll talk later. . . . Get up early. . . . Mike? . . . Stay with me, man, we're racing down the mountain."

The second: "Marilyn, this is Mr. Weintraub. . . . One o'clock. . . . Don't . . . don't panic. . . . No, no . . . just wait, just listen. We're opening the show tomorrow night, I mean, tonight, Sunday, 8:00 P.M. Arrange to have an audience. . . . I know it's too late for newspaper releases; that's good. I don't want anyone to know that Ginny's been replaced, understand? Call up all the first nighters. . . . Paper the whole house if you have to, but fill it. . . . Get started on this early. . . . O.K. . . . You're a good secretary. . . . Get some sleep now; we have a lot to do. . . . See you soon. . . . What? . . . Marilyn, I know what I'm doing."

But under his breath, he muttered, "I hope I do," as he pressed his finger upon the telephone's disconnect button. "God, I hope I do."

28

Police Chief Wheeler dropped a copy of the play *The Trespasser* on his bed with a short, exasperated sigh. Nothing. He had read it twice and been overwhelmed by the exciting power of the plot, by a story line filled with startling effects, personal agonies, unexpected humor and shattering understanding of the fullness of life—but in respect to its revealing something new about Sharon Kane . . . nothing. And that upset him. It ran contrary to both his logic and intuition. He had to be missing something, he felt. Well, he'd read it again. Perhaps . . .

"And he was such a delightful young man," Margaret was saying through a yawn. "He said there are actually blankets for water heaters now. Imagine. And he checked the attic insulation, the air conditioner, all the doors and windows for leakage. Of course, they can't say how much energy is actually being wasted in the entire city, but I imagine it's considerable, and this kind of check-up is essential nowadays I think. Matt . . . Matt, are you listening?"

"What . . . huh . . . oh, no, Maggy . . . I'm sorry, dear. . . . There's something . . ." He had removed his pants and was settling thoughtfully beside her under the blanket. Something was disturbing him.

"Oh well, I'll tell you tomorrow. I do think we have to consider what he said though."

"Who?" he asked vaguely. Something *was* there. Piquing him. Trying to surface.

"The energy specialist, dear."

He wasn't listening at all now. He was fastened upon that—something. Formless but forming. What is it, what is

227

it? He felt himself becoming excited. He bit his lip. Pressed a fingernail between two teeth. Dug deeper into his thoughts to help it out. It was shaping now—coming . . . coming . . . And, then, suddenly, there it was! Clear. Simple. Good Lord, he thought. His breath came faster. Could that be it? Is that it? He grabbed the manuscript again. Excitedly. Eagerly. He flipped the cover so quickly it almost tore. Title page. Author's note. Set description. Synopsis of scenes, and then he had it, the page headed "Characters." His eyes zeroed in on what he was looking for:

> JANICE CAMARON: Kris Hanover's girl; sings, dances with his rock band; seemingly strong, assertive, but basically gentle and sincere; would really prefer marriage and children.

Yes. There it was! But could he be sure? It was such a hair —so thin—he might only be guessing. Reaching for nonexistent answers.

"Matt, the light . . . please," Margaret mumbled.

He had eased himself against the headboard. A faint smile of wonderment and satisfaction pulled at a corner of his mouth. It felt right. It made sense. He was suddenly calm. My God, he thought, I don't believe it.

"Matt, the light . . ." his wife protested wearily.

"Yes . . . O.K., dear." And he switched off his night-table lamp.

She rolled over and curled against him. ". . . said we should . . . turn out . . . lights early," she murmured almost asleep.

"Who?"

". . . fine . . . young man . . . ngy . . . spesh . . . liss . . ." And she was gone.

That fine young man, the energy specialist, was outside waiting in a parked Buick, watching the house patiently from a safe distance.

It was Andrew.

When Mr. Jordan had said, "Kill the chief of police and make it look like an accident," Andrew knew immediately how it would be accomplished. He had that kind of facile mind. It had earned him the Silver Star with Oak Leaf Cluster and the Distinguished Service Cross. Captain Andrew Mallory. Honored in magazines. In major news-papers. On national television. Victor of course had read and seen these honors. The captain reminded him of him-self when he was young. Fearless. Decisive. He recruited Andrew even before the conclusion of the Vietnam War. And both men valued the association from its inception. From Victor's point of view there was no one more reliable in his employ. No one more deserving of the privilege of being his "right hand." From Andrew's point of view, de-votion brought and would always bring desirable sultanic rewards. Perhaps even the Jordan empire itself in time. After all, Mr. Jordan could not go on living forever.

Now he saw the light in Matt's room go off. It was a little past midnight. He waited another hour-and-a-half be-fore he acted. Then he removed a five-gallon can, a very small red tank and a roll of silver wire from the trunk of his car. The five-gallon can had been filled with Bar-B-Kwik, a highly inflammable, nonresidual liquid used in out-door barbecuing and obtainable in any Phoenix super-market; the small red tank contained compressed stove gas; the roll of wire was of a thin but strong gauge.

His plan was simple: earlier that afternoon, his energy ploy had gained him access to the house. He had looked the part: blue plastic "hard hat," clipboard, a small toolbox. The city was making free energy inspections to suggest simple conservation techniques that would save the nation considerable energy and the homeowner valuable dollars, he had said. His "check" was thorough. And in carefully selected places, he planted three-inch paraffin capsules filled with gasoline—in the attic insulation, behind drapes, under the bed.

Now he had only to complete the job. Escape would be impossible. It would be a marvelous fire, presumably started by a defective water heater. So common. An un-fortunate accident.

He approached the house from the rear. It was sur-rounded by a six-foot high, rose-colored cinderblock wall. He placed the things he was carrying on the ground near a padlocked chain-link gate. Then he withdrew a silencer-equipped revolver from inside his jacket. He lifted himself over the wall. Boldly. Nimbly. And he dropped into the Wheeler backyard just as Gobo the family Doberman came tearing around the house snarling in his attack. The movement was unbroken. The dog leaped. Andrew stepped forward. There was the soft *whut* of the gun. Gobo hurtled to the grass dead. The bullet had entered his chest and ripped away part of his heart.

Andrew lifted the animal. He carried him to the house and dropped him near the small wooden enclosure containing the water heater. He ran his hands quickly over the body. No egression. The bullet was still inside. He pulled a switchblade from his pocket. The search was deft, dispassionate. He had it. He pocketed the knife again. And the bullet. There would be no evidence at all when Andrew Mallory completed his assignment.

At this moment, Sharon Kane was nearing the Wheeler house, a vivid picture of Andrew in her mind.

He worked swiftly. He went to the chain-link gate and applied a small, metal prod to the lock. One sure twist. It opened. He swung the gate inward. Claimed his waiting items. Closed the gate again. All without sound. Then he placed the open lock on top of the block wall near the gate. He would exit cleanly and replace the lock at that time.

Sharon was walking down the alley, now, approaching the rear gate. She felt herself becoming breathless. Her body was resisting. That subtle pressure—like north-to-north polarity—was becoming more pronounced again. She saw Andrew in her mind's eye unscrewing the cap of the five-gallon can. Wait. And then her breath caught suddenly. She stumbled. Collapsed. Rolled to her back. She tried to rise but couldn't. Her movements were sluggish. Like trying to roll marbles in molasses. She lay there staring at the stars, telling her body with an almost desperate insistence, "Not yet . . . not yet . . . not yet . . ." She tried once more to rise. Failure. Her breathing was becoming stertorous. She stopped all movement and directed her attention instead toward Andrew Mallory.

He felt his hands go dead. What the!— He shook them. They wouldn't respond. He slipped his left hand under his right arm and forced off the glove. He looked at the hand. The fingers had turned to claws. He was horrified. He recoiled. Tripped over himself. Fell to the grass.

But Sharon couldn't sustain her effort and at that moment she lost control of her body almost entirely and blacked out.

Andrew stared at his hand. It was all right again. He pulled off his other glove. Fine. He breathed a sigh of relief. Returned to his task. But now he moved even faster. He laid a line of Bar-B-Kwik along the base of the house. From the heater. Across the rear bathroom. Around the master bedroom. Then he tied the thin wire to the neck of the small red tank and unraveled the rest until it reached the gate. He placed the tank inside the water heater compartment and the empty Bar-B-Kwik can outside the gate. He intended to release the gas and wait outside the property, safely behind the block wall, for an explosion that would surely be touched off by the water heater's pilot light. Then he would pull the small tank free by means of the attached wire. The ignited Bar-B-Kwik would seal the rear window and door of the building, and he would be away with all evidence even before the planted incendiary devices within the house were activated. The resultant fire should be so intense that no traces of the paraffin capsules would remain.

Jordan would be pleased.

Sharon Kane's immobility was brief. While "unconscious" she had actually been fighting to regain control of her rebellious body. Now she was awake again, pulling herself uncertainly to her feet. She teetered. Things were not entirely settled yet. The internal pressure persisted. It took a few moments of special effort. Finally she had it—full possession again.

However, something had happened as she struggled, something outside her range of concentration. Andrew had released the gas from the small, red tank. He was running toward the gate now. All at once, he was jolted to a stop. The way was blocked by a huge, black German shepherd. Attack rumbled in its throat. Coolly, Andrew pulled his gun again. Raised it. Squeezed the trigger. *Whut.* The silencer gentled the crack of death. But the dog did not die! Instead, the bullet sheared it in two, separated it from itself. And now there were two savage animals blocking his way.

He backed up. He was startled. Confused. He raised the gun again. *Whut. Whut.* And four faced him.

Behind him the water heater exploded with devastating force. Fire leaped along the Bar-B-Kwik. The rear of the house was instantly engulfed.

The dogs attacked. Their ferocity was horrendous.

Whut. Whut. Five animals! Six! And then they began to blaze like the fire behind him. Their bodies. All of them. Not *on* fire, but actually fire itself! Ferocious flaming beasts! They were on him in an instant. And he, too, burst into flames.

Inside the house, Matt Wheeler had jumped awake at the first sound of the explosion. Fire and smoke were everywhere. Margaret was rolling off the bed screaming. The bathroom was blazing. Escape through the rear was impossible. He shouted her name. She was on her feet. Flailing the air. Shrieking. Her nightgown had caught fire. He dived over the bed and grabbed her. Threw her to the floor. Fought the fire with the bed blanket. The paraffin capsules began to explode in a line of destruction. Drapes. Dresser. Closet. Walls. The flames devoured the attic insulation. Raced through the air ducts. Erupted in the hallway. The passage was blocked. They were sealed in their bedroom!

Andrew rolled on the grass in agony, an insane torch. The dogs were becoming one with him. Fusing. Blending. He screamed. Kicked madly at them. Fought his way to his feet. Fell. Stood again. He was out of control. His body blazed like tumbleweed. And he lurched and rolled like it in his death struggle. He was blind. Wild. Then finally he lunged and fell with a hideous scream into the flames of the house itself.

Sharon was there now. The struggle to reclaim her body had prevented her from stopping Andrew's setting off the conflagration. But she was there now, and after she drove Andrew into the flames, she stared at the house and concentrated on saving Matt Wheeler and his wife.

The fire had caught his T-shirt. He didn't seem to notice. Margaret was still ablaze. Hair. Skin. He was fighting like a madman to smother it. He pulled her up. Swept her off the floor and looked about wildly for *some* escape. None. There was none. The room was an inferno, and they were dying within the core of the flame.

Sharon struggled to control the fire. To pull it in upon itself. Snuff it out. But she couldn't hold it together. There was too much for her diminishing powers. She felt split in half, one part holding onto herself, the other reaching to gather flames so Promethean they threatened to ignite the air itself. It was hopeless. She switched to another tack. The house. The room. She pulled every ion of energy she could command into a single funnel of force. There was a fantastic turbulence. A roar of wind. Bushes flew. Trees in her path bent and were almost uprooted. Everything was being sucked into a sudden and enormous void.

Inside, Matt Wheeler—holding Margaret's unconscious body in his arms—looked around desperately and let loose one animal cry of agony and despair—

"GOD ! ! !"

The wall of the bedroom blew out. Blew out with a crack of thunder as though it had been wrenched and sucked from its foundations by some gargantuan vacuum cleaner.

And Matt went stumbling and running from the house just as the ceiling and roof caved in behind him. He charged across the lawn. The blanket covering Margaret was burning. His T-shirt was burning. He lunged toward the swimming pool and threw himself with his wife into its saving waters.

"She'll be in the Burn Unit, Chief," the young doctor informed him as the ambulance prepared to leave. His tone was urgent.

"Just a minute," Matt said, "I'm going too." He was wearing a borrowed coat. His arms and back were lightly bandaged. Miraculously his own injuries were limited and relatively superficial. He had been approached by the fire chief as emergency treatment was being administered to Margaret, and his attention had been momentarily diverted.

"It was arson," the fire chief had said. "Evidence everywhere. May not be traceable though. Whoever did it had it all planned. But somehow he got caught in the fire itself. Incinerated. Identification'll be difficult. All we found on the remains was this." And he produced the gun, the switchblade knife and a gold signet ring.

Matt had taken them. "It's all I'll need," he promised as the young doctor interrupted. "It's all I'll need." The quiet repetition of the words was chilling.

He jumped into the ambulance and sat beside Mar-

garet's unconscious figure. They hurtled down the street
with lights flashing and siren howling.

Sharon Kane had not waited. Neither had she revealed
herself to Matt. When she saw him lifting Margaret from
the pool, she knew that he had survived. The fire had
aroused neighbors, and there would soon be a mob descending on the scene. All necessary assistance would soon
be available.

She felt another surge of bitterness. Once more, there
had been needless pain and suffering. Once more, indifference. Callousness. And once more, Victor Jordan had
been the cause of it all. Alex had seen her as the Avenging
Angel. Yes. Yes, how very right he was.

She hurried to the Hyatt Regency Hotel.

29

He was sitting in bed reading. He wore cool, blue satin pajamas of the best quality that money could buy. His hair was combed. The covers over his legs were perfectly spread. Even prepared for sleep, he seemed flawless. He knew that Andrew had gone out to follow his instructions. He was just waiting for his return and his report before retiring for the night.

The suite's front door opened and closed. He heard the sound and assumed it was Andrew. Then the door of his bedroom opened quickly without the customary signal of a light tap, and Sharon Kane strode into his room.

"You've been looking for me," she said evenly.

He flipped the covers and swung his feet to the slippers on the carpeted floor. And even as he donned his silk robe, he kept his eyes coldly upon his intruder.

"We're alone," she pronounced as he went to the door.

He stopped. The hard clip of her voice left no doubt that she was telling the truth.

"Where are—?"

"They're gone. Like Londos and Andrew. And you're all alone now, Victor. All alone."

This was a little more than he could believe. He opened the door and called, "Frank? Earl? Andrew?" When there was no response, he turned again to look at her. "What are you trying to tell me, young lady, that you . . ." He approached as he spoke.

"I've told you, Victor: you're alone. I've stripped you. Cut away your insulation. You're exposed now."

This was insanity. This child—this sweet-faced little slut, telling him that—he didn't believe a word of it. There had to be another explanation for the absence of his men. And even if they were dead, some explanation other than what *she* was suggesting. Such gall, insolence! No one—but *no one*—could ever be permitted to take such liberties with him. His anger mounted swiftly. And as always, he became inversely and conversely cold. Deadly.

She read his thoughts. She was satisfied. The entire matter had to be handled with extreme delicacy. The proper words. The precise nuances. She had to offer perfect provocation. If he were not antagonized enough, he wouldn't make the required drastic move; if he were pushed too far, he might want to take more time to exact his punishment than she could now afford. It had to work now. The final part of her preparations had to succeed in this meeting.

"It's all a game, Victor. It always has been. But it's not played by your rules. . . ."

"You've been a thorn, young lady. . . ." he breathed ominously.

"Everyone is supposed to win, but you don't understand that. . . ."

". . . and you're going to regret this bravado. . . ."

"You buy people and putrefy everything you touch. . . ."

"I promise you that. . . ."

". . . and now you're losing. . . ."

"You don't know how desperately you're going to regret it!"

"You've just lost Ben . . . and your family will cry . . . you've lost your men . . . and they all had to die . . ."

The rhyme startled him. A dead, monotonous singsong. So completely out of place.

". . . you've even lost Dandy and Alex, you see . . . and all that is left now is you and me."

She grinned at him. A cold grin. Mirthless. Menacing.

He felt it again—that sharp, stabbing sensation. His breath caught. It had happened only once before and then, too, it had been in the company of this strange girl. At the theater. When she had leaned over and said, "You can't have everything you want, young man."

"I want you to leave this room immediately," he said evenly.

She nodded as though she understood some deep secret. The grin persisted. Then, with unexpected grace, she crossed slowly to the bedroom door. She turned and looked at him once more. "I could have eliminated Victor Jordan as easily as the others," she intoned. "But I have something special planned for him, something very special, in a very special place." And she left him as purposefully as she had entered.

Alone in his bedroom, Victor worked consciously now to control the hideous sensation that still gripped him. He breathed more deeply. He sat loosely in the soft chair near the bed and crossed his legs. He relaxed his hands on the armrests. Closed his eyes. Tilted back his head. In time, he was all right again. "So that must be fear," he concluded coldly. Resentment boiled. He felt flawed. He had been violated. Violated, he seethed, by a grinning, arrogant bitch. She had precipitated the most disgusting, the most obscene feelings he had ever experienced. Well, she would pay for it. Yes, she would pay. And he would handle *this* matter himself.

Outside his suite of rooms, Sharon Kane considered Victor's reactions. Her smile became colder. She approached the elevators now with a set, determined step.

The challenge had been accepted.

PART V

The Return

"At the Monroe Institute of Applied Sciences in Afton, Va., businessman and inventor Robert A. Monroe claims to have sent 1,400 persons on out-of-body trips over the past seven years. . . . Monroe says he has sent himself and many other explorers to other 'reality systems' where they sometimes communicate nonverbally with 'humanoid and very intelligent beings who know nothing of our physical-matter system.' "

from *Newsweek*
May 1, 1978
Cover Story

30

Victor Jordan remained awake through the rest of the night. Sitting in his large living room, he considered the morning's events. He remembered something in the way she had spoken her last words—the tone, the conviction—and he knew he was in conflict with a most unusual adversary. His outrage was tempered now by the recognition that a Final Solution to the Sharon Kane Problem would require a very special effort on his part. He reasoned coldly. Calculatingly. And by daylight, he knew precisely how he would proceed. He felt better. That settled, he lay upon his bed and closed his eyes for five hours of uninterrupted, tranquil sleep.

Even as Victor was resting, Alex Weintraub was hard at work in his office. By nine o'clock, he was functioning as though his new telephone were glued to his ear.

"Well, when he gets in, tell him Alex Weintraub called. He has my number. And Sergeant Clemmens, tell Chief Wheeler it's important. *Very* important."

He pressed the disconnect button and dialed again. "Did I wake you? . . . Alex . . . Nine o'clock. . . . Have lunch with me. . . . Fine. . . . Meet me at Chez Gerard's at twelve. Felicia, we're having our preview tonight. . . . Wait . . . wait, wait, wait, hold it. Easy. I'll explain when I see you. O.K. . . . Twelve." And he hung up. Yes, he thought, this is going to be some day.

He riffled through the telephone directory. There—he found it. He dialed quickly.

"Good morning." The voice was bright and alive.

"Dr. Townsend?"

"Yes."

"Good morning, sir. This is Alex Weintraub. I was at your home yesterday."

"Of course, Mr. Weintraub. How are you?"

"Fine, thank you. Tell me, sir," Alex got right to the point, "can you see me today? Couple of things I must ask you."

"About our discussion?"

"Related, yes."

"Well, I'm taking the family out soon, and we'll be . . ."

"When are you leaving?"

"In about an hour."

"What if I come over right now? Won't take more than ten minutes of your time."

"Must be important."

"It is to me."

"Come on over."

He rushed from his office, stopping at Marilyn's desk only long enough to say, "If Chief Wheeler calls tell him you expect me at 10:30."

She was in the middle of her own telephone business. She nodded crisply in response.

He smiled at her efficiency. "Should have our audience by the time I get back," he teased.

She scowled, and he laughed as he exited.

Matt Wheeler had spent the night at Maricopa County Hospital.

Margaret had been rushed into the emergency section of the Burn Unit where a team of staff doctors worked desperately to save her life.

At 9:30 Dr. Elias Friedman approached the chief of police in the unit's waiting room. He was exhausted.

Matt jumped up as he saw him approaching.

"She's in intensive care," the doctor informed him. He was gentle. Her condition was not encouraging. "Third degree burns over eighty percent of her body. She's comatose now."

Matt's soul shrank. He had prayed, but even as he did, fear of the worst had nagged like a dark dream. "Will she live?" He dreaded the answer.

"We don't know. She's critical, of course."

"If she does . . ."

The doctor understood. He tried quickly to offer some hope. "We can accomplish miracles today with surgical reconstruction."

Chief Wheeler studied his face. Sincerity and compassion were clearly there. But Matt was not consoled. Instead, ugly feelings began to well within him. He wanted desperately to do something inordinately cruel. To make that bastard suffer as deeply as his poor innocent Margaret was being made to suffer. But it was not to be. All he could feel now were anger and screaming frustration. He collected himself. "May I see her?"

"There's nothing to see, Chief. She's all bandages. Besides, she's unconscious . . ."

"I don't care. I want to see her."

He was taken to her bedside. He stood there silently, perfectly still until one tear fell upon the bandages around her arm. He touched it with a fingertip. That was all.

Then he left to go to his office. If he couldn't do anything to the person responsible for this nightmare he would at least discover who the madman was!

Victor Jordan sat in casual sartorial splendor eating a light breakfast in his room. Coincidence would not explain the disappearance of three tested men engaged in two separate assignments. He saw their failure to return as confirmation of Sharon's statements. But he was unconcerned. Instead he felt especially and pleasantly alive. It was the first time in years he had been alone. Unprotected. His life was in his own hands again. He was totally self-dependent once more. The entire set of circumstances had become wonderfully stimulating.

At ten o'clock he called for his car. It was waiting for him when he appeared at the entrance. Then with his radio offering soothing, gentle music, he went for a pleasant ride into the desert to scout an old abandoned mine he remembered from his youth.

If it were still there it would become the hiding place for Sharon Kane's body.

Matt reached police headquarters as Victor was driving away from the hotel. He swapped the borrowed coat he had worn all night for a complete change of clothing he always kept in his office closet.

The men on duty knew what had happened. They were self-consciously respectful and solicitous.

"Clemmens!" Matt called as he was dressing. He would tear into this search with a vengeance.

Sergeant Clemmens appeared immediately. "Chief?"

"Get that gun and switchblade to lab. I want a full report yesterday, understand?" They were on his desk.

"Yes, sir." He scooped up the weapons. "The ring too, Chief?"

"Leave that."

"Right." And Clemmens was gone like a shot.

Matt crossed to his desk as he stuffed his shirt into his pants. He was fixed upon that ring. There was something about it. The memory teased. Then suddenly he sprang into action. He raced behind his desk and tossed folders aside until he found the one he was looking for. He pulled a stack of eight-by-ten pictures from it. Began flipping them aside in rapid succession. Five photos. Six. Seven. He had it.

"Murphy," he shouted. He broke to the door of his office. "Murphy!"

The surprised patrolman was on his feet and rushing to the call.

"Blow this up."

"Sure, Chief."

"I want this section right here. The hand. Can you bring it out clearly?"

"No sweat."

It was a telescopic of Andrew, standing at the car rental counter in the Sky Harbor International Terminal, one of the many pictures taken of Victor's arrival yesterday morning. His hand was near his face. The ring, while seemingly small, was quite noticeable.

In the living room of Dr. Townsend's house, Alex Weintraub perched at the edge of his chair with the excitement of a wine fancier tasting the rarest of vintages.

"Then you're saying," he was concluding, "our souls may be the things that actually create our bodies?"

It was a stunning idea.

"Possibly," Dr. Townsend responded. "Look at it this way: every cell of the body has all the coded information of the body itself. We know that today; there's no question about it. Well, information has to come from somewhere, and what it usually comes from is intelligence. Intelligence is a nonphysical source. And that nonphysical part of ourselves we often call consciousness or soul. Therefore, the soul may actually be responsible for the creation and shaping of our bodies."

"Then what happens when a person dies?".

"The consciousness or soul departs."

"No, I mean: if consciousness creates the body and then leaves during death, why doesn't the body just disappear?"

"Good question. We don't know. However, we suspect some kind of special bond with the matter it creates. You know, soul in every cell, so to speak. Then, although the main part of the soul separates at death, some of it remains. In time that dissipates, and that's why the body decays."

"Are you telling me a dead body may be leftover soul." Alex whispered.

"Something like that."

Alex was forced to his conclusion. He thought aloud. "Then if a dead body were to be revived by another entity, there could be an effort by the residual soul to repulse it."

"That's an interesting speculation," Dr. Townsend smiled, "and it's quite logical. After all, our cells will accept other matter only when the information of that matter is harmonious with our own. That's why we have trouble with heart and kidney transplants. Rejection. Mr. Weintraub, we can sew a person's severed nose to his chest, and it'll remain alive and healthy with virtually no difficulty at all until we're ready to put it back on his face. But *another* person's nose soon rots and dies. Why is that? The answer may be quite simple: what's really being rejected is not a nose *per se*, of course, but the foreign information, the foreign consciousness, within the cells of that matter."

Alex stood. He offered his hand. "Thank you, Dr. Townsend. Thank you very much."

As they shook hands Dr. Townsend smiled and asked, "What's this all about, Mr. Weintraub? Why such interest in philosophical speculation?"

"It's related to the play—which by the way I'd like you and your wife to see as my guests. We're having our first performance tonight at eight. Can you make it?"

"I wouldn't miss it! Thank you very much."

"Your tickets will be at the box office. Thank you again, Doctor." And he left.

Alex Weintraub drove all the way back to his office like a man in a trance. If this had not actually happened to him he might have disdained any association with ideas such as those he and Dr. Townsend had just discussed. But it *was* happening to him. And the philosopher's information gave credence to everything he had been experiencing. He knew now. He understood: this Revenant—here for a confrontation with Victor Jordan—was being rejected as a foreign element by the residual consciousness of Sharon Kane's body. And that's what she meant when she said she was dying.

But why was he-she-or-it so determined to bring Victor Jordan to terms? Why this man when the world was filled with thousands, perhaps even millions, every bit as bad as he?

He would have to wait just a little longer for the answer to that final question.

It was still there. A narrow, deep shaft left by some hopeful prospector at the turn of the century. In the 1930's, someone had covered the opening with a large sheet of corrugated metal and then thrown some earth upon it.

Victor Jordan was pleased. No one had touched the spot in decades. And no one but he would touch it for decades to come. It would be a perfect grave; her body would rot there in splendid isolation.

He would have to return to Phoenix quickly now. He had decided to dispose of her before the next morning.

"The switchblade had some animal blood. Probably a dog's."

"My Doberman," Matt conjectured.

"The gun was a mess. Prints everywhere and everything useless."

"I expected that. Half the fire department handled it."

"We traced the serial number to a dealer in New York."

"New York? Marvelous. Get me Captain Garvey again. Quick."

"Right, Chief."

"Here's your blowup, Chief." It was Murphy, and the print was still damp.

He grabbed it eagerly.

There it was. Big. Clear. No question about it—the same ring. But still not conclusive.

The phone rang.

"Captain Garvey, Chief."

"Stay on the line, Clemmens. Hello, Wally."

"What's up, Matt?"

"I need another gun check."

"Sure thing. Something hot?"

"I think he tried to kill me last night."

"Who?"

"Jordan."

"What!"

"Clemmens, give him the gun info."

Clemmens recited the particulars.

"How long will it take, Wally?"

"Seconds. Hold on."

Matt counted to only twenty-nine before his friend was on the line again.

"God bless the computer," Garvey said. "Gun belongs to an Andrew Mallory . . ." He was reading. ". . . who is the bodyguard of . . ."

"Victor Jordan," Matt concluded.

"Jesus," Garvey exploded. "Do you have him? Can you make it stick?"

Matt's voice was bitter. "No."

But the image that compelled that bitterness—the tormenting picture of Margaret swathed in bandages, possibly dying or at best facing endless plastic surgery—was suddenly dispelled by a remembrance of the play he had been reading before the fire, the play and that startling discovery he had made about it. And he added with a grim smile, "But don't you worry, my friend, I know just how to get that sonofabitch now!"

"Alex, we're not ready," Mike Ross was storming. "One good rehearsal doesn't make a show and you know it."

"She's dying."

"Who?"

"Sharon."

"What?"

"She may be dead tomorrow and don't you tell a soul what I'm saying, understand?"

Mike was overwhelmed.

"She wants this performance and I want it too," Alex raced. "Look, Sharon was responsible for that great rehearsal yesterday, and we both know it. Well, I think she deserves a chance to do it at least once the right way—lights, costumes, audience, everything—and the rest of the cast needs a chance to see it that way too."

"She's dying?"

"That's right."

The director groaned and flopped to the couch.

"The only thing that concerns me at all about this performance is the technical end of it," Alex continued quickly. "This thing has to be so tight, so clean, so incredibly beautiful, people will have pictures of it in their minds for the rest of their lives."

Silence. Mike Ross was deeply troubled. "What if she dies in the middle of the performance?" he murmured.

"I'm willing to risk that," Alex answered. "Stay with me, Mike."

The director looked at him for a few moments and then jumped to his feet. "O.K., if you want me, I'll be at the theater." His manner was brisk now. Vital. "We'll be running the best damned tech rehearsal you ever heard of, right up to the minute we pull that curtain tonight."

Alex beamed. "You're my man, Mike." And they shook hands like partners initiating some magnificent venture.

The intercom buzzed. Alex flipped the switch. "Yes, Marilyn."

"Mr. Weintraub, the chief of police is out here." Her tone asked a worried: what have we done wrong now?

"Send him in, send him in."

Matt Wheeler and the director passed each other in a hurried entrance and exit.

"Glad I caught you," Matt said as he took Alex's hand in greeting.

"I tried to get you earlier . . ." Alex started, but the Chief cut him off.

"I know. I've been tied up, and I haven't had a chance to breathe. I've got some conclusions, Mr. Weintraub, and let me tell you, they are very, very wild."

"Really? Well, you'd better sit down, Chief, because what I've got for you will probably jolt you off your feet."

In the next twenty minutes, the exchange of information

kept them both gasping. The only things Matt kept to himself were the facts about the clamps. When it was over, they could only sit and stare at each other. What they had traded formed a mosaic of incredible design. They saw it all now. Or almost all of it. Only the final corner of the picture was missing. And that would be filled in tonight.

"Then it's not wrong for me to help her," Alex concluded.

"Wrong? Hell no. You do whatever you can, my friend. I'll stop her when the time is right."

"Stop her? Why?"

"Mr. Weintraub, one look at my wife and you'd know why I wouldn't let Satan himself take Victor Jordan away from me."

It was 11:30 A.M. She was leaving for her luncheon appointment.

Despite the pleasure she had felt after yesterday's rehearsal, despite her professed indifference to what she had learned about Sharon Kane from Alex, Felicia Ohrman gasped and felt almost faint as she approached her car; Sharon stood there, waiting for her, eyes closed, hands clasped loosely, posture as straight as a ruler—a statue of controlled meditation.

The eyes flew open.

Felicia stopped in her tracks. She was not being manipulated; she was just very anxious.

Sharon opened the door on the passenger's side and took her seat.

Felicia edged closer. She opened her door but wouldn't enter. "What do you want?" she asked.

The voice could hardly be heard. "While we're driving, I'll tell you what I want."

Felicia hesitated. "I . . . I have an appointment with Mr. Weintraub."

"This won't take long." She smiled but there was no life sparkle in it now. A dead smile.

Felicia fretted. She didn't want to be alone with this creature, and yet she couldn't avoid it; she didn't want to miss her appointment with Alex, and yet she knew she couldn't pull Sharon from her car. Despite her anxieties, she got behind the wheel.

They were barely out of the parking lot when Sharon

said, "Except for Mr. Demerest, you are the one who is most afraid of me; that will change in time. At this moment, you are the one I need."

"What . . . what do you mean?"

"We're previewing tonight."

"I was told. Are . . . are you responsible for that?"

"It was Alex Weintraub's decision." A half truth. "And your job now is to get Victor Jordan to the theater."

"Why?"

"You'll know soon enough. Alex has told you much so far. He'll soon tell you all."

"Even if I wanted to," Felicia resisted feebly, "how could I get him there?"

"You'll find a way." Again that empty smile. It was unnerving. It ended discussion.

They were sitting in Chez Gerard's. He considered it wise to have lunch there. The careful gentility of the restaurant, he believed, would discourage any emotionalism resulting from the information he intended to reveal. However, he was surprised. The precaution proved to be unnecessary. Felicia listened very carefully to the full story and, instead of registering fear, she responded now with fascination. "So that's it," she breathed. Now she understood, and her understanding dispelled her fear. "Oh Lord, what that girl has been going through."

"Then it doesn't bother you to know you'll be performing with a person who's already dead?" He found it interesting that he had been able to reveal that fact to her now. Apparently, Sharon believed it was time.

"Are you insane, Alex? Of course that bothers me. How could that not bother me?" Felicia answered. "But now that I know the whole story—well, somehow it's different."

"Marvelous," Alex murmured as he took her hand. "Yes, indeed, when this thing is over, we're going to get married and jump into bed for a year."

"She wants me to get Jordan to the theater tonight," Felicia revealed suddenly in what was almost a whisper.

"She does—!" Alex breathed. "Well, I was wondering how she intended to accomplish that."

"I may feel different toward her now, Alex, but I don't know if I want to become any more involved in her plans than I am right now."

"Leesh, whether we like it or not, we're *all* involved, and all the way."

"Then you believe I should do what she wants?"

"I understand what you're thinking; that's the exact question I asked Matt Wheeler. And I'll give you the answer he gave me: do whatever you can, for the time being."

She stared at him for a few moments. And then very slowly she nodded her head in acquiescence. "Have the maitre d' bring us a telephone," she said softly.

Victor Jordan had stopped at the Empire Hardware Store on Grand Avenue before returning to his hotel rooms. He had purchased a small piece of one-inch doweling, which he had had the salesman cut into two four-inch lengths, a small file, a pair of pliers, a yard of bare copper wire, a pair of snug work gloves, a thin, rubber poncho and a three-by-five-foot strip of heavy plastic.

In the parking lot, he had spread the plastic neatly across the bottom of the car's trunk. There must be no trace of blood when I return this vehicle, he thought.

In his hotel suite, he fashioned the copper wire and dowels into a sinister garrote. The dowels, of course, were the handles. The wire, secured snugly within a nonslip wedge that he had filed around the center of the handles, was as deadly as a well-honed blade. It would slice as it strangled and with sufficient force could probably sever a head from its torso.

He studied his handiwork and was satisfied. After its service, it could be dismantled simply and disposed of with no difficulty at all. Ideal.

His telephone rang. He went to it. It was Felicia Ohrman.

"This is a pleasant surprise," he said.

"You'll find I'm one who always pays her debts," she responded warmly. "You were candid with me yesterday, and now I owe you dinner and an evening of conversation." There was a faint promise of something more than conversation in her voice.

He detected it. His thoughts raced. How could he fit this into his own plans?

"We're having our preview performance at eight tonight," he heard her say. "Please be my guest and after the show, you may take me someplace for dinner."

"And after dinner?" he asked rather pointedly.

"Oh . . . your suite for a drink . . ."

He saw her again on his bed. Nude. Lovely.

He was not the kind of man to allow that—no matter how desirable—to interfere with another purpose. However, it suddenly occurred to him how perfectly he could fit this into his disposal of Sharon Kane. Miss Ohrman would be quite helpful.

He accepted her invitation. And after a few more comments, he said, "Until tonight, then. I'm looking forward to this with keen anticipation, Miss Ohrman." Then, very gently, he replaced the receiver in its cradle.

Well, this was exactly what he needed: first, it informed him of the whereabouts of his intended victim—as a performer, Sharon Kane would obviously be at the theater, too —and then, it provided him with the necessary cover.

He lifted the receiver again and dialed the Sorry Spike.

"Mr. Canto called a while ago to say he won't be in before the dinner hour," a mellifluous female voice informed him. "And I'm sorry, sir, but we're not permitted to give out his home number."

"But he's unlisted," Victor objected, "and I do want to speak with him. I'm his uncle."

"I'm sorry, Mr. Jordan." The voice was uncertain now. Troubled. The sound of dilemma.

"Then you call him," Victor suggested. "Just tell him his Uncle Victor is waiting to hear from him. I'm at the Hyatt Regency."

"Oh yes, sir . . . yes, sir," the voice pounced on the solution eagerly, "I'll do that right now."

Ben returned the call immediately.

"Uncle Victor!" He was excited with pleasure. "It's so good to hear your voice."

"You sound well, Ben."

"I am. Fine. Really."

"I saw Mother and Father yesterday."

"Oh? How are they?"

"They're distraught but otherwise all right. They told me about the trouble and asked me to . . ."

"Uncle Victor, please," he cut him short.

"Just one question, Ben—do you still love her?"

Ben Canto remembered his evening with Sharon—the closeness, the warmth, the marvelous lovemaking—and he answered with the deepest conviction, "More than ever before, Uncle Victor."

The words cut Victor Jordan, just as she knew they would. Ben's love was working for her. Yes, Victor thought coldly, this will be settled.

"All right," he covered pleasantly, "I'm in favor of anything that will make my favorite nephew happy."

"I'm your only nephew," Ben teased.

"That's why you're my favorite."

They laughed. The slight tension quickly vanished.

"I was hoping to see you before I leave Phoenix," Victor said with warmth.

"I'd like that."

Then as though it were a fresh idea, Victor suggested, "Why don't we have dinner tonight, and you bring your lady friend." He refrained from offering any indication that he had already met Sharon. "Dining is the only civilized way to get to know someone."

"Well, I don't know . . ."

"If she's half what you believe, I'll be happy to intercede with Mother and Father in your behalf."

"That's very kind of you, Uncle Victor, but . . ."

"You're not against a reconciliation are you, Ben?"

"No. Certainly not."

"Good. Then let's plan something light. Light and late. Say, eleven o'clock. I'm going to the theater tonight to see a charming actress perform. She's a friend. I'll bring her along. You bring your lady, and we'll have a lovely evening together."

"O.K. I'll see if I can contact her. This is rather short notice."

"I'm sure you can succeed at anything you set your mind to, Ben."

"I'll get to her, Uncle Victor. Yeah, this sounds good. I'll have them prepare something special for us at the restaurant."

"Excellent. I'm eager to see the place. Until tonight, Ben."

"I'm looking forward to it. Have a good day."

"Thank you, Ben. I shall. Indeed, I shall."

"It was easier than I thought it would be," Felicia said with some surprise to Alex as she hung up.

He smiled. "Never underestimate the power of a possible orgasm."

Alex reached for the telephone. "Only one more thing to check," he murmured as he dialed.

It rang twice before it was answered.

"Where do we stand?" he asked abruptly.

"You'll be glad to know, Mr. Weintraub, we have a full house."

He sighed in relief. "You're an angel, Marilyn, a living angel." He hung up and looked at Felicia again. "Well," he said, "everything's ready from our end."

Felicia nodded. "Oh, by the way," she remembered teasingly, "our Mr. Jordan also said he has an exquisite surprise for me."

"Really?" Alex responded. His thoughts were distant. "It looks like we're in for an explosion of surprises tonight . . ." His voice trailed off. He was trying to imagine the events that would occur at the Sunset Playhouse before the close of that final curtain.

It would be her last day in this world. She needed a respite now from everything that could weaken her further. The unrelenting rejection by her body was keeping her vigilant against premature separation. She tried now to get through the rest of the day by quietly roaming about the city's loveliest park. The surroundings proved to be exactly what she needed. And for awhile, she even felt strong enough to lift the normalizing restrictions she had placed upon her senses. Again, as at her rebirth, she was bombarded with the pageantry of life. She wallowed in it. And as she lay on the cool grass, watching everything and everyone swirl around her, she observed with some dismay, "So few of them truly appreciate the whole challenge of living."

31

"Fifteen minutes . . . fifteen minutes . . . fifteen minutes."

Gofer Richard Skolar was making the curtain announcements tonight. He had completed his check. Everyone had signed the call sheet. No one was missing. Now at five-minute intervals, he hurried down the passageway, tapping on doors.

"Fifteen minutes, Miss Ohrman . . . fifteen minutes, Mr. Dark . . . oop—'scuse me . . ." He dodged around other production personnel scurrying to complete last-minute details.

A spirit of excitement prevailed. Everything was charged. Everyone was tense. Eager. Apprehensive.

Outside in the house, even the audience's babbling had a special edge. The calls to announce an earlier preview—so sudden, so unexpected. Why? The air buzzed with anticipation.

Mike Ross gave final instructions to his stage manager. It had been one wild afternoon. But he felt confident. Light levels were perfect. Gel intensities ideal. Fades had been orchestrated like a concerto. Sound cues were needle-sharp, and musical transitions pure velvet. He was ready. Technically the show would work. But what about the performers? He started his round of encouragement.

"Fifteen minutes, Miss Kane. Hi, Mr. Ross. Good luck tonight."

"Thank you, Richard."

The gofer continued down the passageway tapping and calling.

Mike stopped at Sharon's dressing room first. He hadn't seen her arrive. He hadn't heard anything more from Alex about her. He was deeply concerned. "Sharon?" His fingernails tattooed lightly on the door.

"Yes?"

When he saw her, he didn't know what to believe. He had been told she was dying. But she looked all right. Fresh. Vital.

It was a facade. The internal struggle to retain possession of her body had become so intense, so draining with each passing moment, that she was actually extremely and precariously weakened.

"How are you?" he asked.

"Fine," she lied with a smile.

"Hey, I see you've removed your bandage. Good."

She flexed her fingers. "Works like new."

"What was it, a sprain?"

She answered in her oblique fashion. "I have remarkable healing powers."

He forced himself to grin. If Alex were telling him the truth, her response was woefully ironic. "Well, Miss Kane," he tried to be cheerful, "ever dream you'd be a star?"

She looked at him strangely. "As a matter of fact, yes."

"Good. Because tonight, it'll become a reality." He became serious. "Good luck, Sharon; knock 'em dead." And he leaned in and kissed her lightly on the cheek.

He was gone barely two minutes when Matt Wheeler knocked.

"Come in."

He did. He was somber. He closed the door behind him and slipped the bolt quickly into place. "Better if we're not interrupted," he said. There was a rolled program in his hand.

"I've been expecting you, Chief."

He turned and looked at her for a moment. His head was cocked as though he were considering where to start. "We identified Mussum and Jaddis this afternoon."

Her little odd smile didn't waver.

"Did you have anything to do with Andrew too?" he asked.

"I was there."

His words were slightly choked. "Couldn't you have helped Margaret?"

Her smile dissolved. "I did what I could."

They watched each other: two strong personalities, each bound to the other by a tie that was now clearly understood, each not fully trusting the other because that tie was so intensely personal. Matt considered for a moment the possibility of quickly digging his thumbs into her throat. She smiled slowly, a cool, inscrutable smile.

Is she reading my mind? he wondered. And he switched his thoughts sharply to the reason for coming to her dressing room. He unrolled the program he was carrying and spread it on her dressing table. "I understand now why it has to be Victor Jordan and no one else," he said. An electric silence filled the room before he spoke his next words. "You were Chana Ramirez."

He pointed at the program's cast listing. The name of her character had been neatly framed. Below it and within the frame, he had printed another name:

> JANICE CAMARON
> YÑEZ CAMARÓN

"I am called Revenant," she answered softly.

"Yes. And I looked that up: *a returning spirit*. It fits you now, but your real name was Yñez Camarón and you hated it. So you took another. Didn't you . . . Chana?"

She looked at the rectangle with the names. "You found it in the play," she murmured admiringly by way of admission. "You're very clever, Chief."

He moved closer. "We want the same thing," he said.

Her answer was, "Not quite." A simple rejection that suggested something unusual and terrible.

"I want to help you," he insisted. It was an offer churning with need.

She knew what he was thinking, though. His need was also for revenge, and it filled the dressing room like a powerful gas. She could smell his intention to get in her way. Well, she would have to deal with that later. At the moment, she needed his assistance. "All you have to do is keep him in the theater until the final curtain," she said.

He nodded agreement and started to leave.

"And, Chief," she stopped him. The silence ticked. "Remember—he belongs to me."

A picture of Margaret flashed in Matt Wheeler's mind and a strange, dark thought veiled his eyes.

"Ten minutes . . . ten minutes . . . ten minutes."

Richard Skolar stepped before Victor Jordan. "Sorry, sir, but no one's allowed backstage before the performance."

"That's all right, Richard," he heard Alex say.

"Oh, certainly, Mr. Weintraub, certainly." He turned to Victor again. "Sorry, sir, excuse me." And he continued down the passageway. "Ten minutes, Mr. Maynor . . . ten minutes, Miss Ohrman . . ."

"This becomes quite exciting," Victor observed. He was carrying a small flower box.

"Always," Alex agreed. "Glad you could make it."

"I'm delighted. By the way, I want to offer my regrets concerning the death of the playwright. Has there been . . ."

"That's very thoughtful of you," Alex cut him off. "But that's one subject no one wants to think about tonight."

Victor nodded. "Then let me thank you instead."

"For what?"

"Taking a chance on Dandy."

"There were times I thought I'd made a mistake, but it'll work out all right now, I'm sure."

"Mr. Weintraub, the point is, you honored one of my requests."

There was a slight, significant pause before Alex answered, "Well, you helped me once. Now, we're even."

"Yes. But I wonder, Mr. Weintraub, would you honor another request?"

Alex was being tried. He sensed it. After another pause, he said, "Mr. Jordan, you took your chances with my motion picture. But somehow your, let's say, position in the world made me look upon your losses as a debt I owed. To be honest, I was intimidated. Well, I'm not afraid of you anymore, Victor. Honor another request? I doubt it. As I've said—we're even."

He could have responded with a simple no. But he felt, if he were really to be free, ever to breathe easily again, he had to say it all, and to his face. God, he felt better now. Lighter. He was actually happy that Jordan had decided to appear in the dressing room area. It was over. Finally. There was nothing more between them.

But Victor Jordan blinked slowly. "It's a terrible thing for some people to be that sure of themselves, Mr. Weintraub," he whispered ominously. "Excuse me. I'd like to wish Dandy well." And he stepped around Alex without another word and passed down the hallway, glancing at name cards on the dressing room doors.

"Hi, Mr. Jordan," Dandy perked, seeing him in the large, brightly lighted mirror. He was effecting some final makeup touches. "Come on in. Have a seat, have a seat."

Victor was aware of something immediately. An easier manner. A diminution of deference. Like Weintraub, Dandy Maynor seemed to have undergone a change in attitude toward him. "I've come to wish you well."

"Hey, thanks. Thank you very much." He continued sitting, working at the makeup. At another time, he would have stopped everything. He would have stood and given Victor Jordan his full attention.

Victor thought: it appears the Kane girl has spoken the truth. He tested his conclusion. "This play is an important step, Dandy," he began, "but my next plans for you . . ."

"I'm going back to music," Dandy interrupted.

Victor stared at their images in the mirror. His charge wasn't even looking at him. Busy. Busy. Touching his makeup. Here. There.

"We'll see," Jordan responded coldly.

"Nothing to see. I'm going back. We'll talk about it later."

Thwack. A verbal slap. There was actually a note of dismissal in the words.

Victor opened the door. His eyes had narrowed. Yes, indeed, they would talk about this later. "Good luck tonight, Dandy," he said solemnly.

"What? Oh yeah . . . thanks . . . thanks a lot, Mr. Jordan."

"Five minutes . . . five minutes . . . five minutes," Richard Skolar was calling.

Victor passed Sharon Kane's door. His anger rose. Interference. In his business. His family. His life. Well, it would soon end.

He arrived at Felicia Ohrman's door.

"I'll be only a minute," he apologized as he opened it. He was a model of graciousness and aplomb.

"Come in," she insisted. "Please."

He offered her the small box of flowers. "I'm sure, in contrast, your performance tonight will make these seem like weeds."

"I love flowers," she said as she opened the box. Orchids. She smiled appreciation. "A lovely surprise."

"You'll find my other surprise even more pleasant."

"Are you going to reveal it now?"

"Would you like that?"

"Yes, I think so."

"Very well." He paused just a moment for effect. "I own the new Prado Complex being constructed in New York at this time. Are you acquainted with it?"

"Everyone is."

"A $200,000,000 undertaking. Hotel. Restaurants. Shops. Offices. And it will include a legitimate theater as well. The best in the city."

"You're telling me things I already know," she said.

"I know," he grinned, "but the surprise is that I'd like to name the theater after you. And for that privilege I believe you deserve a permanent suite of rooms in the hotel and a significant percentage of the theater's yearly gross. Also, I'd like to open with a play written expressly for you by one of the leading playwrights of the day. And I'd be happy to finance the production in its entirety. I hope you'll consider this your home theater where you may perform at any time in anything of your choice."

She was speechless.

"A pleasant surprise?" He knew it was.

She recovered quickly. "Mr. Jordan . . ." she began.

"Victor," he corrected her.

She smiled magnificently. "Victor, that is an actress's dream come true."

"Places, please . . . places, everyone . . . places . . . curtain in three minutes . . . places, please . . ."

Jordan extended his hand.

She took it.

"There are many details even more interesting than those I've mentioned," he promised. "We'll discuss them at dinner."

"Victor," she beamed, "I wouldn't miss your dinner for the world."

"And I should get to my seat now," he concluded, "because I wouldn't miss your performance for the world."

The hallway became an artery now. Everyone connected with the performance drifted into it to join the flow to the stage.

Victor had left for the lobby by way of a side door.

"Good luck."

"Thank you."

"Break a leg!"

"You too!"

Calls of good wishes snapped through the air at no one in particular and for all in general. Faces were wreathed in the nervous happiness of heightened anticipation.

"Miss Kane . . . Miss Kane." Richard Skolar caught her as she came from her dressing room. "For you. Said it was important." And he was halfway down the hall before she could open the envelope.

A hastily scribbled note read:

Sharon—
Something terrible's happened. I *must* see you for a minute! My car is near the palm trees.

Love,
Ben

The fingertips of her right hand ran circles over the paper as though they were testing its texture. Her mouth pulled into a satisfied smirk. She tossed the note on her dressing table and started down the hallway—against the traffic.

"Come on, baby, let's go!" Dandy was grinning at her.

"Be there soon." She edged away.

"Hey, curtain's in two minutes."

"It's O.K.," she called. "I don't make my entrance for three minutes after that." She disappeared through the side door and emerged from the theater.

She hurried toward a stand of palm trees. When she reached the trees, she stopped between two cars. It was relatively dark, and no one seemed to be present. "What is it you want, Victor?" she addressed the air.

The garrote swung swiftly before her face and bit like a whip into her neck. She felt it jerk and wrench and stop the air to her lungs. Her neck tore open. Formaldehyde gushed from her throat. Poured down her chest. She felt the wire sawing against the clamps. She kicked. Lashed with her feet. Thrashed her arms to grab at his face behind her, his hair, his ears—anything. But she couldn't reach him.

"You . . . must . . . learn . . . your place . . ." she heard him grunting as he tugged and pulled. Her feet came off the ground. The wire sliced through her gullet, split her larynx. She tried to twist around to get at him, but he held her fast. Twisting. Wrenching. Her thrashing began to slacken. Her clawing became spasms. And then, after one shattering moment of suspension, her body went limp.

Victor Jordan moved swiftly. He lifted her. Dumped her into the trunk of his car. He placed the garrote on top of her body. Removed the gloves he was wearing. Then the rubber poncho. These, too, were placed on top of her body. After this, he snapped the lid shut and brushed his hands. The entire action had taken no more than two minutes.

He ran his hands smoothly over his clothes to see if they were damp from what he believed was her blood. They were not. All had gone exactly as planned. He smiled with self-satisfaction. He took a deep breath. And he walked briskly toward the lobby.

Victor made it to his seat seconds before the house lights dimmed. He had just enough time to settle himself comfortably and to respond pleasantly to the elderly lady at his left.

"I understand there's to be no intermission," she had said.

"More than likely, they want to sustain the mood," he smiled.

"It's supposed to be an amazing play," she gushed. "Full of surprises."

"Let's hope it lives up to its publicity." And he waited for his own "surprise"; he expected the show to start and then a frantic search for the missing actress to take place. This would be followed by a closing of the curtains, the introduction of house lights again, and the troubled announcement canceling the evening's performance. Everyone would indeed be surprised. And he would then visit Miss Felicia Ohrman in her dressing room and assuage her disappointment and consternation with an earlier-than-planned dinner engagement—one she would certainly accept in light of the extraordinary career proposal he had already made. Later, if he should be questioned by the police for any reason, both his nephew Ben and an award-winning star would undoubtedly attest to his calmness throughout the evening, as they also bore witness to his whereabouts. Tomorrow he would dispose of the body. It was perfect.

The curtains parted. The show began.

The applause greeting the first view of the set dribbled away only to rise again as Felicia Ohrman made her entrance.

"Leonard, I'm glad you could come," she said anxiously to Elliot Dark as she crossed to where he was standing.

"I'm here," he responded in character, "but I don't know if I can help you."

The mood was set quickly. Agitation. Distress. And after only a few lines, the audience sensed that special performance acuity which always forecasts the most rewarding of theater experiences.

At the rear of the house, Police Chief Matt Wheeler blocked the aisle like a redwood tree, his attention focused on the back of Victor Jordan's head.

Alex Weintraub appeared at his side. "Everything all right?" he whispered.

Matt nodded. "He just made the curtain," he answered, his voice barely audible.

"He was backstage with Felicia till the last minute."

The front doorbell rang onstage. Mrs. Oze crossed to the door. She opened it. And Sharon Kane walked into the play as though nothing whatever had happened to her.

Matt Wheeler gripped Alex's shoulder. Victor's head had jerked as though he were just hanged.

"Hello, Janice," Mrs. Oze greeted her. "You're early."

JAN: "Mrs. Oze . . . Hello, Leonard."
LEN: "Hi, Jan."
JAN: "Is Kris here yet?"
OZE: "No, but he'll come, don't worry."
LEN: "If I know my brother, not even sex could make him miss this meeting."

The scene continued. Setting the mood. Fleshing the characters. Establishing the central point. But Victor Jordan couldn't concentrate on what was taking place. His first thought was that he had killed the wrong girl. He ran the events rapidly through his memory. Saw the details—all of them—as graphically delineated as any on film. No—he had killed her! No doubt of that. He looked at Sharon onstage. But it was *she*. Unquestionably. How could she be up there? This was incomprehensible! He began to feel those strange, ugly sensations that she had generated in him twice before.

He found it increasingly difficult to remain still. His composure was cracking. He had to get out of the theater. Away from these circumstances. He eased from his seat and made his way up the aisle.

Police Chief Matt Wheeler blocked his path.

Their eyes locked.

"Get back to your seat," Matt muttered.

Jordan paused. His back stiffened. What was going on here? "Excuse me," he murmured coldly. And he took two more steps forward.

Matt came up against him. "You tried for me last night, Mr. Jordan," he hissed, "and you got my wife instead. Now, if you're not back in your seat in one minute, you scum, I'll kill you right where you're standing."

He felt the stubbed barrel of a police special in his belly. He hesitated. Stared into the implacable gaze of his long-time enemy. It was there—smoldering anger, fierce determination. A thin film of sweat broke over Victor's upper lip. He turned and made his way back to his seat just as Sharon Kane spoke the line: "Nobody escapes. Nobody. Because everything you do counts, and you're not allowed to think only of yourself." And he had the eerie feeling she was directing the words specifically at him.

The play picked up momentum. It caused gasps. Laughter. Sighs. Tears. It was everything it had been in rehearsal and more—a magnificent affirmation of life, a belief that everyone has genius within him and limitless powers of self-expression, a call for the assertion of basic goodness over evil, and a view of endless life through the repeated process of living and dying. And the audience was elevated by it. Swept away in waves of pleasure and understanding.

Victor Jordan was being affected, too, but in an entirely different way. He watched in mordant fascination. And thought of escape slipped and hid somewhere under the quivering of his nerve endings. This play was being directed at *him!* There was something about the character of Janice, something hauntingly familiar, agitatingly foreboding. She held his attention like a vise. And the more she spoke, the more he felt those horrible, degrading sensations surfacing again. They spread within him. They intensified. In time, they were almost unbearable. Suddenly, his brain exploded in a thousand simultaneous memories. Killings. Maimings. In this life. Past lives. A continual chaos of horror and agony for which he had been responsible. And he saw it. He saw it in that moment—his roots in the deep recesses of time—his soul's corruption—his Being's choking, cancerous growth! Something like a scream began to build, and he fought to retain his self-possession. He glanced up the aisle. Wheeler was still there. No escape that way. Then how? *There*. Yes. As soon as the curtain closed, he'd get out. Through the stage. Then Janice spoke from his past. Words slightly changed, but words that only he had known! The voice seemed to change in his ears. It did! He heard it. He saw her again. Pictures flipped in his mind. Scenes. Sounds. A quarter of a century flashed in an instant:

JAN: "Well I'm twenty-three-years old and I don't have anything and I haven't gone anywhere either! Oh, Kris, you're my man, my life, my soul, and I love you with my entire heart!"

KRIS: "It's all right, Jan ... I know ... I know."

JAN: "Then you're not angry with me?"

KRIS: (*Laughing*) "It's all right ... I understand."

JAN: "I would do anything for you, anything you want— anything! Only don't make me go through that again —please, Kris, please."

KRIS: "Easy ... easy ... you won't ever have to worry about that again. I promise."

It was Chana Ramirez in his mind. Her words. Her face. Her feelings. But where did they come from? How did they get into this play? A chill of dread rushed like ice through his body. He had to get into the street! He couldn't think clearly in here anymore. He had to get away. Far away. From this play. That girl. Those words.

The curtain closed to thunderous applause. The audience was on its feet. Calling. Cheering.

He held himself in check. Soon. Soon. The lights would go up. The people would leave. Soon. Soon.

And the bows went on. The actors radiated. The curtain opened and closed with dazzling regularity.

Still at the rear of the house, Alex Weintraub was beaming and cheering along with everyone else. But suddenly he hit Matt Wheeler's back. He had detected something. On that last call—Sharon Kane. "She's missing!" he barked. "She's missing. She didn't make that last call."

"Get backstage," Matt ordered. "I'll watch him."

Alex turned and rushed for the lobby.

The curtain finally closed for good. But even before it did, even before the house lights came up and the audience began to glut the aisles, Chief Wheeler saw Victor Jordan head for the exit near the stage. And he charged after him into the mass of oncoming traffic. People glared. Frowned. Complained loudly. But still he pushed through them like a man possessed. "He's getting away," he kept muttering with growing frenzy. "He's getting away. . . . *He's getting away. . . .*"

He reached the exit. Leaped up steps and through a curtained archway. He found himself offstage in the wing. He looked around wildly. Nowhere. Jordan was nowhere to be seen. He cursed. Punched the air angrily. And then he hunted frantically for the stage door, the backstage entrance to the theater. Just as he located it, Alex Weintraub came running up.

"Gone," Alex informed him breathlessly. "Not in her dressing room. Not backstage. She's gone."

"He got away too," Chief Wheeler growled.

"Where do you think he is?"

There was a sharp hitch in tempo. Then very slowly, Matt Wheeler said, "I think I know." It was dawning on him. "I think I know. Come on!"

By the sixth curtain call, Sharon Kane felt so weak she thought her moment of death had arrived. The effort to heal herself of the gruesome throat wound that Victor had inflicted, the energy required to free herself from the trunk, to switch so quickly to a "bloodless" blouse, to complete the entire performance, had sapped her to the point of collapse. The terrible internal struggle, inexorable and steadily intensifying, demanded consistent and direct concentration. And digressions into these other areas had allowed the body's consciousness to gain advantage. If she had not left the stage when she did, she would have died before the close of the final curtain. She recognized her needs. She had to find a few minutes of quiet, of solitude, some place she could come to grips with this insistence within her, this powerful confrontation of souls.

Victor Jordan had cut backstage toward the rear exit. Outside, the cool night air struck him like a wave, but he felt no refreshment. He felt pursued; he wasn't sure by whom or what. His thoughts were tumbling in a mélange of memories and fear. Who was she? Who was she!

He reached his car quickly. The trunk lid was up. The sight of it was horrifying. He rushed to the rear of the car and stared at the bodiless space. He grabbed the garrote, the poncho, the plastic floor covering. They were wet. Drenched with the slickness he thought was blood. A faint whimper escaped him. He slammed the trunk lid. Jumped into the driver's seat. Fumbled with his keys. As soon as the engine turned over, he tore from the parking lot with the desperation of Faustus trying to escape his fate.

He raced down Camelback Road. West. Toward the freeway. He wasn't returning to his hotel. He wanted to get farther away than that. Tucson. Mexico. Eventually his home in Venezuela where he would be safe to come to an understanding of all that had occurred. He tried to think of something other than Chana Ramirez. But the best he could do was Matt Wheeler: he knew about last night . . . Andrew must be in custody . . . probably told everything . . . that explains Wheeler's presence in the theater . . . but then why didn't he arrest me? Why did he want me back in my seat to see that play—that play! He couldn't escape the images of Chana Ramirez, the sound of her voice, the words of his past coming from the mouth of Sharon Kane.

He hit the freeway going seventy. And his intention to turn southeast for Tucson disappeared in a surge of countering command. He found himself going north, instead! "What the hell—" he erupted. Then his blood froze when he heard her voice say calmly in his ear, "Hello, Victor, I'm still with you."

She had been on the floor behind him. Resting. Pulling together the desperately needed last-minute control. And now she was staring grimly at him through the rearview mirror.

"How do you know where he is?" Alex shouted as the chief of police sped toward the freeway, lights flashing and siren wailing.

"She's missing. She's got to be with him. If she's with him, she's in charge. And if she's in charge, I know where she's taking him."

He flipped on his police radio: "Chief Wheeler here, Chief Wheeler. I want every patrol car on the west side of town to hightail it to the Black Canyon Freeway. Stop a silver, Mark VI Lincoln Continental, license number TMF 631. Driver is a man in his early fifties. Exercise extreme caution."

They were racing through light traffic, weaving sickeningly around cars that were holding at the order of the screaming siren.

"But what if you do find him?" Alex asked. "You can't stop her."

"She can't have him," Chief Wheeler spat. "I'll stop her. I know how. I'll stop her."

"Only death can stop her. But even if you could, you don't have anything on Jordan that'll hold him."

"Mr. Weintraub, I'm betting that by now he'd confess to the assassination of Abraham Lincoln to get my help."

They cut into the freeway and headed north.

Victor strove frantically to assert his will. It was hopeless. His mind was mush. He was conscious. He was aware of everything. But he couldn't take command of his own actions. All he could do was whimper in agonizing frustration and shudder at the killing terror within him.

"Who are you?" he shouted. "What do you want of me?"

"You'll see," she said weakly. "You'll see." Every word consumed precious moments of life.

He felt his foot slam the accelerator. The car leaped ahead. Eighty. Eighty-five.

A police siren sounded behind them.

Victor glanced at the rearview mirror.

The patrol car was in pursuit, lights flashing, siren howling like a demon.

A ray of tormented hope made Jordan laugh and cry simultaneously.

Sharon closed her eyes and tried to hold on. The Lincoln picked up more speed—ninety . . . a hundred and ten. It tore past the few other cars on the highway as though they were standing still.

The patrol car hung on, and as they passed a freeway entrance, Victor saw two more police cars join the chase.

Sharon fought to keep Victor Jordan under her control. In no time, they were at New River and into the desert of their old love-ground. As on that night twenty-nine years ago, a full, white moon turned the sky sapphire, and the air had its October bite.

Sharon sat perfectly still. Eyes closed. Lips compressed. They were only two miles from the large, flat rock where she had died as Chana Ramirez, and she could see it clearly behind her lids. But everything was becoming almost impossible for her now. She no longer detected sensation on her skin. She existed no longer within her corium cells.

A police car appeared before them out of nowhere. The others still followed doggedly. The Lincoln swerved crazily around the blockading patrolman, kicking dust, barely missing him.

Pavement had become gravel. Gravel, dirt. And dirt was now a wild, flat land of rocks and desert brush.

Victor heard the car crunching the flora. He felt the jarring of the rocks. But he could only hunch over the steering wheel as though he were trying to tear it from its post. And strangled, gagging noises came from deep within his throat.

Hold! she told herself. Soon! Almost there! Her hands were going dead.

Fifty yards . . . twenty . . .

The Lincoln hit the large, flat rock like a stone skimming water. It sailed. Veered in midair. Flipped over. Plowed the desert with a horrific roar.

The dust fallout in the night air was a shroud. But even before it settled, she was pulling herself and Jordan from the wreckage. Toward the rock. The rock. The large, flat rock. "You owe me, Victor," she was saying. "You owe me . . . twenty-nine years and a life . . . twenty-nine years and a life . . . twentynineyearsandalife . . ."

"Who are you?" he screamed.

They were on the rock now. On their knees.

"Mi amor," she laughed, her arms pinning him close, "don't you know your love? Don't you know your love?"

He stared at her.

Her features began to quiver. Weaken. Recede. And Chana Ramirez came out of her eyes. Her skin. Her hair. Shimmering over the body of Sharon Kane. "Twenty-nine years and a life twentynineyearsandalife . . ." she chanted over and over and over again.

He recognized her. A searing pain knifed his mind. The terror he felt was indescribable. *"You're dead!"* he screamed.

And it was almost true. As Sharon she could hold on only moments more.

"You killed me twenty-nine years ago, Victor . . . I want those years from your life . . . twenty-nine years . . . twenty-nine years . . ."

His skin began to shrivel. Flesh began to sag. His hair dissolved. Vision blurred. And suddenly he was an old man. His fear, his agony, had turned him suddenly into an old, old man.

"SHARON!"

She heard the voice.

It was Chief Wheeler's. He was running toward them. Shouting. Screaming. "No. Don't. Don't!"

With her last strength, she pulled Victor Jordan to his feet.

"Grab her throat!" Matt was screaming. "Choke her. Choke her!"

And Victor Jordan felt his hands coming up and his fingers wrapping around her neck. They pressed. They squeezed. They wrung her throat with his last shreds of strength.

But nothing happened.

Instead, a smile came to her face. And she laughed and laughed. A cold, triumphant death-laugh. "You had to know the fear," she whispered. "The fear." She held him closer. "Years for years—and now a life for a life. You owe so many people a life, Victor, but most of all—*me!* You owe me a life, *mi amor.*"

In the cold glare of the moon, Matt Wheeler and Alex Weintraub saw a strong, blue light radiate and pulsate around the figures. A luminescence of astonishing intensity. It swirled like smoke. It seemed to consume.

And then in that gauzy instant, in that glowing, incandescent moment, he was gone. Victor Jordan was gone! Like Londos's head and Mrs. Oze's objects, Victor Jordan was no longer of this world.

She collapsed to the rock just as Alex and Matt reached her. There was only the faintest flicker of control left in her. She smiled up at them. The face and body of Sharon Kane, but the soul and mind of Yñez Camarón.

"You robbed me, Chana," Matt said with quiet bitterness.

"He was mine all along," she whispered. "You knew that, Taxi."

It took a moment, but he finally dropped his head in grudging agreement.

She looked at Alex Weintraub. "Do you like my play?"

He smiled. "You know I do."

She smiled in return. "I was a star," she breathed. "For one night at least, I was a star. Goodbye, my friends. . . . You were both very helpful. . . . Everyone was. . . . Maybe we'll meet again when you come to my world . . ."

And she died.

32

Calvary Chapel.

Her Aunt Ada Rouche, coming from the bed to which she had been confined since the body's disappearance, and her aunt's few friends were in attendance again.

But also present now were some of the cast and production people of *The Trespasser* and the members of Fire and Air.

Howard Demerest moved through the small group with nervous skill. All he wanted was a speedy, trouble-free conclusion to this personal horror.

As for her body—he hadn't touched it. Too afraid those dead eyes might open and stare at him again. Curtis, his assistant, had completed the preparations. And they had puzzled him. He had reopened her neck as a precautionary measure. Just to be sure that everything was still in order. But he discovered the clamps far removed from their original positions, actually off the vein and artery and on the other side of the windpipe.

He had thought about that. Strange. Clips did occasionally loosen a bit . . . but what could possibly have dislodged them and moved them so far from their original positions? Only thing I can think of is some massive force, he speculated. Yet, there was no damage, and the vein and artery had somehow been rejoined. Yes, very strange. He couldn't understand it. But knowing how upset Mr. Demerest had been made by this particular funeral, he didn't mention his findings to anyone—especially, to his employer. And what no one ever knew was that those clamps would, indeed, have stopped her. If only Victor Jordan had not been that brutal at the Sunset Playhouse—if the clamps had not been dislodged by the monumental violence of his act, if they had been in place during those last desperate moments of her control—he would have stopped her, he would have won. But he was gone now—transported, ironically, by the force of his own insistent cruelty.

Howard Demerest wasn't the only one who couldn't look at the corpse again. The Reverend Paul Nelson wouldn't even appear at the mortuary. He was at home, in turmoil, being attended by his patient wife Clovis. It would be a long time before he would be enticed by the body of another woman.

In his place, a new pastor from another church officiated.

Demerest glanced across the room, hoping he would start the proceedings soon.

The pastor looked up. Their eyes met. He read the message and nodded.

Demerest was grateful. He touched a button on the side wall, and gentle melodious chimes sounded a signal to the mourners.

They followed the minister dutifully into the chapel.

"Ginny's out of the hospital," Alex murmured as he settled into a chair next to Felicia Ohrman.

She raised her eyebrows in surprise.

"Mike just got here. She called him before he left his place," he explained.

"How is she?"

"He says fine. Hands are perfect."

She nodded toward the casket. "Well, she said it would be that way. But what I can't understand is why Ginny was in that church in the first place. She's certainly not religious."

"She was helping her minister." He smiled suggestively.

"Ohhhh?" She understood. "We've only been in town a few weeks, Alex, how'd that happen?"

"Apparently, he came to the theater one day to see if we'd do a benefit for his children's fund; Ginny was there. . . ."

"Ladies and Gentlemen, friends of the departed," the new pastor began, and everyone in the room quickly became silent. "Every death must enhance life, or living is in vain . . ."

It was a fine eulogy. He touched on goodness and under-

standing and love, and he spoke with a sincerity that canceled the fact of his never having met the deceased.

His offering concluded, he shook hands with the few
who advanced to congratulate and to thank him.

Alex Weintraub and Chief Wheeler met near the door of
the chapel.

"Are you going to the cemetery with us?" Alex asked.

Just then Matt's driver came rushing over. He tried to be
polite, but his manner was obviously governed by a matter
of great urgency. "Chief . . . Chief Wheeler . . ."

"Excuse me," Matt apologized, and he took Sergeant
Finley aside.

Alex saw Matt's head snap. And then the Chief raced
from the chapel with his driver in close pursuit.

33

The doctors appeared in the corridor.

Matt hurried to them. And as they rushed down the hallway, Dr. Friedman, the head of the Burn Unit, tried to explain. "Chief Wheeler . . . I . . . I . . . your wife was burned over eighty percent . . ."

They burst into the Intensive Care Unit.

Margaret was sitting in bed, beaming.

Matt threw himself at her, and they laughed and cried as he covered her face with kisses.

"But she was burned . . ." Doctor Friedman was protesting in amazement. "She shouldn't be alive . . . and now she's perfect. . . . There isn't a mark on her body."

Matt cut him off. "I know, Doctor. You don't have to say a thing."

And then something caught his eye. It was in the corner of the room. Up high. Near the ceiling. An amorphous, undulating, gentle, blue glow. He watched it. And he understood.

"Thank you," he whispered so softly no one else heard. "Thank you . . . thank you."

The Return 277

Ben's smile broadened. "We'll talk about it," he said

34

Nothing about Sharon Kane appeared in the papers; Matt Wheeler had been very careful about that.

But after she had been buried, Ben Canto learned about her death from two sources. The first was Dandy Maynor who felt compelled to visit him to find out why he hadn't been to the funeral, inasmuch as he, Ben, had been her friend and part of that "night of the stabbing" at the Sorry Spike. And the second, only minutes after Dandy had left, was his mother, Marta, who called to tell him about a terrible dream she had had the previous night, one in which his young lady had been killed.

Coming so soon upon Dandy's information, Marta's dream had a profound effect upon him. It was as though Sharon were trying to reach him through his shock.

He dropped everything and went to her grave.

Remembrances. Remembrances. All of them warm now.

"I never wanted her to die, Ben. I'm sorry." It was his father's voice. Solemn. Sincerely regretful.

He turned and saw his parents.

Nothing more was said as he looked again at the grave.

Later, they went to the Sorry Spike. His parents were impressed with what he had done.

Jorge Canto rested a hand on his son's shoulder. "You have a wonderful place here." His voice became gruff. "Terrible name, though."

"Really?" Ben grinned. "I like it."

"No," Jorge waved a hand. "Should be something else."

"Like what?"

"Oh, I don't know . . . something like . . . Golden Spike

276

Northwest. Something like that." And then he added hastily, "Of course, you would continue to run it; obviously, you know what you're doing."

Ben's smile broadened. "We'll talk about it," he said. Clearly, he was not averse to the idea.

35

The Trespasser opened at the Mark Hellinger Theater in New York three weeks after its Phoenix premiere.

A week of advance advertisements read:

ALEXANDER WEINTRAUB
presents
FELICIA OHRMAN
in
THE TRESPASSER
a play by
ANTHONY KROZIER
also starring
ELLIOT DARK
DANDY MAYNOR
GERALDINE PRESTON
and directed by
MICHAEL ROSS

But two days before opening night, a change occurred in the credits. Anthony Krozier's name was mysteriously deleted. And in its place appeared the name: Chana Ramirez. It lasted one day, and only a few of the most astute theater people on the Broadway scene noticed it.

Some questions were asked at the newspapers, but no one could answer them.

The reviews were unqualified raves. However, the one that appeared in the *New York Times* was the best, and it sparked the long lines at the box office:

No Intruder, *"The Trespasser"* Belongs
by
Walter Brooks

Very moving, clearly written and beautifully performed, "The Trespasser," a play by Anthony Krozier, opened last night at the Mark Hellinger Theater.

This is no fluff. It is straight drama of the most rewarding kind. Felicia Ohrman plays a troubled psychic, eminently successful in making objects —and ultimately people—disappear, but dismally unsuccessful in bringing them back. It is not magic. Their voyage, if you will, is to another world. Into this premise is injected an ambivalent relationship between two brothers and the anxious influence of a young and beautiful girl. And as the story unfolds, we are treated to some of the most imaginative and stirring surprises ever to be presented on the American stage.

It went on to praise each and every aspect of the production and to predict Tony awards for everyone connected with it. But its most memorable lines were in its conclusion:

There is a sad note to this: we've learned that the author, Anthony Krozier, died before he could enjoy the glory of last night's performance. It's sad to think of how many more plays of this caliber we may have lost by his untimely death.

But we should rejoice, too, for at least we have "The Trespasser," his legacy. If you miss it, there will be a gaping hole in your life; if you see it, you may never be the same.

36

Alex Weintraub, of course, was ecstatic. And one morning while in bed with Felicia, he felt the production secure enough to bring up an old point: "Let's get married next week."

She curled up against him and purred sleepily, "No . . ."

"Yes, we're getting married next week."

Another happy purr. "No–o–o–o . . ."

"Why not?"

"Because illicit–y is felicity . . ." And her hand glided in a slow caress down his chest, over his belly, under the cover and to its mark.

Hmmmmmmmm. Well, he wouldn't argue the point just now.

37

Officially, it was over. The necessary reports had all been filed. Of course, they didn't tell everything: stolen corpse of Sharon Kane . . . perpetrator(s)—*unknown;* death of Anthony Krozier . . . reason—*unknown;* death of Domitro Londos . . . perpetrators(s)—*unknown;* deaths of Earl Mussum and Frank Jaddis . . . perpetrator(s)—*unknown;* whereabouts of Victor Jordan—*unknown.*

For the record, so many unknowns.

But for the privileged few, there were no mysteries. The file on Chana Ramirez, victim and trespasser, was finally closed, and they knew.

Indeed, they knew.